THE
BLOOD-DIMMED TIDE

MICHAEL LISTER

PULPWOOD PRESS

Paperback ISBN: 978-1-947606-48-7

Books by Michael Lister

(John Jordan Novels)
Power in the Blood
Blood of the Lamb
Flesh and Blood
(Special Introduction by Margaret Coel)
The Body and the Blood
Double Exposure
Blood Sacrifice
Rivers to Blood
Burnt Offerings
Innocent Blood
(Special Introduction by Michael Connelly)
Separation Anxiety
Blood Money
Blood Moon

Thunder Beach
Blood Cries
A Certain Retribution
Blood Oath
Blood Work
Cold Blood
Blood Betrayal
Blood Shot
Blood Ties
Blood Stone
Blood Trail
Bloodshed
Blue Blood
And the Sea Became Blood
The Blood-Dimmed Tide

(Jimmy Riley Novels)
The Girl Who Said Goodbye
The Girl in the Grave
The Girl at the End of the Long Dark Night
The Girl Who Cried Blood Tears
The Girl Who Blew Up the World

(Merrick McKnight / Reggie Summers Novels)
Thunder Beach
A Certain Retribution
Blood Oath
Blood Shot

(Remington James Novels)
Double Exposure
(includes intro by Michael Connelly)

Separation Anxiety
Blood Shot

(Sam Michaels / Daniel Davis Novels)
<u>Burnt Offerings</u>
<u>Blood Oath</u>
<u>Cold Blood</u>
<u>Blood Shot</u>

(Love Stories)
<u>Carrie's Gift</u>

(Short Story Collections)
North Florida Noir
Florida Heat Wave
Delta Blues
Another Quiet Night in Desperation

(The Meaning Series)
<u>Meaning Every Moment</u>
<u>The Meaning of Life in Movies</u>

For Aimee Walsh

My first best friend and the best little sister anyone could ever have!

THANK YOU!

Dawn Lister, Aaron Bearden, Jill Mueller, Tim Flanagan, Micah Lister, Bryan Mayhann, Sheriff Mike Harrison, Dr, D.P. Lyle, Judge Terry Lewis, Lexi Street, Bill Peterson, Michael Connelly, and the many, many friends, family, and Good Samaritans who helped us during the storm and its aftermath.

Thanks for all your invaluable contributions!

THE BLOOD-DIMMED TIDE

NEWS HERALD SPECIAL REPORT

Hurricane Michael Devastates Florida's Gulf Coast from Panama City to Apalachicola

By Merrick McKnight, *News Herald* Reporter

Hurricane Michael first made landfall on October 10, 2018 at approximately 1pm CDT near Mexico Beach, Florida, a coastal town of just over 1000 people, known for its quiet, laidback, small-town charm and its picturesque and pristine beaches.

First there was the wind—howling, shrieking, angry winds of over 155 mph. Then there was the rain—pelting, slanting, sideways, blinding rain. And there was the storm surge—a massive water monster of a storm surge that swallowed its prey whole.

Though much of the Panhandle has been affected,

particularly from Panama City to Apalachicola and over 70 miles inland, Mexico Beach was struck by the notorious front right quadrant of the eye of the storm, and you can tell.

The destruction and devastation were quick and pitiless and nearly total.

Buildings blew down as if made of papier-mâché, leaving little but floating piles of splintered lumber behind.

What the wind didn't destroy, the tidal surge washed away.

This is the first time in recorded history that such an intense storm reached landfall this late in the year. But that's not nearly all that is unique about Hurricane Michael.

Hurricane Michael is one of the strongest storms to ever hit the United States and the strongest ever on record in October.

Michael intensified quickly, fueling itself with the Gulf of Mexico's unseasonably warm waters as it tracked from the coast of the Yucatan into the Gulf of Mexico.

And the superstorm didn't give Floridians much time to prepare. Just a few days before it made landfall on Wednesday afternoon, the storm was a loosely organized system. It wasn't until the Saturday before the Wednesday that it hit that forecasters even mentioned that the system had a good chance of forming into a major storm, but none came anywhere close to predicting what it became.

By Wednesday evening, over 388,000 homes and business were without power. The cleanup will be considerable, the rebuild daunting.

TAMPA BAY TIMES DAILY DISPATCH

By Tim Jonas, *Times* Reporter

Hurricane Michael slammed the Florida Panhandle on Wednesday with 155-mph winds and a 10- to 14-foot storm surge. Flooding is already taking place in much of the area and more is expected as the system makes its way into Georgia. Be cautious. Even after hurricanes move out of an area, they often leave rivers rising and streams overflowing in their wake, and flood waters can take weeks to recede.

FLORIDA STORM WATCH

By Gabriella Gonzalez, *Herald* Reporter

Flames lick at the dark sky as fires burn in the coastal town of Mexico Beach, Florida. And they will continue to. There is no one to put them out. Mexico Beach is ground zero for Hurricane Michael. Vehicles are stacked on top of each other like a child's toys. Wooden steps lead up to beach houses on stilts that are no longer there. The beaches are flat, their dunes all washed away.

The death toll is rising and officials warn they expect the fatality count to continue climbing as search-and-rescue efforts dig deeper into the rubble left in the wake of Michael. An untold number of residents defied orders to evacuate, and for now we're left to wonder how many of them lie lifeless beneath the obliterated seaside community.

PROLOGUE

The swelling, roiling sea rises above its appointed rim.

A tsunami-like torrent rolling in.

The sea rushing ashore.

Beach cottages and seaside mansions washing away like sandcastles at high tide.

Mere anarchy is loosed upon the world,

The blood-dimmed tide is loosed, and everywhere

The ceremony of innocence is drowned;

The angry, menacing wind roars in, and with it decimation and destruction.

The falcon cannot hear the falconer;

Things fall apart; the centre cannot hold;

Toppling enormous oaks like ancient watchtowers in the pitilessness of time.

Shearing, splintering, and bifurcating tall two-decades-old slash pines like dry twigs.

Slinging steel and stone structures like wet cardboard boxes containing the stored accumulation of a lifetime.

Tossing vehicles like toys.

Turning and turning in the widening gyre;

Crushing mobile homes like empty soda cans.

Cutting a bloody path through North Florida, leaving everything leveled in its wake.

Snapping power poles. Severing electric lines. Leaving the mutilated landscape shrouded in the utter lightlessness of outer darkness.

Completely cut off from the world outside this mortally wounded one, an apocalyptic nightmare comes to fruition.

Soundless. Sightless. Unmoving. Dying in the dark.

Surely some revelation is at hand;

What will rise out of this chaos and confusion? What evil is drawn to feast on the battered remains of the reeling and vulnerable?

When a vast image out of Spiritus Mundi

Troubles my sight: somewhere in sands of the desert

A shape with lion body and the head of a man,

A gaze blank and pitiless as the sun,

A predator pulled by the pain and injury of distressed prey to storm-ravaged killing fields.

The darkness drops again; but now I know
That twenty centuries of stony sleep
Were vexed to nightmare by a rocking cradle,
And what rough beast, its hour come round at last.

1

Judge Wheata Pearl Whitehurst looks like what she is—an aging lightered knot of a Southern hardwood hippy. In that way she not only resembles the historic Potter County courthouse we're in but is better suited to it and it to her than any other judge in the area. She is a tough, stubborn, feisty, mostly genial, slightly scattered grandmother in her mid-sixties. Her round-through-the-middle, bird-like figure is mostly hidden beneath her black judicial robe, but a few rolls can be seen within the folds. Wispy strands of her strawberry-blond-fading-to-gray hair have escaped her headband to wiggle in the wind from the air-conditioning vent on the ceiling directly above her.

She looks down on her courtroom from an unusually

high bench, a light dusting of powder visible on her pale face.

Though she eventually takes in the entire courtroom, she starts with the jury.

The jury, eight women and four men, are mostly middle-aged and white, except for one black man and two black women, and though they all know me to varying degrees, they have thus far largely avoided making eye contact with me.

"Ladies and gentlemen of the jury," the judge is saying in her characteristic husky smoker's voice, "now that you have taken an oath to serve as jurors in this trial, permit me a few moments to share a few Wheata Pearls of wisdom that will get us off on the right foot, so to speak. Let me first say that though our town and county weren't really affected by the hurricane, much of the area around us was—and I'm sure we all know someone, a friend or family member, who was. This is a difficult and trying time for this region. We will be mindful of that, but because it is possible that some of the cases from the affected area might be tried in our courthouse, we must move forward, and we must do the best job we all can. It's more important in times like these than at any other.

"Now, it is my intention to instruct you on most of the rules of law, but it might be that I will not know for sure all of the law that will apply in this case until all of the evidence is presented. However, I can anticipate most of the relevant law and give it to you at the beginning of the trial so that you will better understand what to be looking for while the evidence is presented. If I later decide that different or additional law applies to the case, I will tell you. In any event, at the end of the presentation of the evidence, I will give you the final instructions upon which you must base your verdict. At that time, you will have a complete written set of these instructions, so you do not have to memorize what I am about to tell you."

Though she only mentions the jury, the penetrating gaze of her small green eyes scans the entire courtroom, pausing especially on counsel, plaintiffs, and defendant, making it clear that her *pearls* are intended for everyone.

The grand old courtroom is all polished dark woods, maybe walnut or mahogany, and smells like an old well-worn saddle—the result of Old Joe, the janitor known equally for his devotion to this hallowed hall and his devotion to Murphy's Oil Soap.

The large, echoey courtroom takes up the entire second floor of the red-brick and white-columned building that occupies the very end of South Main Street. Built back when form was elevated above or at least equal to function, the courtroom, like the courthouse and even the town, is like something out of *To Kill a Mocking Bird*. So is Wheata Pearl Whitehurst, come to that.

As the judge goes over the laws that apply to this case, I reflect again on what it's like to be on trial. I would be uncomfortable with this much attention no matter the circumstances, but for it to be so negative, so critical of my every action and the motives behind them is without question the most awkward, uncomfortable, and sustained emotional unease I've ever experienced.

In most civil cases where a cop is sued for wrongful death, the agency or department he or she works for is also sued, but for some reason—one that will no doubt come out in trial—Derek Burrell's parents chose to sue me and me alone. So in addition to my feelings of severe self-consciousness, I also feel an equally intense sense of isolation.

As difficult as it is for me to be here for all the obvious reasons, there's the added issues of the Hurricane Michael aftermath. It has only been two weeks since landfall. My hometown of Wewahitchka, the county I serve as a sheriff's investigator, and the prison where I serve as part-time chaplain all lie in ruins, in various degrees of devastation and decimation, and I want to be there helping with the recovery effort and investigating the multitude of missing persons cases we have as well as the increased crime occurring with the influx of transient and itinerant workers flooding the area. Instead, I'm here on trial in Pottersville, which was just outside the storm's path and missed most of the damage.

"I know a lot of judges frown on a lot of pre-trial instructions, but I've always found you can't go wrong giving people as much information as possible and letting them know exactly what you expect. It works with raising kids and grand-parenting grandkids, so why not with all God's children? Since I'm the ringmaster of this particular circus, let me start by telling you what I'm like and what I expect. I'm like your eccentric old grand-mother who has lived long enough to become set in her ways and not give a damn what anybody thinks of her or her ways. Like your kindly old granny, I'm mostly agree-able, and I'm genuinely pulling for you to be and do your best, but . . . I can become very cantankerous if you mess with me or get on my bad side."

As she pauses here, the creaking of wooden seats and the settling of the old building can be heard above the hum of the air-conditioning. The majority of the creaking comes from the predominately empty gallery behind us. Because many of those who would like to be here could potentially be called as witnesses, they aren't permitted to attend. That leaves a few curious townspeople, a few friends and family for the plaintiff and a few for the defendant, and the few from the school system that can't be called as witnesses. It also leaves a few reporters—all local and regional accept the two from the *Miami Herald* and the *Tampa Bay Times* who happened to be in the area covering the aftermath of Hurricane Michael. Near them is Merrick McKnight, a friend and true crime podcaster who is covering the case for the *Panama City News Herald*.

Merrick recently moved to Panama City and took the beat reporter job after he and my boss, Reggie Summers, broke up.

Since Dad and Merrill will be called to testify, only Verna, my dad's wife, and Jake, my brother, are here to support me today—and this is the only day they plan to be here until the verdict is delivered.

"I know I'm giving you a lot of information," Wheata Pearl continues. "And the truth is I'm just getting started —there's far more to come. But it's important, vital even to this sacred procedure. Please listen. Please pay attention. I'm sure you've seen and heard and read plenty about court cases in books, on TV, and in the movies, but those aren't always factual and sometimes are downright dangerous, so I'm going to tell you what's going to happen in this trial and explain it to you.

"In a few moments, the attorneys will each have a chance to make what are called *opening statements*. In an opening statement, an attorney is allowed to give you his or her views about what the evidence will be in the trial and what you are likely to see and hear in the testimony. After the attorneys' opening statements, the plaintiffs will bring their witnesses and evidence to you. *Evidence* is the information that the law allows you to see or hear in deciding this case. Evidence includes the testimony of the witnesses, documents, and anything else that I instruct you to consider. A *witness* is a person who takes an oath to tell the truth and then answers attorneys' questions for the jury. The answering of attorneys' questions by witnesses is called *giving testimony*. *Testimony* means statements that are made when someone has sworn an oath to tell the truth. The plaintiff's lawyer will normally ask a witness the questions first. That is called *direct examination*. Then the defense lawyer may ask the same witness additional questions about whatever the witness has testified to. That is called *cross-examination*. Certain documents or other evidence may also be shown to you during direct or cross-examination. After the plaintiff's witnesses have testified, the defendant will have the opportunity to put witnesses on the stand and go through the same process. Then the plaintiff's lawyer gets to do cross-examination. The process is designed to be fair to both sides."

She pauses a moment, and after sweeping back her loose strands of hair with one hand while taking a long sip of coffee from her large ceramic rattlesnake coffee mug with the other, she clears her gargley smoker's throat and continues.

"It is important that you remember that testimony comes from witnesses. The attorneys do not give testimony and they are not themselves witnesses. Sometimes the attorneys will disagree about the rules for trial procedure when a question is asked of a witness. When that happens, one of the lawyers may make what is called an *objection.*

"The rules for a trial can be complicated, and there are many reasons for attorneys to object. You should simply wait for me to decide how to proceed. If I say that an objection is *sustained,* that means the witness may not answer the question. If I say that the objection is *overruled,* that means the witness may answer the question. When there is an objection and I make a decision, you must not assume from that decision that I have any particular opinion other than that the rules for conducting a trial are being correctly followed. If I say a question may not be asked or answered, you must not try to guess what the answer would have been. That is against the rules too."

Long before these instructions to the jury, the judge had given the attorneys and, through them, their clients and witnesses, instructions regarding the scope of this trial. Since the school shooting at Potter High is part of an ongoing and very high profile investigation, we are not allowed to identify or discuss who we believe to be responsible for the incident or any other aspects of that crime. The scope of this trial is only about Derek's death and the role I played in it, and we've all been warned not to talk about anything else related to the case—in or out of court during the trial.

"After you hear the final jury instructions, you will go

to the jury room and discuss and decide the questions I have put on your verdict form. You will have a copy of the jury instructions to use during your discussions. The discussions you have and the decisions you make are usually called *jury deliberations.* Your deliberations are absolutely private and neither I nor anyone else will be with you in the jury room. When you have finished answering the questions, you will give the verdict form to the bailiff, and we will all return to the courtroom where your verdict will be read. When that is completed, you will be released from your assignment as a juror."

She pauses again and takes another pull from her rattlesnake mug. As she does she scans the courtroom, her small, intense eyes searching for anyone not paying attention, challenging anyone to dare to deign the appearance of boredom.

"Are y'all still with me?" she asks in such a way that it seems more like a demand than a question. "We're almost done with this part, so hang with ol' Wheata Pearl just a wee bit longer. Before we begin the trial in earnest, I want to give you just a brief explanation of rules you must follow as the case proceeds. Your number one job as a juror is to keep an open mind. You must pay close attention to the testimony and other evidence as it comes into the trial. However, you must avoid forming any final opinion or telling anyone else your views on the case until you begin your deliberations. It is important that you hear all of the facts and that you hear the law and how to apply it before you start deciding anything. And you must, you must, *you must* consider *only* the evidence. Only you get to deliberate and answer the verdict questions at the end of the trial. Discussing and deciding the facts is your job alone."

She gives the entire courtroom her full attention. "Again, see me as your crazy old grandma who treats all her grandkids the same," Judge Whitehurst says, "one who insists on manners and civility, who is fair and does her best to be unbiased, but who is also a hornet's nest you don't want to be sticking your hand into. Get my meaning? There will be no grandstanding in my courtroom. There will be no discourteousness. There will be no cheap tricks or whorehouse parlor games. And the only drama will be that which accompanies the suspense of waiting for the verdict. Understand?"

Everyone in the courtroom nods earnestly. Judge Whitehurst has been heard and understood.

She turns back to the jury. "Now, let me just say . . . We all have the good fortune of living in this fine small town. That means we mostly know each other—or at least know of each other. You are going to know or have connections to the plaintiffs, the defendant, the witnesses, and the attorneys in this case. I do. There's no way around it. Your job is to not base any of your conclusions or ultimately your verdict on any of that. It must be on the facts in evidence alone. Nothing else. It doesn't matter what you think of the plaintiffs or the defendant or their counsel or me or any witness. Understand?"

Again they all nod their understanding.

"And when it comes to evaluating that evidence," she says, "remember that, unlike in criminal cases, in a civil case like this one, the plaintiff has the burden of proving their case by a preponderance of the evidence, which is different than in a criminal case where the prosecutor's case has to be proven beyond a reasonable doubt. Not so here. Let me repeat—in a civil case like this one, the plaintiff only has the burden of proving their case by a preponderance of the evidence—just the slightest tipping of the scales in the plaintiff's favor."

I can feel the anxious aching hollow at the center of my core begin to expand.

Her emphasis on this reminds me of just how stacked against me those scales really are.

Next to me at the defendant's table, Anna, my wife and attorney, reaches over and puts her hand on my leg—under the table, out of view of the jury and most everyone in the courtroom. Having her here with me, representing me, is the only grace I've so far found in this entire awkward and painful process.

"Okay, now," Judge Whitehurst says, "I have only two more things to say to you and they're both incredibly important. First, this an extremely serious matter. Before you sit two broken, grieving parents who have lost a child. Across from them is a man whose very life in many ways is in your hands. Give these proceedings the gravity they deserve. Be very careful and thoughtful and deliberate. Second . . . I want to remind you of something I said before. You're about to hear opening arguments. It's vital that you remember that unlike everything else you hear during this case, these opening arguments are not facts. They are not evidence. They are merely what these lawyers intend, plan, *hope* to prove during the course of the case, not proof itself. That's why we'll be hearing only opening arguments today and will wait until tomorrow to begin the presentation of the plaintiff's case. I want you to have a clear-cut distinction in your mind between the two. Understand? Okay. That is all. Let's begin."

2

"Ladies and gentlemen of the jury," Gary Scott says, "Judge Whitehurst is right. What I'm about to say to you is not evidence. What I or Ms. Rodden say in our opening isn't proof of anything, but it *is* what we intend to prove."

Scott is a smallish, mid-fifties man with olive skin, a full head of fluffy, longish black hair, and a slight but unmistakable wet, nasally whistle quality to his voice. As if having arrived at the courtroom from a different era, he is wearing a dark gray three-piece suit with black ankle boots and a wine-colored tie with an oversized matching pocket handkerchief.

"And what I intend to prove is that the defendant, John Jordan, is guilty of wrongfully depriving Derek Burrell, a minor, of his life."

Those words, which will haunt me every day for the rest of my life, are the most difficult I've ever had to hear.

Derek's parents, Bryce and Melissa Burrell, the plaintiffs in this case, sit at the table across the aisle from me, where Scott is standing. They have the shrunken appearance of the broken, as if slowly imploding is causing them to incrementally collapse in on themselves. Their sunken faces and hollow eyes—and the distant, unfocused stares that emanate from them—speak to the dry husks of human beings they've become since experiencing the loss of losses.

"Now, as Judge Whitehurst said," Gary Scott continues, "this is a small town. I know Mr. Jordan. I went to school with him. I was a few years ahead of him but I knew him back then, and though he no longer lives here in Pottersville, I still know him today. We were never close, never big buddies or good friends, but I knew him then and know him now to be a good man. And he's not just good. He's likable. But likability doesn't prevent someone from being responsible for their actions. And good people do bad things all the time. Good people can have bad sides or personal issues that cause them to do bad things. Good people—even chaplains and sheriff's investigators—can be negligent, they can act in such a way as to actually kill an innocent human being, even a child. And that's what we believe a preponderance of the evidence in this case will prove—that Mr. Jordan acted recklessly, irresponsibly, and negligently, and that negligence caused the death of high school student Derek Burrell, which has inflicted unimaginable damage onto his parents, Bryce and Melissa Burrell."

He pauses here and takes a sip of water.

"Ladies and gentlemen, we are a nation governed by laws. Without them there would be anarchy. And no one is above those laws—no matter how much they think they might be. Not the president. Not Congress. Not the rich and powerful. And especially not those charged with upholding those laws. Especially not them. And the truth is, most of our brave men and women who protect and serve in the various law enforcement agencies in our nation are good, honest, hard-working people doing a difficult and too often thankless job. But there is a small percentage of cops—I say small, but it's far, far higher than it should be—who cross the line, who go rogue, who treat the gun and badge like a free pass to do whatever they want to. These are cops who for whatever reason— ego, testosterone, superiority complex—believe they *are* the law, believe because they're the ones doing it that it's okay, that it's lawful. They disregard all the policies and procedures and act like gods. Some do it because they're on a power trip and are abusing that power because they can. They're getting back at every girl who rejected them in high school, every boy who bullied them, and they don't ever really even think about or even care that what they're doing is wrong. But others, and I believe Mr. Jordan fits into this category, are far, far more dangerous, because they *do* think, they *do* consider, they *do* ponder, and they come to believe that they are better than the law, that they are above it and everyone else, that what they're doing is the work of God. These true believers, if you will, are far more dangerous and do far more damage than other out-of-control cops, because they feel like they have a mission, a sense of purpose, a sense of righteousness about everything they do. These are zealots. These are militants. These are the radicalized and they are walking around with all this power, with a gun and a badge and a sense of self-righteousness, all of which causes them to believe they can operate with impunity. That's how you get cops killing kids. These officers no longer protect and serve. They abuse and destroy. Not because they're monsters. Because they believe they are gods."

The jury is implacable, impossible to read, but Scott speaks as if he's feeding off the encouraging energy of his audience.

"When it comes to determining whether someone is negligent, if they're responsible for the actions they've taken, I find that it helps to put those actions in context. And the thing to look for, ladies and gentlemen, is a pattern. And there is a pattern of violence in the career of Mr. Jordan. There's a pattern of recklessness and death. I know career cops—patrol officers, detectives, deputies, investigators, sheriffs—who retired after twenty, thirty years, sometimes even more, and who never once even drew their weapon. And yet the defendant sits here today a still relatively young man, and he has not only pulled but used his weapon numerous times. That's a pattern, ladies and gentlemen. A history of violence if you will, that sheds light on the actions Mr. Jordan took on the morning of April 20, 2018—actions that resulted in the death of a stellar young man with his whole promising life before him. You'll hear how other law enforcement professionals with far more experience than Mr. Jordan would have responded to the situation. How, if Mr. Jordan had acted more professionally, more cautiously, Derek Burrell would still be alive today, in his first semester of college, enjoying a loving relationship with his new girl-friend. What I'm saying to you is that the events of April 20, 2018 weren't inevitable. They were the result of actions taken by a rogue cop cowboying about with no regard for the precious lives at stake, or for the pain and suffering a loss would cause for the poor parents forced to bury a child. One person is responsible for that—the defendant, John Jordan."

Of the competing critical voices in my head, Gary Scott's words sound remarkably like one of them.

"Too many people in power—and people who carry a gun and a badge and have the weight of the authority of the laws of our land and the constitution behind them have very real power in this country—too many of these people too often abuse that power."

Is that what I've done? What I do? I try to think over my actions—and not just in this case that I'm on trial for, but my investigative actions in general.

"In fact, do you know how much some people with power will abuse the power entrusted to them? I'll tell you how much. Just as much as the people will allow. Ladies and gentlemen of the jury, you are the people, you are *We the People*, and you have power over this rogue cop who so blatantly misused and abused his power, the power entrusted to him by law-abiding citizens for the purposes of him protecting and serving them. But he did neither. Not for the students of Potter High School. Not for Derek Burrell. Not for Bryce and Melissa Burrell. Their son is dead. And Mr. Jordan killed him. These are the facts. They are undisputed. What we are here to dispute is Mr. Jordan's responsibility, his culpability for his killing of this innocent child. We believe that after hearing the evidence during this trial, you'll reach the same conclusion we have—that Mr. Jordan acted irresponsibly and recklessly and with a negligence that I would call criminal, and that he is fully responsible, fully culpable, and must pay for his actions. And that's the only punishment we are able to mete out in a civil case. We very literally make the guilty pay. And we do this because those behind the blue wall of silence failed to exercise oversight and accountability, because those in the criminal justice system likewise failed to stand up for a slaughtered young man whose blood will forever stain the halls of his high school. The only hope of any justice at all for Derek, for his parents, for our community is within this case and the verdict you reach. I want to thank you in advance for the great job you are going to do. Unlike Mr. Jordan on that fateful Monday morning in April, I know you will be careful and thoughtful, deliberate and just. Thank you."

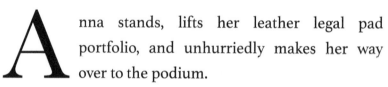nna stands, lifts her leather legal pad portfolio, and unhurriedly makes her way over to the podium.

She exudes calm and confidence, strength and stateliness, and if I were Gary Scott I'd already be considering dropping my case.

Her tailored, fitted navy pants and blazer are stylish and modern and hint at her athletic beach volleyball body. Her longish dark hair is down in sleek waves, and she is breathtaking.

Her composure seems to suggest that she is as comfortable here in this moment as at home in her sexy drawstring pajama pants and soft cotton tank that I find so irresistible.

Even if she weren't my wife I'd want her as my

attorney—and if she were just my attorney then I'd want this trial to last forever.

"Ladies and gentlemen, first I want to thank you for being here. I truly appreciate your civil service in such an important case—especially in a time when so much of the region around us is struggling and suffering. This case, and therefore your service, is far, far more weighty than you've probably yet realized—and not just to Mr. Jordan and his family, but to our society as a whole. We are blessed to live in a nation of laws. We are fortunate that we as citizens actually have oversight in the way we are policed. That's rare in the world, and that makes what you're doing truly significant."

For the past few years, the first years of our life together, Anna has been in mom mode. Her focus has been on our small children and our home and little else. And this after suffering severe trauma while pregnant and a difficult, premature delivery. And before she had fully recovered mentally, emotionally, or physically from that, her ex-husband began stalking and harassing her. She has not only been away from work and the public sphere but it has been an extremely challenging time. So for her to have the poise and confidence and skill on display here today shows just how incredibly strong and resilient she really is.

"Speaking of John's family . . ." she says, "among the many mistakes and inaccuracies plaintiffs' counsel made during his opening statement was my name. My family name was Rodden, but my married name is Jordan. I'm Anna Jordan, and I have the honor of not just being John's attorney, but his wife. And as his wife and as his lifelong friend before that, I know John Jordan better than anyone, and I can tell you without hesitation, reservation, or qualification that John is far and away the best person I've ever known. He is a man of honor. A man of compassion. A man of extraordinary decency. He has spent his life helping others—as a minister and counselor, and as an investigator. He's a man who has spent his life in pursuit of justice, and no one in this courtroom today wants justice more than John."

She pauses but doesn't take a sip of water or even look down at her notes.

During her preparation for this case, she shared with me that she was going to address the fact that she wasn't just my attorney but my wife as openly and honestly and as early in the case as she could. She also said that, given our relationship, she was going to refer to me as *John* instead of *Mr. Jordan* or *Investigator Jordan*—something she believed would have the added benefit of further humanizing me with the jury.

"Skeeter," she begins, but stops and starts again. "Sorry, *Mr. Scott*—Skeeter was his high school nickname. Mr. Scott had to acknowledge to you, though it didn't do his case any favors to do so, that John is a good man. And he is right. John is. But where Mr. Scott's narrative went off the rails completely was his suggestion that John has some sense of superiority or a god complex about what he does. Just the opposite is true. John is truly humble. I'm not talking about the false humility of a certain type of public figure, but the true humility that causes him to continually remain open and searching for truth and answers, to always seek the input and advice of others, to continually question his own assumptions and conclusions. He's the opposite of the self-righteous man on a self-imposed mission with a sense of certainty and impunity that Mr. Scott described. And throughout the course of this case you will hear from the women and men who have supervised and worked with John, those who are truly in a position to know, and they will tell you that what I'm saying is true. And with regards to this notion of John being a rogue cop . . . In the decades I've closely observed him as a detective, I've never seen him investigate a case he wasn't asked to. Just as he was in this one. There's nothing *rogue* about John. Now . . . John is a non-conformist—as Emerson noted, what man who is truly a man, isn't?— but this doesn't mean he just does what he wants to with no oversight or input. It means while gladly accepting all that, he doesn't become guilty of the group-think that is so dangerous to what is true and right. And again, we will demonstrate all of this as we put on our case and give an answer to the baseless charges that John was negligent or reckless in any way."

I could be imagining it—or more likely projecting it —but it seems to me that the jury, not to mention the judge and the rest of those present in the courtroom this morning, are far more engaged with Anna than they were with Gary Scott. The feel of the room is different, and there appears to be more eye contact and nodding of heads.

"The actions John took on April 20, 2018 were brave and intelligent and saved lives, but they also resulted in the death of a young man. A fine young man, who was obviously brave and heroic himself, but who, as the young so often are, was misguided in his efforts. As difficult as it is to say, as painful as it is for his friends and family to hear, it was the misguided and reckless actions of Derek Burrell, *not* John Jordan, that led to this tragic accident. And that's what it is—a truly heartbreaking and tragic accident. And I can tell you that apart from Derek's parents, Bryce and Melissa Burrell, no one is more heart-broken about this tragic accident than John. It's under-standable that Bryce and Melissa are devastated and looking for someone to blame for what happened. And of course they want to blame someone—anyone—but their son for what happened. We all would. But that's why you're here. You, the jury, have to look past the pain and heartbreak and unimaginable loss to see the truth of what happened. And the truth of what happened is that in the middle of a school shooting, Derek Burrell bravely, heroically, but mistakenly rushed to his truck, grabbed a weapon—something that was illegal to have on school grounds—rushed back into the school and began firing that weapon. And in addition to whoever else he fired at, he fired at John. He fired first. He fired more than once. And even believing that Derek was the active school shooter—and if you think about it, he was, just not the one who was there to kill fellow students—John still tried just to stop and not kill him. Unfortunately, one of the rounds ricocheted off of Derek's weapon and hit and killed him."

When she pauses there is only the low hum of the air-conditioning. No coughs. No creaks. No rustling of paper.

"The pain of losing a child has to be nearly unbear-able," Anna says. "John and I have three children of our own, and we can very easily put ourselves in the place of the Burrells. We can empathize with them, and our hearts genuinely do break for them—John's especially. More than you can know. Feeling compassion for them as we do, we can imagine the desire to lash out, to look for someone to blame, someone to get back at, to destroy if possible. And though we can imagine that, I hope if we were ever in their position—a position none of us ever want to be in—I hope we would resist the urge to try to inflict pain on someone else out of our pain. Again, I *get* the temptation to do so. But . . . I hope you as the jury can feel for the Burrells without feeling the need to make an innocent man pay for what they're feeling."

"You have no idea what I'm feeling," Melissa yells from her seat at the plaintiff's table.

Anna looks over at her, looks directly at her, showing nothing but understanding and compassion, but says nothing, merely waits for the judge to address the situation.

Judge Whitehurst says, "Ms. Burrell, I'm going to excuse that outburst because, like Ms. Jordan has just said, we all feel for you, but you need to remember that you brought this case, you asked for this, and that means you're going to hear and see things during the course of this case that you're going to want to react to, but you simply can't. I'm trying to my best for you and your family, your son, and Mr. Jordan. That's my sacred duty. And as part of that I can't allow outbursts in my court. You don't have to be here for this. You can step out any time you need to. But if you're going to be in here you have to withhold your reactions just like everyone else. Understand? You don't think Mr. Jordan wanted to respond to the things Mr. Scott was saying about him? I guarantee he did. But he didn't. And neither will you."

Melissa, who is crying softly, nods her head.

"We're sorry, Your Honor," Scott says, half standing,

holding his suit coat to his midsection as he does. "It won't happen again."

"See that it doesn't, Counselor," the judge says to him, then to Anna, "Please proceed, Ms. Jordan."

"Thank you, Your Honor." Anna returns her attention to the jury. "What Ms. Burrell just did is completely understandable. No one can know what she's going through. Not me. Not you. No one. But that outburst is the very thing I was talking about. She and her husband want to lash out, to strike back, and they've chosen a good man to do it to. A man involved in the terrible tragedy and horrible accident that took their soon, yes, but a good and innocent man nonetheless."

Melissa Burrell's pain is palpable, her outburst heartbreaking, but Anna couldn't have handled it any better.

"Speaking of innocence. Did you realize that every time a law enforcement officer uses his weapon, there is an investigation? Every single time. And unlike what Mr. Scott suggested, it wasn't conducted by the women and men of John's own agency, not those behind Mr. Scott's imaginary blue wall of silence. No, John's actions were objectively and thoroughly investigated by the Florida Department of Law Enforcement—a state agency with a stellar reputation that conducts investigations like this one all over the state. And with all their experience and expertise and with no allegiance to John or his department, but only to the truth, they cleared him, determining he was innocent, concluding that this was a tragic accident. And I'm confident in this trial you will reach the same conclusion."

She pauses here to give weight and resonance to her words and the point they are making.

"I'll just leave you with this," she says. "After law enforcement officers waited outside of Columbine and Parkland and other places while children were being killed inside, a brave officer didn't hesitate to run into the firing line of Potter High School. He's a hero. Not a villain. And he was fired at—more than once—by a large young man with a shotgun who was refusing to comply with his lawful orders to put down his weapon. And all of this was after John had been told by another law enforcement official that Derek was the shooter they were after. Context is everything, and these are the circumstances surrounding this shooting. During a school shooting, a very large young man with an illegal shotgun was actually firing at a police officer—that's two crimes being committed—and the experienced officer only returned fire. Didn't shoot first. And he attempted to merely wound the shooter so he could disarm him and save lives. As sad and tragic and upsetting as the death of Derek Burrell is . . . it's not due to any negligence on John's part. It's wrong that Derek is dead. But that isn't the same as John being guilty of wrongful death. I wish Derek would have remained in his classroom like he was instructed to do. I wish he had never climbed out that window and gotten his gun and come back in and started shooting. I wish he hadn't shot at John. But if anyone is to blame for any of it . . . it is the school shooter who started this massacre in the first place, not the brave officer who put his life on the line to help save the lives of our high school students and teachers. Thank you."

TAMPA BAY TIMES DAILY DISPATCH

Hurricane Michael in Real Time

By Tim Jonas, *Times* Reporter

Much of the affected areas still have no cell phone signal, no running water, and no electricity, and many residents are still unaccounted for and could be alive beneath the massive piles of rubble and debris.

Drone and helicopter footage dramatically reveal the few handfuls of structures still standing in Mexico Beach, where the monster storm made landfall.

The Florida National Guard is working its way into the most impacted areas with 13 helicopters, 16 boats, and 1,000 high-water vehicles.

Florida emergency officials say they have rescued

nearly 200 people and checked 25,000 structures since Hurricane Michael crushed portions of the Panhandle last week.

In a briefing at the state emergency operations center in Tallahassee on Friday evening, authorities said they had wrapped up their initial rapid searches and had begun more-intense searches including inspecting collapsed buildings.

Mark Bowen, head of emergency management for Bay County, said "Everything that people depend on for their daily lives has not just been disrupted, it's been absolutely destroyed."

Many of the injured were taken to hard-hit Panama City, 20 miles northwest of Mexico Beach. Gulf Coast Regional Medical Center treated some, but the hospital evacuated 130 patients as it ran on generators after Michael took out power, part of its roof, and shattered its windows.

According to the US agriculture department, Hurricane Michael severely damaged cotton, timber, pecan, and peanut crops, causing estimated liabilities as high as $1.9 billion. Michael also disrupted energy operations in the Gulf of Mexico as it approached land, cutting crude oil production by more than 40% and natural gas output by nearly a third as offshore platforms were evacuated.

Michael was the most powerful storm to hit the

United States in more than a quarter of a century, and the single most powerful to strike the Florida Panhandle. Striking like a coiled serpent, Michael sprang quickly from a weekend tropical depression to a Category 5 storm by the time it came ashore.

4

The drive back from Pottersville is slow and depressing.

The hurricane-ravaged landscape looks war-torn and post-apocalyptic.

The thousands and thousands of acres of planted slash pine forests lie decimated.

Downed trees in every direction, most of them snapped in half. Their top halves lean down to the ground or onto other trees, the splintered place that still tenuously connects them to the base looks like exposed slivers of broken bone partially protruding from skin split open by the violence of the break.

What less than two weeks ago was a vibrant timber crop worth billions now resembles a giant, jagged thorn bush thicket in a lifeless wasteland.

Pottersville was on the outer northwest wall of the storm and received very little damage, and we're now driving in the direction of ground zero of one of the most powerful storms to ever hit the continental United States.

The slow-moving traffic on the rural two-lane highway not only has far more volume than usual, but the vehicles that make up the increased inertia are the type that tend to decrease speed—trucks of every imaginable shape and size towing trailers of every imaginable shape and size, vans full of volunteers, semis loaded down with supplies, ambulances, cop cars, military Humvees, and TV news trucks. And the rusted, junker clunkers of out-of-work contractors, repairmen, and roofers looking to be the first to capitalize on both the desperation of the situation and the insurance and FEMA checks footing the bills for the first fledgling attempts at recovery.

"You were even more magnificent than I imagined you would be," I say, "and my imagination set the bar impossibly high."

In the seat next to me, Anna smiles, pats my arm, and thanks me.

"It was something to see," I add. "You're such a gifted attorney. Thank you so much for what you're doing for me."

"How was it for you?" she asks. "Had to be hard to hear the things Skeeter had to say."

I frown and give her a small nod because I can't think of anything to say that wouldn't sound either dramatic or flippant.

"How did you feel about how it went?" I ask.

"Juries are difficult to read. It's so easy to be wrong, but . . . I felt like it might have been a good beginning for us. It's just opening statements and won't mean as much as literally everything else, but . . . I was pleased overall. I definitely have some ring rust but I'll get back into trial shape soon."

"I don't think you have any ring rust at all," I say, "but if you do—not only did it not show, but poor Gary Scott doesn't stand a chance. I mean, really, how the hell do you improve on that?"

"You're sweet and biased, and whatever we do we can't underestimate Skeeter. He's deceptively good and he rarely, rarely loses a case."

Her words land like a digging body-blow that takes my breath away, as the very real possibility of losing this case comes down on me.

I know she's right. I know that the jury will see the grief and devastation of the Burrells and want to exact some sort of retribution on their behalf. I also know that regardless of the circumstances and mitigating factors, I am responsible for Derek's death, and I am the one they will want to make pay.

"Hey," Anna says, "we haven't lost yet. Don't go there."

"Can't help it," I say. "It's pretty much where I live these days."

"I know and I'm so sorry. I'm sorry that it happened. I'm sorry that you have to live with it. But just keep reminding yourself that all you did was return fire at someone who was trying to kill you. He was in the wrong. Not you. His actions created this terrible tragedy. Not yours."

It's sweet of her to say, but it was my actions too, and we both know it. I can't rationalize it. Can't justify it. Can't escape it.

At a certain point along the highway, all the leaning and fallen trees begin to lean and land in the opposite direction.

We have been told that the direction of trees is dependent on which side of the eye of the storm they were actually on, that the two sides of the storm spin in different directions. Air moving northward on the east side of a hurricane acquires clockwise spin while air moving southward west of the storm acquires counterclockwise spin.

The change in the direction of the leaning and fallen trees is surreal and jarring, but so is every other aspect of our environment these days.

"Where are we?" Anna asks. "We've traveled this road thousands of times but I have no idea where we are on it.

It's so disorienting. It's like we're in an episode of *The Twilight Zone*."

"We've entered another dimension . . ." I say. "*A dimension not only of sight and sound but of mind.*'"

"It really is what it's like."

We both look around at the storm-altered world in silence for a moment.

Eventually, Anna glances at her watch. "What's your plan when we ever get back?"

It's early afternoon on an unseasonably warm Tuesday in October—one day shy of two weeks since Hurricane Michael forever altered the landscape and our lives. We are out of court earlier than we had expected.

"Touch base with Reggie and follow up on the new missing persons reports. You?"

"I have some more work I need to do for tomorrow," she says. "Think I'll leave Taylor with the sitter a little while longer so I can get it done."

"If I get done early I'll pick her up," I say.

"Dinner at seven okay?" she asks. "I was gonna see if Carla and John Paul could join us."

I nod.

Even in this new post-apocalyptic landscape, even while on trial for the wrongful death of an adolescent boy, we have children to care for, domestic duties to coordinate.

Single mom Carla Pearson and her infant son John

Paul are part of our unofficial extended family and often join us for dinner.

"You sure?" she asks. "It's fine if you're not up for it after today."

"No, I'd like to see them. Need to actually. Just wish Johanna could be there too."

Johanna is my daughter by a previous marriage who is only with us on the weekends, holidays, and summer break, and I miss her every moment she's not here.

"I know," Anna says, "but she'll be here this weekend. Just a few more days."

Before I can respond my phone vibrates in my pocket. I pull it out and hand it to Anna to read to me since I'm driving.

"'Call me as soon as you're out of court,'" she reads. "'We've got another.'"

I wonder if she means another missing person or another body, but I don't have to wonder long. Within moments my phone starts vibrating again.

5

The hydraulic arm of the grapple truck is still extended, the claw dangling some twenty feet above the piles of debris on 2nd Street below.

This strip of 2nd Street, between Church Street and Lake Grove Road, is residential, but the old firehouse and city hall can be seen in the next block.

Traffic in both directions is stopped, restless and nosey drivers leaning out of their windows, impatience and ill-tempers intensifying more quickly in the cauldron of the post-storm environment.

The grapple truck is a super heavy-duty dump truck with a white cab and a black bed that resembles a huge, high-sided industrial dumpster. Attached to the back is an enormous hydraulic grappling claw capable of lifting large sections of giant trees. This particular type of truck is known as a double because it also pulls a trailer that looks identical to the truck's bed.

These enormous truck-trailer combos can be seen racing up and down the roads around here at all hours since shortly after the storm. The debris removal process in place involved these vehicles picking up all the trees and limbs and building material debris that citizens can pile at the edges of their property next to the road. These contracted cleanup trucks aren't allowed on private property.

For nearly two weeks now, neighbors have been helping neighbors, and volunteer groups like the evangelical organization Samaritan's Purse have been helping everyone, with the cleanup. Together they chop and cut and saw and drag and haul and pull the millions of branches and the thousands of trees mangled by Michael to the edges of every commercial and residential piece of property in the area. And almost as quickly as the piles are picked up, they are replaced by others.

There's not a street in Wewahitchka, Port St. Joe, Mexico Beach, or Panama City that isn't lined with detritus of the demon storm that unleashed hell on earth here.

When I pull up, Reggie is waiting for me. As usual of late, she is flanked by Raymond Blunt and Phillip Dean, two of the cops from Sarasota assigned to her.

Blunt is a meaty middle-aged man with deeply

tanned skin, coarse salt-and-pepper hair that never moves, and intense green eyes. He's never without the flat gold chain around his neck and the gold nuggets pinky ring on his right hand, as if they are as essential to his identity as the badge on his belt. His silent partner, Phillip Dean, is a tall, thin forty-something man with pale skin and a hairless head. They are two among many cops from around the state who have been here since the storm, aiding and assisting, protecting and serving.

As I walk up to where they're standing, Reggie is telling a couple of deputies to tape off a larger area and redirect traffic and asking Ray and Phillip to go deal with the gathering crowd.

As they move off to carry out her orders, she looks at me. "How'd it go today?"

I shrug. "Anna was spectacular, but if the jury buys into Gary Scott's narrative it won't matter much how good she is."

"They won't," she says. "The good guys are going to win this one."

The traffic in both directions is slowly turning around and drifting away.

"How many missing persons cases we got right now?" she asks.

Since the storm, we've had a rash of missing persons reports filed. Some were just loved ones from outside the area requesting wellness checks on those they were still not able to get in contact with, but many were for people who are actually missing—either displaced by the storm or their dead bodies yet to be recovered. Some victims were washed out into the Gulf during the tidal surge. Others remain beneath rubble heaps or inside debris-covered vehicles.

In addition to dealing with the aftermath of the hurricane, my court case, and trying to wrap up the investigations into the murders of Father Andrew Irwin and Joan Prescott, I have been trying to help on the many missing persons cases, but have been falling way behind.

"Ten active, I believe," I say.

"It's nine now," she says, and nods up toward the dangling grappler claw.

I follow her gaze to the tangled, jagged web of limbs caught in the claw and see human limbs mixed in with them—at least an arm and two legs are visible.

The pendulous limbs of a person peeking out of the branches suspended above us is disorienting and discordant, and I have to refocus several times to take it in.

The soiled and tattered jeans and the dirty, misshapen sneakers appear to be the ill-fitting and unwashed garments of a homeless person. Between the gaping opening of the sneaker and the faded and frayed bottom of the jeans on the right leg, the DIY-looking tattoo of a solid black circle with arrows coming out of it in every direction is visible on the filthy ankle.

"ME's investigator and FDLE crime scene are on the way, but they're going to be a while," Reggie says.

In addition to the torn-up terrain of the post-Michael landscape and the additional traffic, all agencies are operating in critical mode right now and have more to deal with than they can handle. This is truer of the medical examiner's office and its makeshift portable morgue than any other agency.

"I'm thinking we let Jessica get pictures," Reggie says, "and go ahead and bring the grappler down and see what we're dealing with. More likely than not it's an accidental death related to the storm."

I nod. "All they're going to do is bring it down once they get here."

She calls forensics officer Jessica Young over, and has her take pictures of the pile of debris the body had been a part of, then the body in the grappler from beneath, and then we call the operator back over to his truck and have him lower the arm, bringing the grappler to hang just a few feet off the ground.

As a deputy escorts the operator back behind the cordon again, Reggie, Jessica, and I ease in toward the grappler to take a look.

"That's . . . PTSD Jerry Garcia," Reggie says. "He wasn't one of our ten, was he?"

I shake my head. "We've been looking for him," I say,

"but no one turned in an official missing persons report on him."

"No one would, would they?" she says, a shade of sadness in her voice.

PTSD Jerry Garcia is the nickname for one of Wewahitchka's more colorful characters, a fringe figure with mental issues who resembles the Grateful Dead guitarist.

I find the creativity, accuracy, and ubiquity of nicknames in Southern small-town culture fascinating. If a kid doesn't pick up a nickname from his family or while in school, then it happens on a barstool in a local drinkery, at the intersection of idleness and inhibition. This latter was the case with PTSD Jerry, who had moved to town only recently.

Often heard babbling to himself and occasionally acting out like someone with shell shock, PTSD Jerry Garcia drank to excess and slept rough, but avoided altercations with law enforcement and functioned well enough to survive in an indulgent small town. Though not officially a missing person, a bartender at the Saltshaker Lounge had notified us that she hadn't seen him since the hurricane and asked if we'd keep an eye out for him.

"He smells like an old kerosene engine," Reggie says.

In addition to the sickly sweet fetid stench of decay, the pungent odor of alcohol is present.

It's obvious that's he's been dead for a while. What isn't obvious is how he died. What little visible damage to his body that can be seen could have been made by the grappler claw and doesn't appear to be the kinds of wounds that would be fatal.

Reggie says, "Is it possible he was stumbling around drunk and decided to climb inside this pile of debris to sleep and somehow got killed—more debris being piled on crushing him or something?"

"It's possible," Jessica says. "There's no obvious signs of that kind of severe trauma, but it's hard to see him and we have no idea what the back of the body looks like. Probably take the autopsy to know for sure."

I step closer and examine the body more intensely.

Like the Grateful Dead guitarist, PTSD Jerry Garcia has a full head of thick gray hair and a big gray beard. Unlike the famous front man, our Jerry's hair was always greasy, always framing a grimy face. There are other differences also. Our Jerry is—or was—a good bit younger than the original, smaller and thinner too.

His smaller, thinner body is mostly hidden by the large steel grappler and the tree debris it holds inside the tight clench of its iron fist, but there's no blood visible and no severe signs of violence—nothing obvious that can't be explained by the damage done by the grappler and limbs. His soiled, ill-fitting clothes are crumpled in a few spots that they shouldn't be and at least one of his legs is bent back in an unnatural position.

It could easily be an accidental death, and yet there's something about it that gives me pause.

I can't quite identify what it is, but something, perhaps subconsciously, is linking it to another victim I had seen recently.

Last Friday, a week and a half after the storm, I had been called to an old collapsed cottage on St. Joe Beach where a cleanup crew found the body of Philippa Kristiansen, a twenty-something waitress from Shipwreck Raw Bar. Like PTSD Jerry, we couldn't be sure if her death was accidental—we're still waiting for the autopsy results.

"What're you thinking?" Reggie asks.

I tell her.

"Please tell me they're not connected," she says. "Except by the storm."

"Probably what it is," I say. "But . . ."

"*What?*" she asks, her voice full of impatience and dread.

"The house Philippa was found in . . . It wasn't hers. We can't figure out why she was in it."

"Lots of people took refuge in whatever was still standing during the storm," she says. "Seems I recall you doing that. Maybe the place she was staying in became uninhabitable or she thought it was about to be and she runs into the one she was found in and . . . sadly it falls down on top of her."

"That's what we were thinking at first," I say. "Until . . ."

"Until what?" she asks. "I haven't received an update."

"We've got a witness that swears Philippa survived the storm," I say. "Says he saw her long after the storm had passed, long after the house she was found in had been destroyed."

6

Otto E. Hausmann is a tall, thinnish older man with pale skin and fine red hair going to gray. For reasons I don't understand, everyone calls him Pete.

He's pleasant and polite, and when he smiles it pushes up his black-framed Buddy Holly–style glasses.

"I hope you're here to tell me what exactly's going on?" he says as I near his front porch.

His small home is made of dark brick that looks like slate and sits some twenty-five feet back from 2nd Street and the sidewalk that lines this side of it. Like every other house in the area lucky enough to still be standing right now, its roof is missing a number of shingles and its yard is missing nearly all of its trees.

He stands up from the wooden rocking chair he had

been in and meets me at the bottom step with his hand extended.

The pile that PTSD Jerry was found in was on Pete's property, so while Reggie deals with the medical examiner and FDLE, I have walked over to find out what he knows.

"I'll tell you what I can," I say, "but I'm here to ask questions more than give answers."

"Least you're honest about it. Come on up and have a seat. Would you like some iced tea or a cup of coffee? Glass of water?"

There's something about him that I associate with the Midwest—a hint of it in his accent perhaps, maybe his manner and bearing, or it could be his politeness and hospitality, which though are similar to the South, are somehow also different.

I accept a glass of water and we sit in the two University of Missouri rocking chairs on the porch—each painted yellow and black with the school's tiger logo across the back.

Though he's new in town and I have no idea what brought him to Wewa, I've heard that his family was in the oil and gas business wherever he relocated from, which based on his rocking chairs I'm guessing might be Missouri.

"Can you tell me about the piles of debris on the edge of your property out by the street?" I say.

"We were told to drag everything out there and the city would have it picked up. Is that not right?"

"No, sir, it's just right. How long have your piles been out there?"

"Well," he says, pushing his glasses up on his nose. "I started dragging the smaller limbs and branches out there a day or two after the storm—soon as I got word the city would be picking it up. But . . . at my age . . . I can only do so much before I'm hunting one of these rockers and a glass or bottle of something cold. So I've just been doing a little at a time, here and there. The nice church people came with chainsaws a couple of days ago and cut the fallen trees into manageable pieces and carried them out there for me."

The "nice church people" are volunteers with Samaritan's Purse, an evangelical organization created to help people in extreme crises. Since shortly after the storm, they have been set up in the parking lot of First Baptist on Main Street, their many volunteers helping locals in a variety of ways—from distributing supplies to cleaning up debris.

"So you've added a little each day, starting with the smaller, lighter limbs, and the volunteers with Samaritan's Purse came a few days ago and cut the bigger stuff and tossed it on top?"

He nods. "That's about the size and shape of it."

"Do you know the older gentleman with the big gray beard who walks around town talking to himself?"

"Looks like Jerry Garcia? People call him PTSD? I don't know him but I know who you're talking about, of course."

"His body was found in your center debris pile."

"What? No. Please tell me you're not serious," he says. "How can . . . His body? You sayin' he's dead?"

"I'm afraid he is."

"And he was found in with my trees and limbs?"

I nod. "Any idea why he would be in there?"

"None whatsoever. Absolutely not."

"Was he around at any point while you were dragging the limbs out or while the Samaritan's Purse people were here?"

"Not that I saw," he says. "I'm trying to recall the last time I saw him. Had to be before the storm. Can't recall seeing him since . . . though might have done. Everything's so chaotic."

"Yes, it is. Anyone else live here with you who might have seen Jerry or . . ."

"Just me, I'm afraid."

"Did the Samaritan's Purse volunteers use a tractor or any heavy equipment?"

He shakes his head. "Just wheelbarrows and tarps. They'd pile the tarp with the debris and then several of them would drag the tarp around front and throw the logs and things onto the pile."

"You and Jerry ever have any kind of conflict?"

"What? No. I only spoke to him a few times—and that was just waving to him from my porch. Bet I've never been within ten to twenty feet of him. Ever. But . . . asking a question like that . . . I mean, surely it was just an accident, right?"

7

I notice Reggie stiffen a bit and run her hand through her hair.

A thick-bodied tomboy who dresses down and rarely wears makeup, yet is naturally attractive, even pretty in an unfussy way, it's funny to see Reggie act in any way that shows concern for her appearance.

I turn and follow her gaze over to the small crowd gathered on the other side of the crime scene tape and see that Merrick McKnight is among the reporters and onlookers. He and the other reporters are talking to Raymond Blunt, who is on this side of the cordon beside Phillip Dean who, as usual, isn't speaking.

"He was at the trial today," I say.

"Who?"

I let out a little laugh. "Are you nervous to see him?" I ask. "I thought you were the one who broke things off."

"It's complicated."

"I read somewhere that things with former lovers can be," I say with a smile.

"That's helpful," she says. "Thanks. And I *hate* that term."

"What term is that?"

"Lovers," she says. "We were *lovers*," she adds, drawing it out and making her voice sound like a '70s WASP newly initiated in the Free Love movement. "He's my *lover*. We're former *lovers*."

"Well, when you say it like that . . ."

"It doesn't bother you?"

"I have a different context," I say. "A much older one."

"Oh, yeah, what's that?"

"Ancient religious poetry," I say. "Hebrew Bible. Song of Songs. Rumi. 'Lovers don't finally meet somewhere, they're in each other all along.'"

"I don't know," she says. "Sounds the same to me."

"Well, it's not," I say. "Not even in the same realm. But I'm about to step over and speak to your former *lover*. Would you like to join me?"

She punches me in the arm, and we begin to drift over toward him.

"And I'll buy you lunch if you work *lover* into the conversation," I say.

"I'll buy *yours* if you don't," she says.

"I was just tellin' these fine, outstanding members of the press that we'll release information to them as soon as we have any to release," Ray says as we walk up.

"Hey, Reggie," Merrick says. "How are you?"

Ray's thick eyebrows raise and he gives a sideways glance to the familiarity and even intimacy with which this particular fine, outstanding member of the press addresses the sheriff.

"*Hey*," she says. "How'd you do during the storm?"

"Both my apartment complex and the *News Herald* building got hit hard."

"So you need a place to stay," I say.

"How's it going, John?" he says.

"You tell me," I say. "What'd you think of the opening statements?"

"Anna ate his lunch," he says. "Don't you guys agree?"

He turns and looks at the *Miami Herald* and *Tampa Bay Times* reporters and photographers standing nearby.

National media coverage of Michael—especially post storm—has been next to nil. But the *Tampa Bay Times* has had its reporter and photographer in the area since just before landfall, and the *Miami Herald* wasn't far behind, and at this point about the only non-local and regional coverage we're getting is from them.

"We're objective journalists," the only woman in the

small group says. "We don't have opinions. But if I did I'd say your wife is a badass and really mopped the floor with ol' Skeeter."

"John, Reggie, this is Gabriela Gonzalez," Merrick says. "She's a reporter for the *Miami Herald*. And this is Grover Arnold—her photographer."

The tall, pale, soft *Herald* photographer says, "Well, I don't exactly belong to *her*. Though she certainly acts like I do."

"Sorry," Merrick says. "Didn't mean—"

"Just fuckin' with you dude," he says. "It's all good."

"And that's Tim Jonas and Bucky Swanson from the *Tampa Bay Times*," he says, nodding toward the smallish, boyish-looking Tim and the old, grizzled, hippie-looking Bucky.

"I'm his photographer," Bucky says, nodding toward Tim. "And I *do* belong to him."

Tim says, "You know what they say . . ." his intense blue eyes twinkling in a way that make him look even more boyish. "When in North Florida . . ."

"People still own people up here, don't they?" Bucky says.

"This is our last day here," Gabriela Gonzalez says to Reggie, "but I'd love to do a feature on you. Not many female sheriffs anywhere, but especially not in the Deep South."

"Where people still own people," Bucky says.

"As much as I hate stuff like that," Reggie says, "I'd consider doing it if it'd keep y'all here. Y'all are about the only coverage we're getting."

"Our editor pulled us after the first week," Bucky says, "but once we got home and saw the dearth of attention this clusterfuck was getting, young Tim with the big brass balls told him we were coming back up here even if it meant we wouldn't have jobs when we finally returned home again."

"No way he'll let us stay much longer either," Tim says. "Big balls or not. And I hate it. Nobody outside of here really understands what's going on inside here. Nobody's talking about it much and there's gonna be no significant help if our coverage doesn't move the needle some. We've seen it before—initial help to deal with the emergency crisis and then . . . very little help to actually recover and rebuild."

"What have you got?" Merrick asks, nodding over toward the grappler.

"Not sure yet," Reggie says. "We're waiting on FDLE."

"Is it a suspicious?" he asks.

"It's a *off the record*," she says, mocking him playfully. "But the truth is we don't know enough to be able to say anything for sure yet."

"Give us *something*," Merrick says.

"I told you I would as soon as I could," Raymond

Blunt says as if he's been appointed media liaison instead of crowd control.

Observing everything and everyone, wordlessly, implacably, Phillip Dean looks down from his high vantage point in a way that feels invasive and more than a little creepy.

"Yeah," I say. "It's the least you can do for a former lover."

Reggie's lips twitch and she tries not to smile.

"A do what now?" Gonzalez says.

"You couldn't tell?" Ray says. "I could tell. Just by the way they spoke to each other. Cops know people. Thought reporters did, but . . . guess not."

Beside him Phillip smiles but doesn't say anything.

"You been holding out on us, Merrick?" Tim Jonas says.

"Thanks, John," Merrick says with a smirk.

"It's an awkward time to bring this up," Reggie says to Merrick, "but if you and the kids need a place to stay, you know y'all are always welcome with us."

The other reporters and photographers react with whoas and whistles.

"Thank you," he says. "That's really good of you."

"Talk about an exclusive," Bucky says.

"Again, thanks, John," Merrick says.

I start to respond but stop as I see Randa Raffield step up to the crime scene tape about twenty feet away.

Merrick and Reggie follow my gaze.

"What the fuck?" Merrick says.

"I'm gonna go find out," I say.

"I'll call Liberty to see what's going on and radio our deputies to grab her if she tries to run," Reggie says.

8

"Hey, John," Randa says.

She is a mid-thirties white woman with pale skin, auburn hair, and impossible-to-read green eyes.

"Randa," I say. "How are you?"

"I'm good," she says. "Really good. How are you?"

Since I arrested Randa, she's been housed at the jail in Liberty County—the facility all female inmates from Gulf County are housed in because we have a male-only jail here.

"What're you doing here?" I ask.

"Heard you had a body," she says, nodding toward the grappler. "Just wanted to see what was going on."

"But how—"

"Oh, you mean . . ." she says. "I'm a free woman now,

John. I was acquitted. I mean, we both knew I would be, right, and it finally happened. Took a while, but . . . that's to be expected. What was it Dr. King said? 'The arc of the moral universe is long, but it bends toward justice.'"

I smile at that.

"I know. I know. It's a bit grandiose to quote King, but I did get justice. Just like I hope you will in your trial. How's it going, by the way? I wanted to be there this morning but it didn't work out."

The subject of a popular true crime podcast and many online conspiracy theories and irrational rabbit holes, Randa Raffield was at the center of one of the most compelling and fascinating missing persons cases of the past two decades.

On Thursday, January 20, 2005, the day of George W. Bush's second inauguration, Randa Raffield, a twenty-one-year-old student at the University of West Florida, crashed her car on a secluded stretch of Highway 98 near the Gulf of Mexico not far from Port St. Joe. The location of the wreck was hundreds of miles from where she was supposed to be. Moments after the accident, Roger Lamott, a truck driver hauling fuel, came upon the scene. Randa refused his help, asked him not to call the police, and said she preferred to wait alone for the towing service she had already called. After pulling away, Lamott called the police anyway. Seven minutes later when the first Gulf County sheriff's deputy arrived, Randa was gone, vanished without a trace. And she stayed gone until a couple of years back when Merrick McKnight and Daniel Davis started a true crime podcast about the case and asked for my help investigating it.

One of the more complex and complicated people I know, I still have no idea whether Randa is a damaged vigilante avenger or a psychopathic serial killer. What I do know is that she's both interesting and dangerous, and that life was simpler while she was incarcerated.

"What're you still doing here?" I ask. "Figured you'd be long gone the moment you got out."

"This place really grows on you, you know?" she says. "I was already thinking about staying—actually, thought we might work a few cases together or something—but now with the storm . . . I figured I'd stick around and help with the recovery. It'd give me a chance to give back."

My phone vibrates and I pull it out and glance at it. It's a text from Reggie saying that the Liberty County jail said Randa had been released after her case was dismissed. Evidently the state's attorney's office had concluded they didn't have enough evidence to bring the case to trial and, after trying to bluff Randa into taking a deal didn't work, had to dismiss it. They meant to inform us but then the storm happened and well . . .

"There's plenty to do," I say.

Reggie walks up and says, "You've never struck me as a manual-labor kind of girl."

"I'm full of surprises," she says. "How are you, Reggie? I actually wanted to talk to you about possibly coming to work for you. As you know I've been a bit of an armchair —or what is it they call it these days, oh yeah—*citizen detective* with a pretty good track record. Even bested ol' John here a time or two."

"I'm pretty sure he got the best of you every time," Reggie says.

"Well, either way, I think I'd like to try my hand at official detecting. I certainly have unique experiences and perspectives."

"Sure," Reggie says. "Drop by my office after we've recovered from the hurricane a little more and we can discuss it. We'll get you set up with a psyche evaluation and some of the other prerequisites."

"I noticed you haven't made an arrest in the Father Irwin and Joan Prescott cases," Randa says. "Maybe I could help with those."

"We're going to make an arrest," she says. "As soon as the initial crisis is over and we have a functioning DA and courthouse again."

"Randa fuckin' Raffield," Merrick says as he and the other journalists walk up behind her.

"Hey Merrick."

"Haven't seen you since you kidnapped my best friend," he says.

"I keep tellin' everyone . . ." she says. "I didn't kidnap

anyone. Daniel and I just went on a little getaway together. He could've come back anytime he wanted to—and eventually he did."

"Hi, Randa," Gabriela Gonzalez says. "I'm a reporter for the *Miami Herald*, and I'd love to do a feature story on you."

"But unfortunately she's leaving tomorrow," Tim Jonas says. "But I'm gonna be here for a while, so I could really give your story the time it deserves. I'm Tim Jonas and I'm with the *Tampa Bay Times*, by the way. Florida's largest newspaper."

"Wow," Randa says. "Y'all really make a girl feel good. What about you, Merrick? You don't want in on a piece of this action for the *News Herald*?"

"Want no part of it," he says. "And I wish you didn't even know I worked for the *News Herald*. Stay away from me, my friends, and my family."

"You came over to me, Merrick," she says. "Not the other way around. But don't worry, I won't be showing up at the *News Herald* trying to see you. Of course, from what I've heard there's not a lot of the *News Herald* left. And you have my word that I won't take Daniel along on any more excursions—no matter how much he begs me."

"Well, we've got to get back to work," Reggie says, trying to conceal her annoyance. "We'll have a press release ready for y'all later this afternoon."

"We'll be looking forward to it," Gonzalez says. "And

maybe later you and I could sit down for a quick interview."

"I have some thoughts on what happened here," Randa says, nodding toward the grappler and holding out business cards to me and Reggie. "Give me a call if you'd like to hear them."

9

"She already has business cards," Anna says. "How long has she been out?"

"Not long at all," I say.

"Unbelievable."

"Really is," I say.

We are in our kitchen. I'm at the stove making dinner. She is at the table preparing for tomorrow.

"She still fixated on you?" she asks.

"I'm not sure she ever was, but . . . didn't seem to be. She did mention maybe working cases together. She actually asked Reggie for a job."

"Can you imagine?" she says. "Randa with a gun and a badge."

Carla has taken Taylor and John Paul for a stroller ride to Lake Alice Park. We will eat when they return.

I've just gotten off the phone with Sam Michaels, my FDLE friend in Tallahassee, letting her and Daniel know that Randa is out of jail, though I'm sure Merrick has already notified Daniel.

We're getting a later start on dinner than we wanted to and I got less done this afternoon because of how long it took with the ME's investigator and the FDLE crime scene unit.

I'm trying not to disturb Anna, but when she initiates conversation I tell her things I remember from my day. As I stir the spaghetti sauce into the browned ground beef, I tell her about Reggie and Merrick's interaction.

"Really," she says. "She actually invited him to stay with her?"

"And she meant it."

"But in a *I want you back* or a *I'd do this for anyone after the storm* kind of way?"

"I'm not sure."

"Think he'll take her up on it?"

"No idea," I say, "but I hope he will."

She stops what she's doing and looks up at me with a smile on her face. "You hope they'll get back together, don't you?"

"Of course, I do," I say. "You don't?"

She smiles. "My husband the romantic."

"What's not to love about love?" I say.

"Where you're concerned my dear?" she says. "Absolutely nothing."

"Speaking of . . ." I say. "What's your stance on the term *lover*?"

LATER, after dinner and giving Taylor a bath and putting her to bed, Anna and I are in our own bed, each of us sitting up, propped on pillows against the headboard, our work on the bed in front of us.

Anna is still working on the case.

I am looking through the files of every death we've had in Gulf County since the hurricane. Both the Philippa Kristiansen and PTSD Jerry Garcia cases not only seem suspicious, but make me wonder if perhaps other deaths deemed accidental might not be.

At this point, Philippa's death seems more suspicious than Jerry's, but it's possible that neither of them are, that they're both what they appear to be—accidents caused by the storm. But I can't be sure, and it's causing me to look at all the deaths during and after the storm differently.

As usual when in the bed with Anna, especially when she's in her soft, sexy pajama bottoms and cotton tank top, I'm finding it extremely difficult to concentrate on anything but her.

She smells so good, her quiet breathing so deep and

rhythmic, and through the soft fabric of her tank top I can make out the faint impression of her nipples.

"Thank you again for how very hard you're working on this case for me," I say.

"Truly my pleasure," she says. "I literally can't imagine entrusting it to anyone else."

"Me either."

"You finding anything interesting?" she asks without looking up.

I shrug. "I'm just not sure. I just keep thinking that a hurricane is the perfect time for making a murder look like an accident. I'm probably reading too much into this, but some of these deaths seem so much more suspicious than they were believed to be by the investigators at the time."

"What did the ME's investigator say about Jerry?" she asks. "I wish we knew his real name."

"I know. We're working on finding out what it is. She said that we'd have to wait for the autopsy for any kind of determination but that the trauma to the body, which included a fatal blow to the back of the head, could've been done by a 2x4, a baseball bat, or the limbs in that pile. But the FDLE crime scene unit discovered blood and other biological matter on at least one of the limbs, which seems to indicate that striking his head on it is what killed him."

"So . . . his is most likely an accident, but you think there could be others that might not be?"

"Maybe. I don't know. I'm probably just trying to keep my mind off the trial."

"I might be able to help with that," she says.

"There's no might about it, but . . . I'd hate to take you away from your work on the case and . . . I'm not sure I can afford the additional billable hours."

"*Hours?*" she asks with a wry smile.

"Okay," I say. "Well, at least *several minutes.*"

NEWS HERALD SPECIAL REPORT

Opening Arguments heard in Potter High School
Shooting Wrongful Death Suit

By Merrick McKnight, *News Herald* Reporter

Opening arguments were heard yesterday in the
wrongful death suit brought against Gulf County Sheriff
Investigator John Jordan by the parents of Derek Burrell.
Bryce and Melissa Burrell claim that John Jordan was
negligent in his duties when he shot and killed their
seventeen-year-old son Derek in the hallway of Potter
High School during the school shooting that took place
there on April 23, 2018.

The judge in the case is the honorable Wheata Pearl
Whitehurst. The plaintiffs are represented by attorney

Gary Scott. The defendant is being represented by Anna Rodden Jordan, who is not only an attorney but also the defendant's wife.

The trial is expected to last a little over a week. Check back here for daily updates.

10

"Mr. Glenn," Gary Scott says, his nasally voice whistling slightly. "What is your current position?"

"I'm the sheriff," he says. "Here in Potter County."

We are back in court the next morning, at the very beginning of the plaintiffs' case. There are more people in the courtroom today, and among them is Randa Raffield, who sits on the same row, though on the opposite end, as Merrick, Tim, Bucky, and the other reporters. She is striking—even from this distance—the contrast between her deep auburn hair and extremely pale skin making her stand out among those seated in the gallery. I have no idea what Randa is up to, but her presence here has to cause far more anxiety for Merrick than it does for me. He and Daniel were obsessed with her and her case so intensely and for so long, and then for it to resolve the way it did and then have her back in his life—even just sitting on the same row in a courtroom as him has to be as difficult as it is surreal.

Today in addition to the print journalists, there are a few regional TV news reporters—not allowed to have their cameras inside the courtroom, they sit taking notes like all the others.

I'm not surprised that Scott is calling Hugh Glenn or that he's starting with him, but I am interested in what he's going to say. He is close with both Scott and the Burrells, and I wonder to what extent that will determine what he has to say. Of all the testimonies to be given, this is the one that Dad most wants to hear and I wish he could be here for it.

"Sheriff Glenn, thank you for being here today," he says. "And as sheriff you're the chief law enforcement officer of the county. Is that right?"

"Yes, sir. I am."

"And what does that mean exactly?"

"Well, that I have complete jurisdiction and that the only one over me is God."

Scott laughs at that like it's the funniest thing he's ever heard. "Is it fair to say that no one is allowed to come into this county and practice law enforcement without your permission?"

Glenn gives a kind of half-shrug half-nod and says, "Yeah, I guess that'd be fair to say."

"Could you take a moment and just tell us a little about your law enforcement background? How long have you been sheriff and what did you do prior to that?"

I feel fairly confident that Glenn is not going to mention that he was one of the laziest and least motivated deputies Dad ever had.

"I've been sheriff of Potter County for about the past three years."

"And who did you defeat in the election to become sheriff?"

"The long-time former sheriff here, Jack Jordan."

"And what if any relation is he to the defendant?"

"It's . . . he's his father."

Though he doesn't seem particularly nervous, Hugh Glenn is awkward, many of his phrases coming out stilted, their words in unusual or unnatural orders.

"I actually worked for him for a number of years before becoming sheriff. Rose up through the ranks in the department. I was a deputy mostly, and I loved it. But it is the honor of my life to serve as sheriff. My proudest accomplishment. I love our community . . . the great people here."

"So, is it fair to say that the Jordans are your political enemies?"

He shakes his head. "No, I wouldn't say that. I try not

to have any enemies. And honestly, both Jack and John have never been anything but gracious to me—even in defeat. No, we're not enemies. I wouldn't say that."

"That's good to hear," he says. "Though just because you don't consider someone to be an enemy doesn't mean they feel the same way, does it?"

"Objection, Your Honor," Anna says. "Not only does it call for Mr. Glenn to speculate as to what other people may or may not feel, but it's inflammatory and he knows it."

"Sustained," Wheata Pearl Whitehurst says from the bench. "Play nice, Mr. Scott. Don't make me have to tell you again."

Today several strands of the judge's straw-textured and strawberry blond-colored hair flutter in the wind from the vent above her, but unlike other times she makes no attempt to press them down.

"Sorry, Your Honor," he says.

He takes a moment to gather himself, taking a sip of water as he does.

"Sheriff Glenn," he continues, "when exactly did you hire the defendant?"

"I'm sorry?"

"When did you hire Mr. Jordan to work for the Potter County Sheriff's Department?"

"I don't understand. I didn't."

"Does Mr. Jordan work for your department?"

"No, sir, he doesn't."

"Do you mean now?" Scott asks. "Surely at the time of the shooting he—"

"No, sir, John has never worked or me. As far as I know he's never worked for the department—not even when his dad was running the place."

"So you're saying that at the time John Jordan shot and killed Derek Burrell, he wasn't working for the Potter County Sheriff's Department?"

"No, sir, he wasn't."

"Well then can you tell us what he was doing there? Why he was even involved in the shooting?"

"I'm sure he was just wanting to help."

"'Wanting to help,'" he says. "Did you know he was going to be there that morning *helping*?"

"No, sir, I didn't."

"You didn't?"

"No, sir."

"But you're the chief law enforcement officer of the county—right under God. And you had reason to believe there was going to be a school shooting, right?"

"We did. A deputy of mine found some evidence and based on everything we knew, we believed that the shooting would take place on Friday, April 20."

"Did you ask Mr. Jordan to help with the investigation or the task force that attempted to stop the shooting that y'all thought was going to happen on the 20th?"

"No, sir, not exactly."

"What do you mean 'not exactly'?"

"Well, what I mean is he was involved and I knew it and I even discussed the case with him, so . . . just like I did with a lot of the others helping us out, but I didn't ask him to be involved . . . is what I mean. We had several different agencies involved in an attempt to stop the shooting before it happened on the day we thought it was going to occur so that no one—especially a student— would be injured or killed, and John was involved as a part of that."

"But a student was killed, wasn't he?"

"Unfortunately, yes, sir. He was."

"And it was Mr. Jordan who killed him, wasn't it?"

"Yes sir, but—"

"Please just answer the questions you're asked, Sheriff."

"Yes, sir."

"If you didn't ask John Jordan to be involved in the case, who did?"

"I'm not sure exactly. I don't . . . My understanding is that the deputy who discovered the notes that made us think there might be a shooting in the first place may have mentioned it to John or his father, the former sheriff."

"So you're telling us that John or his dad got involved without your invitation or permission?"

"Well . . ."

"Just yes or no, please."

"Well, yes, I guess, but . . . I mean, if you're gonna put it like that and those are my only options."

"I really don't think there is any other way to put it," Scott says. "Sheriff, isn't it true that in most civil suits like this one where a law enforcement officer is involved, the agency that officer works for is a co-defendant?"

"I believe so, yes."

"Do you know why that is?"

"I believe it's because the agency or municipality behind it has deeper pockets—more for the plaintiffs to potentially get."

"Yes, that is correct. Just so. So can you tell me why the plaintiffs in the case aren't suing the Potter County Sheriff's Department or the Gulf County Sheriff's Department?"

"Objection," Anna says. "Calls for speculation."

"Sustained."

"Well, that's okay," Scott says. "We'll get to hear from Derek's parents themselves why they chose to only sue Mr. Jordan."

"Your Honor," Anna says, "Counsel is testifying, not asking questions."

"Sustained," the judge says again. "Mr. Scott, do you have any other questions for this witness?"

"Just one, Your Honor," Scott says. "Sheriff Glenn,

given everything you know about the defendant and especially after the actions he took at Potter High School that resulted in the death of Derek Burrell, if Mr. Jordan applied for a job in your department, would you hire him?"

"No, I don't think I would."

11

"Mr. Glenn, you testified that you are right under God when it comes to law enforcement in Potter County," Anna is saying.

"It was just a way of explaining that each sheriff is the chief law enforcement officer in his county."

"Or hers."

"Huh? Oh, yeah, well, are there any female sheriffs in the state of Florida?"

"There are," Anna says. "There's Reggie Summers in neighboring Gulf County."

"Yeah, I guess, but she was appointed. I meant—"

"And there's Sheriff Susan Benton of Sebring who has been elected for three terms so far."

"Sorry," Glenn says in way that makes it obvious he's not. "Don't call the politically correct police on me."

"There is no such thing," she says, "but if there were and it were in Potter County it would be under your jurisdiction, right?"

"Right."

"So, you have jurisdiction over Potter County, but who's really in charge?"

"I am."

"I know you were voted into the office, but I'm asking who actually runs it."

"I do."

"But you know what I'm asking. Who's really in charge?"

"I do know what you're asking and the answer is me," he says. "I don't . . . I'm in charge."

"Well, who did you appoint to run the school shooting task force?"

"I did it. I had plenty of help. But I ran it."

"How many meetings—official or not—did you have about trying to stop the potential school shooting at Potter High?"

"I'm not sure exactly," he says. "Quite a few if you count them all."

"Of the main meetings with most of those assisting with the attempt to prevent the shooting from happening, how many was John at?"

"Most, maybe all of those main ones."

"Did you ask his opinions, involve him in the discussions and the decisions?"

He nods. "I did, some, yeah."

"You're the chief law enforcement officer in the county, you're in charge of your department, you're in charge of the school shooting task force, John is at the meetings, and you involve him and ask for his input, but you're going to imply that he was just there, that you didn't invite him to participate, that he didn't have your explicit or implicit permission, even blessing, to be involved?"

Glenn clears his throat.

"And Sheriff, before you respond, let me just say that during the defense portion of the case, I'll be calling as witnesses several people present in those meetings."

"I didn't mean to imply he was just there or didn't have my permission," he says. "I merely answered the question did I invite him to participate in the task force, and I did not."

"But you knew that someone who worked for you had asked him to participate?"

"Yes, ma'am, I did."

"And you never asked John to leave, did you?"

"No."

"On the contrary, you asked for his opinions and actively enlisted his help, didn't you?"

"I . . . I asked everyone at those meetings for their input."

"But did you ask John specifically?"

"Yes."

"Now, let's go back to this notion of jurisdiction for a moment," she says. "You said that you have jurisdiction over Potter County, is that correct?"

"Yes, ma'am, I do."

"Does that mean no one else has jurisdiction?"

"Right."

"So when I leave here today, if I decide to speed down one of the streets of Pottersville, you're telling us that a Florida Highway patrol officer can't pull me over and write me a ticket?"

"Yes. I mean, no. They can."

"They're not in your department, not under your jurisdiction," she says.

"But that's on the road," he says. "They have jurisdiction on the roads."

"Okay, well could a game warden pull me over for speeding?"

He hesitates but then nods slowly. "Yes, ma'am. They could."

"What about the Florida Department of Law Enforcement, could they come into Potter County and investigate —you for instance?"

He nods but doesn't say anything.

"We need a verbal response for the record, please," Anna says.

"Sorry, yes, they could."

"Sheriff Glenn, are you familiar with Florida's mutual aid agreement?"

"Yes, ma'am."

"What is it?"

"Ah, basically it's an agreement between all the sheriff's departments in all the counties in Florida."

"An agreement for what?"

"Basically it says that if a law enforcement officer sees a crime being committed, he has the right to intervene—even if it's not in his county."

"Not in his normal jurisdiction?"

"Right."

"And the agreement says that he's afforded the same rights and protections an officer from that county receives?"

"And the responsibilities too," he says.

"Is the answer to my question yes or no?"

"Yes. It's yes."

"Thank you. Now . . . Just one more question for you. If you were at a sheriff's conference in Orlando and you stopped to refuel that big black SUV you drive and you saw a robbery in progress inside the convenience store, would you intervene, try to save lives, attempt to stop the perpetrators, or would you say, not my county, not my problem?"

"I'd intervene," he says.

"Thank you."

"But I'd try to do it without injuring or killing any of the innocent bystanders."

Hugh is clearly trying to land one last punch for the plaintiffs.

Instead of asking the judge to correct him or direct him to only answer the questions she asks, she shows not even the slightest irritation at his insolence.

"You said you'd *try* not to injure or kill anyone—"

"Right."

"Does that mean you couldn't guarantee it in that situation?"

"Well, you can . . . you could try real hard."

"Do you have any evidence to suggest that John didn't try real hard to save lives, to protect everyone but the shooter in the school that day?"

He shakes his head. "No, ma'am."

"Have you ever been in an active shooter situation?" she asks.

"No, ma'am," he says, and actually knocks on the wood of the jury box.

"But if you were . . ."

"I'd protect the lives of the innocent and put the shooter down."

Anna nods and pauses for just a moment.

"And what is the official law enforcement definition of an active shooter?"

"Just what you'd think it was," he says, some of his confidence and swagger back. "Someone with a gun shooting at civilians and/or law enforcement."

"I see, and based on that definition, was Derek Burrell an active shooter?"

12

During the recess for lunch, while Anna works on the case, I check in on Taylor and Johanna then briefly touch base with Reggie before calling the ME's office.

I had asked for prelim autopsy results as soon as they had them, and I had missed a call from one of the investigators while we were in court this morning.

His name is Leno Mullally, and he's a youngish, slightly offbeat and socially awkward investigator with the office.

"I'm at lunch," he says. "You mind me talking with my mouth full?"

"Not at all," I say. "I'd say I'd let you eat your lunch in peace, but I don't have long and then I'll be back in court all afternoon."

"No problem. I wouldn't know how to eat lunch in peace anyway. I really wouldn't. Especially these days. It's like a war zone."

"Yeah, I was surprised to get your message, but I really appreciate y'all getting to it so quickly."

"Just how the bodies bounce sometimes."

That's such an odd remark, I'm not sure how to respond.

We are quiet an awkward moment, which consists mostly of me listening to him chew.

In the absence of conversation I imagine what he's eating. In my imaginings it's exotic and pungent, leftover from a meal he made for himself the night before.

"Well," he says finally, "I can tell you . . . there's not much I can tell you. This is a strange one. The body is banged up pretty bad. Got all manner of injuries, but mostly internal. There are very few lacerations, abrasions, or even brushing on the skin. It's mostly blunt force trauma, and it occurred so close to when he died that his heart stopped and therefore blood flow stopped and therefore not much bruising. And there was very little blood loss because of how few lacerations there were. Meaning whatever hit him wasn't sharp, which fits with the large, rounded tree limb we found the blood on. That came from a particularly nasty blow to the back of the head, which is what killed him—fractured his skull and gave him a massive subdural hematoma. Like I say, it's likely it happened as a result of the limb striking him or his head striking the limb. What I'm saying is that I can't really say it wasn't caused by the tree limb—or that all his injuries weren't caused by the pile of limbs he was found in, though to be honest I can't really figure out how exactly it would happen. It'd be one thing if it had just happened. If he had just died and there was blood everywhere and fresh injuries—then we'd know it happened when the grappler lifted him and the debris. But with him already being dead—and I'd estimate he'd been dead a while—it's hard to see how just being in the pile of limbs could have resulted in the trauma to his body. And yet his blood and brain matter was found on one of the limbs and the fixed lividity fits the position his body was found in. So . . . I don't think it was moved after death—at least not hours after death. I'll tell you this . . . if someone did kill him and put him in there . . . they did a damn good job of making it impossible to prove it wasn't an accident."

"Okay," I say. "Thank you. I really appreciate it. Can you give me an estimate of how long he's been dead?"

"Best guess is between forty-eight and seventy-two hours."

"And there are no injuries inconsistent with an accident caused by those limbs?"

"No, not really. I don't know. It just seems a stretch that they could've done it, but . . . I can't say they didn't."

"Okay. Thanks again."

"There is one other anomaly . . . and it could've happened in the pile or as he was being picked up by the grappler, but . . . his right tibia bone was broken . . ."

I recall the unnatural way his right leg bent to the side at the bottom.

"It was broken after death," Mullally is saying. "The only bone that was broken. And the more I think about it the more I think it confirms accidental death. It'd be very difficult for a person to do—and why would they after he was already dead?"

13

"I 'm Randal Todd. My stepmom was the art teacher at Potter High School."

He's a tall, thin, fair mid-twenties man with very faint freckles and short, wavy light brown hair. Sincere and soft-spoken, he's likable and easy to empathize with.

I didn't know Janna all that well, and apparently I didn't even know her as well as I thought I did. I had no idea she had a stepson.

"*Was?*" Gary Scott asks, his emphasis on the word increasing his voice's nasality.

"She was killed in the school shooting that happened here last spring."

I'm surprised Scott has called Janna Todd's stepson to testify, and I'm wondering what he can possibly offer as evidence that wouldn't be hearsay.

"I'm so sorry to hear that," Scott says. "You have my deepest sympathies. So the makeshift task force investigating and trying to prevent the school shooting failed to prevent it from happening and failed to keep students and faculty from being killed."

"Yes, sir."

"Now, Randal, did your stepmom have a second job?"

"Yes, sir. She did. When she and my dad split up, she needed to make some extra money, so she started bartending at the Oasis."

"What is the Oasis?"

"Kind of like a sports bar here in town."

"How well are you acquainted with the place?"

"Pretty well."

"Are you a big drinker?" Scott asks, as if he doesn't know the answer already.

Randal lets out a low laugh. "Actually, I don't drink. I've seen firsthand how stupid some people get when they've had too much."

"So, if you don't drink, how can you be well acquainted with this drinking establishment that your stepmom worked at?"

"I worked there too. Still do."

And now I think I know why he has been called to testify, and as my heart begins to simultaneously beat faster and sink into my stomach, I wonder if Anna has figured it out and is prepared. She has talked to me about many aspects of the case, even had me help prep her for some of the witnesses, but not this one.

"Doing?" Scott asks.

"Lots of different stuff, but mostly I'm a barback."

"A what?"

"What's known as a barback. I back up the bartender —mostly restocking. Changing out kegs. Reloading the coolers. Making sure the bartender has everything she needs."

"Did you and your stepmom work the week of the school shooting?"

"Yes, sir, we did. Every night that week."

"What, if anything, do you remember about it?"

"I remember the defendant coming in and drinking with some of the other cops and people involved in the investigation. Heard them talking about it. Plus Janna told me about it."

A new wave of guilt crashes over me, a new level of embarrassment and self-consciousness. My face feels like I have a sudden sunburn, and my heart races as beads of sweat pop out all over my body.

I remember a lot about that night, but I don't remember this young man being there.

"You saw the defendant drinking alcohol? The week of the shooting?"

"The night before."

"The night before?" Gary asks in surprise. "Are you sure?"

"Positive. It surprised me and Janna 'cause he's an alcoholic and usually doesn't drink."

For a variety of reasons, only some of which I'm even aware of, alcohol has not been an issue for me since shortly after the shooting. It's odd and strange and wonderful and in some ways inexplicable, but after decades of playing a prominent role in my life—whether I was drinking or not—alcohol, its use or abuse, alcoholism, the fetishizing of liquor and its power, is no longer an issue for me. At all. But that wasn't the case during the time that Randal is testifying about.

"And you're absolutely certain that the night before the shooting you saw the defendant drinking alcoholic drinks at the Oasis?"

"Absolutely positive."

r. Todd," Anna begins, "let me start by saying how very sorry I am for your loss. I mean that. John and I both are."

"Thank you."

"I saw firsthand how hard John and the others worked to prevent any of this from ever happening. Were you and your stepmom close? Even after she and your dad divorced?"

He nods. "Yes, ma'am. We were. She was always more like a cool older sister to me than a stepmom."

"I figured you must be," she says. "Makes this even that much harder. Sounds like y'all had a very special relationship. She was quite a talented artist as well. I've seen some of her work. I understand she was a good teacher too."

I know Anna means every word she's saying, and I'm glad she's taking the time to empathize with this young man who lost someone he cared about. I also know she's not doing it as part of some cross-examination strategy and isn't going to try to use it to any kind of advantage whatsoever.

"She was. All that. And more."

"Such a shame," Anna says. "So tragic for her life to be cut short the way it was. Such a loss."

"Really was."

"You mind if I ask you . . . I hadn't planned on doing this and it just occurred to me, but . . . who do you think is responsible for that?"

He looks confused for a moment. "Her killer," he says as if it should be obvious to everyone. "The sick fuck who shot her in cold blood."

Anna nods. "I just wondered if you blamed anyone else or held anyone else responsible."

He shakes his head. "No, ma'am."

"I know others, including the plaintiffs in this case, think those who were part of what Mr. Scott so dismissively calls the 'makeshift task force' bear some of the blame for not preventing the shooting from happening. But you don't?"

"No, I appreciate all their efforts. I really do."

I believe what he's saying. It's very convincing.

"Even that of John Jordan, who you just testified was drinking the night before?"

"I don't blame him for my stepmom's death," he says. "Even if he shouldn't've been drinking."

"If he was drinking at all, and we'll get to that, you're saying he shouldn't have been drinking in the evening when he was off duty?"

"Well . . . I mean, I guess it's okay when he's off duty. Yeah, I hadn't really thought of it like that. But . . . you know . . . as long as it didn't affect him the next day."

"'The next day,'" she says. "We'll get to that in a moment, but before we do . . . Do you know what O'Doul's is?"

"Sure. Near beer. Like a fake beer for people who don't drink."

Suddenly, I'm back at the bar that night in my mind. I can smell the beer, feel my fatigue and frustration from the day—a day in which we had worked so hard to stop a shooting that never happened. I can hear the jukebox in the background, the quiet conversation, punctuated occasionally by the overly loud laughter of the chemically uninhibited. I can see Kimmy and LeAnn at the table with me, Ace Bowman across the way, and even Janna behind the bar, but I can't see Randal anywhere.

"Does the Oasis serve it?" Anna is asking.

"O'Doul's? Yes, ma'am. Sure do."

"And if that's what John had been drinking that night,

would you still testify that he was drinking alcoholic beverages that might have impaired his ability to do his job on what you testified was the next day?"

"Well, no, but . . . Was he? Is that what he—?"

With that one, simple question—*Was he?*—Anna has undermined everything he has testified to, and the jury takes notice. It's obvious in their expressions and body language.

"What if I told you that that's what the receipts from that night will show and what those who were with him will testify to?"

"Then I'd owe John and everyone here an apology," he says. "I'm not trying to . . . I don't have an ax to . . . I was just answering the questions I was asked. But . . . Janna did say that John took at least one shot that night. I'd bet my life on it."

I remember the shot I snuck while no one was looking—the shot that only Janna knew about, and the bottle I bought later that night. I remember the guilt I felt then, and it just compounds the guilt I feel now. I had been drinking O'Doul's, but that's not all I had.

"Interesting," she says. "Okay. Well, let's talk about *that night*. You're testifying that it was the night before the shooting."

"Yes, ma'am. Stands out on account of losing Janna the next day."

Anna nods. "Well, yeah. That would. But of course, memory is a funny thing—funny and unreliable."

"You saying . . . I'm wrong about the day too?"

His use of the word *too* implies he had been wrong about the alcohol, and though he tries not to show it, Gary Scott's reaction at the plaintiff's table reveals what a blow it is.

"The drinks and the day too," Anna says. "But even if you're partially right and in addition to drinking O'Doul's that night, John had one shot, it wouldn't matter because of *when* it was. And I don't just mean because it was in the evening and he was off duty."

"Objection, Your Honor," Scott says. "Does Ms. Jordan have a question or is she just going to testify for the witness?"

"Sustained," Wheata Pearl says. "Ask the witness questions, Ms. Jordan, or cut him loose."

"Sorry, Your Honor," she says. "And I'm sorry to you too, Mr. Todd. I really was just trying to make this as easy on you as possible. What night are you testifying that John and his coworkers on the makeshift task force came in and did this alleged drinking?"

"Thursday night, April 19, the night before the shooting."

Anna nods as if what he has just said confirms what she thought. "Your Honor, I have two exhibits I'd like to introduce into evidence," she says, handing photocopies to Scott, then the bailiff.

After the judge looks at them and they are entered into evidence with no objections from Scott, she hands them to Todd.

"The first exhibit is a copy of a receipt with an affidavit from LeAnn Dunne stating that this is her receipt from the one and only night that the members of the makeshift task force went to the Oasis. It was the night after what they thought was going to be the day of the school shooting, the anniversary of Columbine. What is the date on the receipt, Mr. Todd?"

"April 20th. But that still fits . . . because the shooting happened the next day after they thought it was going to happen. I remember."

"It happened the next *school* day, but not the next *day*. April 20 was a Friday. John and the group he was with were there on a Friday night. The next day was Saturday, so even if he had had a single shot or many it wasn't the night before the shooting. The shooting took place on the next school day, which was Monday. I'm very sorry to have to ask you this . . . but was your stepmom killed on the day of the shooting?"

"Yes, ma'am."

"She wasn't injured and then died a few days later?"

"No, ma'am. She died at the school."

"The second exhibit you have is your stepmom's

death certificate. I'm so sorry to have to put you through this, but really it's the plaintiffs that are making us do this. Not only that but their investigator or attorney should have looked into this before calling you to testify. What is the date on your stepmom's death certificate?"

He hesitates for a moment, then actually looks at me, shaking his head and apologizing.

An act that only makes me feel far more guilty.

"I'm so sorry," he says. "The date is April 23."

"And just so there's no misunderstanding or confusion about anything," Anna says, "is the Oasis open on Sundays?"

"No, ma'am, it's not."

"So there's no way John was in the Oasis drinking anything the night before the shooting at Potter High School. Is that right?"

It's right and he says so, but as right as it is, as true as it is that I wasn't at the Oasis drinking the night before the shooting, it doesn't tell the whole truth. The whole truth and nothing but the truth is that I had been drinking the night before the shooting—at home, alone, out of the view of bartenders and barbacks and everyone else, hidden in my own little mental isolation cell of shame and self-recrimination.

TAMPA BAY TIMES DAILY DISPATCH

Hurricane Michael in Real Time

By Tim Jonas, *Times* Reporter

As the heat beats down from the North Florida sun's meridian, families huddle under sets and tarps and makeshift tents in a hotel hallway strewn with shards of glass and roofing fragments.

The hotel is damaged so severely it will be condemned. There is no electricity. No running water. But the people here have nowhere else to go.

The night brings a modicum of relief from the heat, but with it the threat of looters and other nocturnal predators.

The residents here are the new post-storm homeless, and though the hotel they're in has huge holes in the roof and is missing windows and doors and huge swaths of it are uninhabitable, they are the lucky ones. Many of their fellow citizens have no shelter at all.

Despite all the efforts of recovery workers and volunteers, post-Michael life in the Panhandle is perilous. Where are you, FEMA? Where is the help, Mr. Trump? Congress? US citizens are barely subsisting on the absolute fringes of existence and are in desperate need of the kind of relief only you can provide.

15

What once was hundreds of thousands of acres of slash pines on a thirty-year rotation is now no more. What remains, the few severely leaning smaller trees and the broken larger ones, looks like the partially cleared underbrush left behind by a dull machete.

In every direction, the destruction resembles the debris field of the hard crash landing of a massive Airbus A380 passenger airliner.

After our eventful day in court we are once again making our pilgrimage back into the war-torn world of our bombed and battered home.

I'm driving, but instead of working in the seat next to me as she has so often been doing lately, Anna is just sitting there decompressing.

"You were brilliant," I say.

"That's sweet, but Gary Scott is lobbing softballs so far. He's testing me before he brings out his real firepower."

"Really?"

"Oh, yeah. He's known for it. If he had gotten these two by me, he'd know he can do anything."

"You're amazing," I say. "Truly. How'd you know what Randal Todd was going to say?"

"I didn't."

"You seemed like you did—like you knew exactly what he was going to say."

"Did a little research when I saw his name on the witness list," she says. "Had Merrill look into him."

Merrill Monroe, a private security consultant and my best friend since childhood, has been serving as a sort of unofficial defense investigator for our shoestring-budget operation.

"When we found out he works at the Oasis I guessed at what they were calling him for," she says. "I prepared for other possibilities also—tried to be ready for anything. Got lucky."

"Luck has nothing to do with what you did today. Brilliance. Skill. Poise. Intelligence. Experience. Compassion. I could go on and on—and none of it would involve luck."

"Well, thank you. You are as biased as you are kind.

But . . . are you okay? Your words and your demeanor aren't exactly lining up."

"It was hard to hear," I say. "All of it. Takes a toll. I'm just drained."

"I'm sorry. I knew it would be. It's so hard to sit there unable to say or do anything while you're being talked about in horrible ways like you're not even in the room."

As we reach the outskirts of our small town, the piles of debris on the sides of the roads change from just trees and limbs to trees and limbs and shingles and tin and siding and appliances and furniture and clothes, as if a bomb exploded in a heavily populated area.

Beyond the piles of wet and battered trash, the hobbled houses still remaining are plywood patched and blue roofed with heavy tarps, the edges of which flap in the breeze.

"And the truth is . . . I feel guilty. I'm physically ill with it."

She starts to say something but then stops, allowing me the opportunity instead to say whatever else I need to.

"He may have been wrong about what he testified to, may not have seen me on the night he thought he did, but—"

"I don't think he saw you at all," she says. "I think he got that info from Janna and said he saw it because otherwise it'd be hearsay and inadmissible."

"Really?"

"Merrill found evidence he was somewhere else that night, but since we didn't need it and it would just complicate things I didn't use it."

"That makes everything you did even more impressive," I say. "Shows such wisdom and good judgment too. It's no wonder I'm so over the moon for you."

"And I, you, but get back to what you were saying before."

"Just that even though he didn't see me the night he thought he did—"

"Or at all."

"—or at all, he was right about what he said. I did drink the night before the shooting."

She nods. "I know you didn't drink much that weekend," she says. "It was pretty packed with nonstop kids and family activities. But I figured you did that Sunday night."

Somehow it's comforting that she knows—has known all along.

I reach over and take her hand.

Suddenly I feel less alone and isolated than moments before.

"Are you saying you were impaired on Monday morning when you reached the school?" she asks.

"I don't know," I say. "I didn't think I was, but . . . what if I'm wrong?"

"Mind if I just ask you a few questions about it?" she says.

"Not at all."

"Did you wake up hungover that Monday morning?"

"I'm just not sure. Maybe. A little."

"Did you drink any that morning?"

I shake my head. "No."

"Did you get up and drink any after we went to bed Sunday night?"

I shake my head again. "No, I didn't."

"So you drank some between, what—ten and midnight Sunday night? And you think you might have been a little hungover Monday morning or in some way impacted by the time you got to the school some nine hours after your last drink?"

"I'm afraid I might have been."

"The evidence that shows Derek was firing at you is incontrovertible," she says. "Agree?"

I nod.

"Would you be dead instead of Derek if you hadn't reacted?"

"At least injured. Possibly dead."

"But because you responded the way you did, you're alive today. Is there anything—anything at all—in your response time that would indicate you were impaired in any way?"

I can't help but smile. It's a smile that's more of an

inappropriate grin given the gravity of our topic of conversation. "My wife," I say. "The brilliant defense attorney. With just a few quick questions you convinced the judge, jury, and executioner inside my head."

"Only because of the answers to the questions," she says. "Only because of the truth that you weren't impaired in any way that morning."

16

Inspired by Jesus's parable of the Good Samaritan in the book of Luke in the Christian Bible, Samaritan's Purse teams have been working in crisis areas around the world for over forty years. A nondenominational evangelical Christian organization, this kind of first responder ministry team uses volunteers to provide spiritual and physical aid to hurting people dealing with war, poverty, natural disasters, disease, and famine.

Since shortly after Hurricane Michael moved out of the area it left so devastated, Samaritan's Purse has been set up in the front yard and grass and dirt parking lot of First Baptist Church on Main Street, working tirelessly to help relieve the suffering of those hit hardest by the storm.

Parked parallel to Main Street, the black Samaritan's

Purse semi-tractor-trailer with its huge logo filling the side lets people in town know who all the orange-shirted volunteers represent. Beyond the eighteen wheeler, a fleet of rented orange and white U-Haul trucks filled with supplies and tools and tarps sit ready to carry the small volunteer teams in various directions each morning, alongside other trucks, trailers, tractors, campers, and tents—and in and among and around them all are the mostly middle-aged white men and women who seem to be in perpetual motion.

"That's the second one," Rob Mills is saying. "Something's going on. We go into some truly dangerous places all around the world and we rarely ever have anything like this happen."

He's the volunteer coordinator for the operation here and is telling me how he's had another volunteer go missing.

We are standing at the corner of East Church and Main. Behind him the all-white church rises up into the soft late-afternoon sky. Like nearly all the churches in the area, First Baptist suffered damage from Michael. Unlike many of the churches in the area—particularly Panama City, Mexico Beach, and Port St. Joe—this one is still standing. The landscape is littered with steeples—many of them partially buried in the rainwater-softened ground they impaled when they were ripped off and flung by the 200-mile-per-hour gusts.

The first Samaritan's Purse volunteer to disappear was a white woman in her mid-fifties from Nashville. She went missing on the first night the initial team arrived, just two days after the storm. Her name is Betty Dorsey, and she left the camper she was staying in next to the church to grab her phone charger out of her car in the middle of the night or early morning hours and was never seen again.

"We're going to be here into next year," Rob is saying. "That means a lot of volunteers rotating in and out. If it's this unsafe we've got to warn them and take additional precautions and safety measures."

The night that Betty Dorsey disappeared, the electricity was still off, the storm-stunned town still in shock shrouded in darkness. The most recent missing person, Rick Urich, is an early forties black man from Indiana.

"When was Rick last seen?" I ask.

"This morning," he says. "He left his tent to go take a shower at the crack of dawn. He's the early riser of our group. Always gets up first. Always gets the coffee going. Always exercises, showers, and has his quiet time first. Usually by the time most of us are stumbling out of our campers and tents, he is sitting on the front steps of the church drinking his coffee and doing his morning devotional. And the thing is, Rick is built. He works out and does circuit training every morning. He looks more like a professional athlete than a cell phone salesman. He wouldn't've gone quietly. He would've fought. It would've been loud and violent, and yet no one saw or even heard anything."

He looks over toward the sanctuary and I follow his gaze.

I'm not sure how old the new section of the Baptist church is. It has been here as long as I can remember. But the truly old section behind it, the one that used to be the sanctuary and is now offices and Sunday school rooms, came all the way from Buck Horn or Blue Gator way, way back, and was rolled the several-mile trip on massive logs cut down for that purpose. Given its connection to the history of our town, I'm extremely grateful it survived Michael's assault.

"How do you know what time it was he disappeared this morning?"

"The guy he shares a tent with, Derry Cerrone, stirred as Rick unzipped the tent and asked him what time it was."

"What time was it?"

"Four-forty-three. We found where Rick had started making coffee in the gym's kitchen—the coffee canister, filters, and bottles of water were on the counter next to the maker, but that was as far as he got."

"And y'all've done a full search of the facilities?" I say. "Made sure he didn't have a heart attack in one of the bathrooms or classrooms or something?"

"We certainly looked for him," he says. "But I can't be sure we searched every possible place. But . . . there are people everywhere around here. As you can see. How could someone snatch a big, strong young man like Rick in the first place—let alone not be seen or heard doing it?"

A deputy had responded this morning and taken the initial report, but she's one of our most lazy and sloppy officers and she wasn't here long enough to have done a proper search.

"Okay," I say. "Let's quietly organize a small group to search the entire area. I need a picture of Rick and I'd like to talk to Derry Cerrone."

WHILE THE SMALL group of trusted volunteers headed up by Raymond Blunt and Phillip Dean, searches the obvious and larger places, Derry Cerrone and I look in the smaller, less obvious places.

Mechanical and storage closets.

Kitchen cabinets.

Camper and truck and trailer storage compartments.

"Rick would have to be chopped up into pieces to fit in some of these places," Derry says.

He's a late-twenties white man with bad skin, hair that looks like he cut it himself, and anger issues. He seems nothing like the other volunteers and I wonder why he's here.

He adds, "We looking for Rick, or his remains?"

"We're looking everywhere for everything—hoping to find clues or evidence or the missing persons themselves."

"There's more than *one*?" he asks.

"How long have you been here?" I ask.

"Since the beginning,"

"And you haven't heard about Betty Dorsey?"

"Oh, forgot about her. Guess I figured she probably just decided to go home. This isn't for everyone. Lot harder than it looks. Helping people is hard. *Dealing* with people is hard."

"Wonder if Samaritan's Purse ever considered using that as a slogan instead of 'Helping in Jesus's Name'?"

"It'd be more honest," he says.

"What made you become a Samaritan's Purse volunteer?" I ask.

"Honestly . . . my dad's a big donor . . . and . . . if I want him to keep donating to me, I have to keep him happy. This is one of the ways I do it."

17

"I'll post a patrol car here," Reggie is saying. "All night every night and as many hours during the day as I can spare—especially early mornings and late afternoons."

She and I are across Main Street from the church, leaning against her vehicle, looking over at all the activity.

"Lot of people," she says. "Need to keep a closer eye on them. And not just because of the two that have gone missing . . . but because whatever happened to them could've been done by another one of the volunteers."

"True," I say. "Would make sense if it was someone who knew their schedules or could just blend in while waiting for one of them to stray away from the herd."

"Yeah," she says, "someone from outside of the group

would have to stand around for hours hoping for an opportunity."

"Doesn't mean they didn't, but it'd be far more difficult."

"Are you thinking their disappearances are related?" she asks. "I mean, they're so, so different from each other. I can't see a single thing they have in common but being a volunteer here—and all that does is puts them in the same vicinity. It doesn't change the fact that they'd never fit the same victim profile."

I shrug. "I'm not sure what to think," I say. "They are way, way too different to be part of a type and yet being taken from the same place under similar circumstances would seem to connect them. I just don't know."

"I'll tell you what I *do* know," she says. "Our little area has been infiltrated by criminals. We've seen such a spike in crime of all kinds. Theft, rape, assault, battery, fraud. It's certainly possible that their disappearances are unrelated."

"I just feel like we've got too many missing persons cases for some or most of them not to be connected. Especially the ones who were seen alive after the storm. I've started digging into them and the deaths we've had—suspicious or otherwise—but I'm having to work through them mostly at night, so it's going slow. But if it's okay with you I'd like to continue that, dig even deeper."

"Of course," she says. "Hell, you've been doing it on

your own time. What *could* I say? But it's very respectful of you to ask. Just do what you can. Let me know if you need help with some of the legwork and I'll get it for you."

Betty Dorsey and some of the other missing persons cases belong to other detectives, and while I don't want to take them away from them or even appear to, I do want to look at them all for connections and patterns we may be missing.

"You mind just letting all the other investigations proceed as they are?" I ask. "Don't even mention that I'm looking at them? I'll just work in the background as I have time."

"Perfect. Everyone is stretched so thin right now they wouldn't care anyway, but I won't say anything. Most of my investigators are still functioning more as deputies than anything else. And I feel bad that you're having to do anything but deal with the trial, but . . . given the state of our world right now and the potential of a . . . of some kind of link between some of them . . . I really need your help. How'd it go today, by the way? Meant to ask earlier."

"Are Merrick and his kids staying with you?" I ask.

She looks surprised and confused at the question but can't help smiling some at the mention of his name.

"Why do you ask?"

"He looked extra tired in court today. I wondered if you kept him up all night."

"Actually, tonight is the first night they're staying."

"He wasn't the only person we know well in attendance," I say. "Randa kept her word and showed up today."

"I wish I knew what she was up to," she says.

"*She* may not even know," I say. "And it's at least possible that she's not up to anything . . . yet. Just observing, waiting, enjoying her freedom. It's interesting to see the lengths Merrick goes to just to avoid having to interact with her."

"Can't blame him," she says. "Only interaction I want to have with her is my fist with her face."

It's an odd comment to hear from an adult—especially one in Reggie's position—but she means it. She'd pummel Randa given the chance. And she'd enjoy it. A seasoned barroom brawler and all around tough *mujer,* my money would be on Reggie regardless of who she was fighting, but against someone like Randa it'd be a massacre.

I'm about to tell her she might yet get that chance when Raymond Blunt and Rob Mills emerge from behind the Samaritan's Purse semi, cross Main, and rush toward us.

"We found him," Rob says.

As if not to be outdone, Ray yells, "Rick. He's back. He's okay. He was just . . . helping someone."

When the two men reach us they breathlessly trip over each other trying to be the first to tell us the news.

Thankfully, Rick Urich joins us a few moments later.

"Sorry for the scare," he says. "I sure didn't mean to put anybody out. Didn't intend to stay as long as I did. A guy came by this morning before anybody else was up and asked for help. His elderly parents were stuck in their home because fallen trees blocked their driveway. He said he had a tractor and chains and saws and just needed a little help. I figured I'd be back before anyone else was up, but either way I was going to call Rob a little later when I knew Rob would be up—but I had no signal and then my phone died. And then we bogged down his truck and trailer and it took us all day to get them out and clear his parents' drive. Again, I apologize."

"No need to," Reggie says. "We're just glad you're okay. And we appreciate what you were doing."

"Next time just wake someone up," Rob says. "And always go out as a team. That's how we do things."

"Got caught up," Rick says. "It won't happen again."

We talk for a few more moments about Rick's adventures and the communications challenges facing us in this new post-apocalyptic landscape, and Rick and Rob drift back across the street to join the other Good Samaritans.

"I had a case like this once," Ray says, "and I'll tell you—"

"Where is Phillip?" Reggie asks.

He shrugs. "Probably still over talkin' to some Samaritans."

"I doubt he's *talking*," I say.

"Well, yeah," he says with a laugh. "Listening or observing. Whatever the hell he does. He's bad to just disappear, just sort of quietly wander off. Anyway, this case I had—"

"Since we're here," Reggie says, "why don't you go interview the volunteers about Betty?"

He hesitates.

"I think fresh eyes on everything could really help," she says. "Especially given your experience."

He smiles and nods and rushes off.

"That's a very good result," Reggie says.

"Getting rid of Raymond or finding Rick?" I ask.

She laughs. "Both, I guess. I bet Phillip was a big talker before being partnered up with him. But I was talking about Rick."

"The best."

"Betty Dorsey's story isn't going to have that kind of happy ending."

18

The bar in the Boatman is so full it's a fire hazard, the loud, raucous crowd constantly stumbling and bumping into each other.

One of only two hotels open in Gulf County, this dilapidated old inn on the Chipola River was built in the late '20s as a fisherman's getaway. A millionaire from Alabama named Jamie Lynn Lee wanted a place he and his fishing buddy friends could spend weekends without their wives, and he didn't care if it turned a profit or even lost money. As it happened, it did neither.

In the process of being restored and reopened by Lee's great-great-granddaughter and her husband who inherited it, it is currently filled with evacuees from Port St. Joe, Mexico Beach, and Cap San Blas, with Duke Energy and Gulf Coast Electrical Cooperative employees, with reporters, contractors, FEMA workers, out-of-town cops and firefighters, Red Cross representatives, and a few families whose homes were destroyed by the storm.

And though Kad Lee and her not-a-handyman husband could charge any price at all, they're still just charging pre-storm prices.

Because the storm has driven so many people from their homes and compressed them together, I'm hoping my visit here will enable me to interview a few different people who before the storm lived more than twenty-five miles apart.

Though living conditions are marginally better now than a week ago—cell service, electricity, and running water have all been to some degree restored—life itself in this hurricane-savaged environment is still difficult, challenging, and anxiety inducing. The people drinking and talking and even occasionally laughing together are tired and dirty and stressed, and are attempting to alleviate some small portion of the apprehension and uneasiness they feel.

Because we're in a state of emergency, Reggie has instituted a ban on alcohol sales, which is why the bar at the Boatman is giving away what they have left and allowing BYOB.

It takes me a few minutes to get from the bar to the table where Feather Stalnaker is waiting for me, and several times along the way my hands and arms are bumped and struck, causing the contents of the two glasses I'm carrying to slosh out onto my hands, onto the arms and backs of those pressing against me, and ultimately onto the already sticky unfinished floor.

"There was a lot more in it when I left the bar," I say as I set the partially filled glass in front of Stalnaker.

"No worries," he says, and lifts the glass toward me.

I tap his glass with mine and sit down across from him.

He looks around the room, and I follow his gaze.

The too small hotel bar is filled with strangers—with only a few exceptions. Raymond Blunt and Phillip Dean sit at a table drinking whiskey with other loaner cops from around the state. Merrick, the *Times* reporters, and a TV news crew from a station out of Panama City are at one end of the bar. Arnie Ward, another investigator in our department, and a couple of Gulf County Deputies stand around a tall table with no chairs near the open entryway that leads to the lobby. Rudy Pearson, Carla's dad and John Paul's grandad who nearly killed my kids during the hurricane, is setting out dinner on a folding table in the far corner. And at the center of the bar, her back to it, taking it all into her mesmerizing green eyes, like a mildly interested anthropologist, is Randa Raffield.

"Think it's bad in here now," Feather says. "Should've been here the first days following the storm—no electric or running water, hellishly hot, and the biggest, meanest mosquitoes you've ever had your blood sucked by."

Feather—his actual name—Stalnaker is a gentle, soft-spoken young man with long blondish hair, one side of which has a braid and a feather in it. As usual, the smooth, deeply tanned skin of his thin, boyish body can be seen through the open vintage leather vest—which along with his too short cutoff jeans shorts and cowboy boots are all I've ever seen him wear, like a kind of unspoken uniform.

"Thanks for the drink, mate," he says.

"Pleasure," I say, nodding in his direction.

He uses phrases like *no worries* and calls everyone *mate*, but his accent is Deep South not English or Australian.

He waited tables with Philippa Kristiansen at Shipwreck Raw Bar in Port St. Joe Beach before it and the small shack he was sharing with three other guys were damaged by Michael. Now he's staying here—in a single room with five other guys.

Though still very much in progress and unfinished, the Boatman shows what it can be—a charming, classic country inn that remains true to its fisherman roots. Nearly everything is genuinely antique, its decor a combination of images of idyllic freshwater fishing and what once had been the breathtaking natural beauty of the area before Michael blew in and blew it all away.

"What's your plan?" I ask.

He shrugs. "Don't really have one, mate. No job. No place to live. No idea why I'm still here . . . except . . . don't really have anywhere else to go."

"Is Shipwreck going to reopen eventually?"

"Eventually, but . . . I won't be able to survive until it does. It'll be months—maybe longer."

He places his drink on the table and pulls out his phone.

"Look at this," he says, swiping through his photos.

He then places the phone in the center of the table facing me and begins to show me pictures of the damage done to the restaurant where he and Philippa had served steamed seafood to tourists.

The poorly taken pictures show not only the damage done to Shipwreck but everything around it.

"Now, look at this," he says. "See that?"

He shows me another picture of the damaged old convenience store building that houses the raw bar restaurant.

"Yeah."

"Now look. Same day."

He swipes to the next picture that shows Philippa Kristiansen surveying the damage with everyone else.

"It's after the storm," he says. "Proves she was alive after the hurricane had come through."

"Yes it does," I say.

"And look . . ."

He zooms into the background behind Philippa. It shows the battered beach flattened by the winds and tidal surge, which no longer has any dunes.

"See? Oh, wait. Sorry . . . *There.*"

He uses his finger to slide the picture over a little to the left. It shows the collapsed beach house that Philippa had been found in.

"Don't have to just take my word for it anymore, mate," he says. "Photographic fuckin' evidence. There she is alive after the hurricane and there's the house she was found in already destroyed."

19

"T his where you're staying?" I ask.

Randa smiles. "You asking as a cop or as a friend?"

I've stepped over to the bar to see if Kad Lee can spare a minute for me, and Randa, assuming I had come to see her, had engaged me in conversation.

"Do you consider me a friend?" I say.

"Of course," she says. "A dear friend. Why?"

I shrug. "Just wondered. We probably have different definitions of what it means to be a friend."

"If you're worried I haven't forgiven you for arresting me, don't give it another thought," she says.

I laugh. "No, that's not what I meant, but—"

"We're all good, you and me," she says. "I understand why you did what you thought you had to. And it all worked out. I'm truly free now—for the first time in a very, very long time."

"Well, I just hope you'll use all that freedom for good," I say.

"I am."

"You can still have a good life," I say.

"I plan to. Already beginning to."

I nod, but not like I mean it.

"And to answer your question," she says, "yes, this is where I'm staying. Not a lot of options around here these days. I'm lucky to have a room. They didn't have one for me at first. Eventually, I'd like to buy a place around here —or maybe even build. I'd like to be on the water. It'd be a dream to live on the Dead Lakes, but I'd settle for the Chipola or the Apalachicola."

Kad waves at me from behind the bar and motions me out into the lobby.

"Take care of yourself," I say to Randa.

"I'm learning to," she says.

As I begin to move away, she says, "Let me know if I can help you in any way. I'm good at solving crime, and I'd be more than happy to help you again. We make a formidable team."

I don't ask what she means by *again* nor why she thinks we've ever been a team—formidable or otherwise—but instead press my way through the crowd and into the small lobby. The lobby is the room closest to being finished, the brick, tile, and mantle of its grand fireplace restored, its hardwood floors refinished, its opulent chandelier and the mahogany banister of the wide, winding staircase that leads up to the guest rooms redone and polished to gleam.

"Open a quiet little country inn, they said," Kad says. "It'll be fun, they said. You might be bored but that'll just give you more time to work on your poetry."

I laugh and thank her for giving me some of what she doesn't have much of right now—her time—and promise to be quick.

"We're taking another look at the death of Charlie West," I say, "and I wondered if you've thought of anything else since you spoke with the other investigator?"

Charlie died a little less than a week ago—on the same day that my friend Brad Price died in a tragic accident while clearing hurricane debris with his tractor. It was also the night that the electricity in town first came back on.

"Oh, no," she says. "Does that mean it may not have been an accident?"

"Not necessarily," I say. "Just trying to be thorough. It's too easy for things to get missed in a post-storm environment like this."

"I bet it is."

"Is there any reason you can think of that would indicate it wasn't an accident?" I ask.

She shrugs. "A few things just seemed odd to me, but I figured y'all know a lot more about this stuff than I do, so I let it go when the other detective didn't seem too interested in it."

In looking at the crime scene photos I noticed something odd as well. The position of the body was all wrong for it to have been an accident—unless it's just the angle or perspective of the photo, which is why I'd like to see the location for myself. But first I want to hear what she found incongruent with it being an accidental death.

"Would you mind sharing them with me?" I ask. "The things you found odd."

"The whole thing," she says. "I mean, he was in great shape and he was young and vibrant. So it's hard to imagine him falling, you know? Plus, the floor of that shower is not slippery at all. I put down way more safety strips than I should have. I was so paranoid about someone falling. And—"

"Do you mind if we go take a look at it?" I ask.

"Well, we don't have any empty rooms, so . . . Or did you mean the actual shower he fell in?"

"It'd be helpful to see the actual one he was found in."

"I guess we can ask the guest if they mind, but . . . I really don't want to remind them someone died here, you know?"

"Tell you what . . . Are all the bathrooms the same?"

"Identical," she says. "Every room."

"Okay, give me just a minute. I think I know what we can do."

I fight my way back into the bar and over to where Merrick and the *Times* reporters are.

"Hey, John," Merrick says, as if he's had a little too much to drink. "You remember Tim Jonas and Bucky Swanson."

Hippie Bucky and boyish Tim, like everyone else I encounter these days, including myself in the mirror, appear exhausted.

"Hey guys, how's it going? I want to thank you for your coverage of what's going on here. Your concern for our area really comes through in your pieces and in your pictures. I can't believe how little attention the hurricane and its aftermath are getting."

"Our pleasure," Tim says. "We can't believe it either. We were surprised the *Herald* pulled Gabriela and Grover back so soon."

"People have disaster fatigue," Merrick says.

"Or just news fatigue," Tim says. "Between the chaotic Trump presidency and the wildfires in California and the million other things bombarding us every single day . . ."

"It's true," Bucky says. "People have no fucks left to give."

"Makes what y'all are doing all the more important,

and I appreciate it. Maybe we can get some attention and get some real help down here. Hey, I've got somebody waiting on me and I need a quick favor."

"Name it," Merrick says.

"Do you have a room here?"

He nods. "Been bunking in with these guys since the *Herald* crew left."

"Could I borrow your key and your room for just a few minutes?"

Tim and Bucky turn to look out into the lobby and Merrick laughs.

"I guarantee it's not how it sounds," Merrick says to them. "No way he's borrowing our room for a quickie with anyone other than his wife, and she's not here."

"I was wondering . . ." Tim says. "We've seen your wife in court and not only is she smokin' hot and wicked sexy and intelligent, but what she's doing for you right now in there is . . ." He trails off as Merrick continues to glare at him.

"No, I'm working on something, and the owner says all the rooms are the same, so instead of disturbing another guest I figured I could just take a quick look at yours."

"Sure," Merrick says.

"As long as when you can you'll give us an exclusive interview about it," Tim adds.

"I don't know when that will be," I say, "but when I can ... sure. I'll only talk to y'all."

As Merrick hands me the key I can feel Randa staring at us.

I take the key and rush out of the bar as quickly as the crowd will allow, and a few minutes later, Kad and I are in the reporters' room, studying the shower.

The rooms of the old inn are small, the bathrooms even smaller than most. In a concession to space, there are no bathtubs, only a small, narrow, white-tile shower stall. The three-sided stall is less than three feet by three feet and is fronted by a plain white shower curtain. Beneath the curtain is a raised tile ridge that comes up off the floor about four inches and is maybe six inches wide. It was on that ridge that Charlie West supposedly hit his head, but based on the crime scene photographs and now seeing it in person, I don't see any way he could have. And I think Kad has reached the same conclusion.

"See?" she is saying. "See how much grip tape is on that shower floor? No way someone slips in there—especially someone young and fit. And see how small the shower stall is?"

"I do," I say.

"That's what I've been thinking," she says. "If you're in the shower and fall ... how do you hit your head on the ridge right here? But I can't see how you could hit it from the outside of the shower either—not with the way the toilet and door and sink are situated."

I nod. "Good point. Anything else occur to you?"

"Nah, guess that's about it."

"Okay, thank you very, very much. That's been extremely helpful. I can't tell you how much I appreciate it."

"You're welcome. I want it to have been an accident. I really do. So I hope I'm wrong. I mean, maybe he collapsed instead of fell over. But if he didn't, if it wasn't an accident, I want you to get whoever came into my place and did something like that."

"We're gonna do our best. Well, I know how busy you are, so, I'll let you get back down to the maddening throng, but if you think of anything else . . . please let me know as soon as you can."

She says she will and turns to leave.

As she reaches the door I say, "And for now let's keep this all to ourselves."

"Nobody will hear anything from me," she says. "This is the last thing I want out there. No matter what it is— accident or . . . something else. I can't even bring myself to say it."

When she is gone, I run water in the shower for a few minutes to get it good and wet. I then take off my shoes and socks and wet my feet. I then turn off the water and get in the shower stall and try to re-create Charlie West's fall.

I fall in every conceivable direction. I collapse several times. I even get out of the shower and walk back toward it to get into it. But no matter what I do, I can't ever come close to landing how West did, and I can't figure out a way for his head to strike the ridge the way it did from any kind of fall.

20

"Please tell me you're not cheating on Anna," Randa says as I descend the last of the stairs into the lobby.

Her straight, longish auburn hair is even shinier tonight, her narrowed green eyes even more implacable.

"I'm not."

Through the open French doors of the bar I see Lucas Burke, an inmate I worked with at Potter Correctional Institution a few years back. He smiles and waves when he sees me and it takes a moment for me to recognize him. I've never seen him not wearing an inmate uniform before and he no longer has the pale prison skin and bad buzz cut that he had back when I knew him.

"That's not what it looks like," Randa is saying.

"Things are often not what they look like."

"Well, I sure hope that's the case here," she says. "And if it is . . . that can only mean one thing . . . you're working on a . . . Is it something I can help with? Staying here puts me in a great position to see and hear things."

"Thank you," I say. "I appreciate that and I'll certainly let you know if anything comes up that we could use your help with."

"That's all I want to do, John," she says. "I'd just really like to contribute to making the world a better place. That's all I've ever tried to do. I hope you can see that. Or at least that you eventually will. I really am one of the good guys."

Merrick, Tim, and Bucky walk out of the bar and over toward me.

"Well, I'll say good night," she says. "I know how much Merrick hates being around me."

With that she disappears up the stairs.

"Get what you needed?" Merrick asks. "'Cause . . . we're exhausted and need to crash."

He's even more unsteady now, his words though not slurred coming out stiltedly and a little too loud.

I nod and hand him the key. "Thanks for the loan of the room," I say.

"No problem . . . just don't forget . . . we get a story out of it."

"I thought you were staying with Reggie tonight?"

"Change of . . . plans."

"His *change of plans*," Tim says, "means ol' Bucky and I have to bunk together again."

"I can give you a ride," I say. "If you're too . . ."

"I've had a little too much to . . ." he says. "I go over there like this . . . and we'll wind up sleeping together for sure and that . . . would just complicate . . . things . . . The kids . . . have gone to Orlando to stay with their aunt for a bit so . . . I'll just . . . hang here with . . . the boys."

"Hey, do me a favor and take a little more precaution," I say. "Be sure to lock your door and look out for each other. Okay?"

They nod.

"We will," Tim says.

Bucky says, "Just here at the hotel or when we're out and about too?"

"Both."

"Is this to do with what you're going to be giving us an exclusive on eventually?" Tim asks, sniffing at the air. "I can smell a story."

"Things around here are just more perilous these days," I say. "In many ways and for many reasons. Just mind how you go and keep an eye on each other."

"We will," Merrick says. "But we want that story."

As Tim and Bucky help Merrick up the stairs, I drift back into the bar and over to Lucas Burke. Though still crowded for its size, the bar has thinned out a good deal, but across the way at a table near the front corner Arnie

Ward is still here—and now he has been joined by Darlene Weatherly. Which, with me, means that all three Gulf County sheriff's investigators are in this one bar— something that can't be a coincidence. I try to catch their eye to wave to them but they carefully avoid looking this way.

"Hey man, how are you?" I ask Lucas when I reach him.

He nods slowly. "I'm okay. I'm . . . doing all right."

Lucas Burke is a twenty-something young man with intense brown eyes and thick brown hair. He's thin and deceptively muscular, the features of his clean-shaven face razor sharp—like the jawline above his long, narrow neck.

"It's good to see you," I say. "Just surprised to see you here."

"I EOSed about six months ago," he says.

EOS stands for an incarcerated individual's end of sentence.

"No, I meant here in the area. Were you here during the hurricane?"

He nods. "That's actually something I need to talk to you about," he says. "Got a minute?"

21

Luc and I make our way over to a table in the far corner and sit down.

"You want a drink?" he asks.

"I'm fine. Thanks."

"I've been meaning to come see you," he says. "But . . . things are so crazy here right now, and . . . the truth is . . . I was trying to talk myself out of it, but seeing you here tonight . . . I knew I had to."

"What is it? Are you okay?"

"You're the chaplain at Gulf CI now, right?"

"There is no Gulf CI now," I say, "but before it was wiped out by the storm I was a part-time chaplain there."

"And you're a detective for the sheriff's department?"

I nod. "We don't have detectives, but yeah, I'm an investigator."

"I had heard that."

"What is it, Luc?" I say. "Does this have something to do with your sister or—"

"You remember that?" he asks.

"Of course."

"That's . . . wow. I can't believe you— Well, I guess I can. You're a standup guy. You gave me water during my time in hell and I'll never forget that."

"I'm glad I was able to help in some small way."

"Thing is . . . I need to tell you something but . . . I really don't want to get myself jammed up over it. I can't. I've got to be free to find McKenzie, but I owe you and there're some things you need to know."

"Okay."

"Things I need to tell you—partly because you're a cop, but they're not the kinds of things I want to be telling a cop. Let me ask you this . . . If I didn't commit a crime— at least not any serious ones—but I was crime adjacent . . . would you have to . . ."

"Tell you what," I say. "Since I can't make any promises without knowing what we're talking about here . . . Why don't you tell me a story—a story with fictional characters, even if they're based on actual people, and hypothetical events?"

He nods. "That I can do."

"So," I say, "once upon a time . . ."

"There was this guy. And he had real shitty parents

and he was taken in by this foster family and they were good people—the best—and they became his family. He's raised in this loving environment by these amazing people and they really love and accept him—the dad, the mom, the older sister and brother. And in time he learns to love them back. Now, this kid he still has all sorts of anger issues and such but he deeply loves these people, his family. And later after all the kids are grown, the sister goes missing. And this angry young man who she loved like her actual blood brother and who was as good to him as anyone has ever been, he can't live with that, can't just let her go, can't say the police are looking, doing everything they can, can't say that as tragic as it is some people just vanish and are never seen again. He has to do whatever he can to find her. No matter what it takes. No matter what it costs him."

I nod. "That story sounds very familiar," I say.

He's talking about himself and the Burke family who took him in and eventually adopted him, and his older sister, McKenzie, who went missing several years ago and has never been seen again.

"Yeah, I knew you'd probably remember that part. Well, anyway, after a stretch in state prison this lost and angry young man continues his search for his sister. It's probably what would bring him to a place like this on a night like this and cause him to run into a man who was genuinely good to him in an environment and situation where he didn't have to be, where not many others were. But this isn't the only time he's seen that good man recently. The good man doesn't know it, but this lost and angry young man saw him the day of the hurricane. I mean right in the middle of the storm when the world was being blown apart around them."

I think back to the storm and where he might have seen me.

"Everything this guy does, he does to try to find his sister. Everything. Some things aren't the best things, but he'll do anything—*anything* that might help him find her."

"She's lucky to have him looking for her," I say.

His eyes glisten for a moment and he blinks and looks away.

"So this guy hears that this bad dude, I mean truly bad dude, may have had something to do with what happened to his sister or at least know something about it. And he hears that this bad man has built this fortress of a mansion right on the beach and that he plans to ride out the hurricane as if what his safe house really is is a courtside seat to the event of the century. And he hears about these other guys—also bad guys, not on the level with the safe house bad guy, but bad dudes nonetheless —who plan to break into the dude's house during the storm and rob him while there is no one else around and no cops to respond even if an alarm goes off or a 911 call gets placed. So this lost and angry young man gets cut in on the ah . . . home invasion—not to steal, not to even help anyone do anything, but only to get his hands on this big bad guy while he's got some backup and can ask him in a less than polite way, a way that might involve some power tools, where his sister is. And though there are many more complications and bad shit that happens, I'll skip ahead to the part where . . . as all this is going down, the angry guy not there to steal to his shock sees this good man who helped him while he was in hell . . . walking out of the storm toward the house with what must be his two small daughters."

Suddenly I'm back in the storm with my girls.

Clinging to Taylor in the front with one hand and to Johanna who is strapped to my back with a belt with the other, I wade through the water slowly and carefully because going any faster would risk tripping and falling and injuring the girls.

Not that I could go much faster anyway. Not with the weight of the girls and the force of the storm.

Because I have the girls, the assault of the rain and the wallop of the wind feels even more brutal and personal.

I can feel Johanna's little face pressed hard against my back, and I'm glad it is, though I wish there was a way to protect her ears from the noise and her head and body from the pelting rain and debris.

I'm not sure how far we've walked or in which direction,

but I nearly step into a swimming pool that already has a white Honda Accord and a red moped in it.

As I change direction to walk around it and blink the rain out of my eyes, I see a large house on stilts—the only one in the area still standing.

All around it, the flattened landscape is covered with the remnants of other houses, but it looks nearly untouched, which can only mean one thing—someone exceeded code and built a hurricane house.

I begin to make my way toward it, allowing myself a faint sense of relief and a modicum of hope as I do.

As I get closer, I see lights and movement inside. Not the overhead lights and lamps that would indicate their generator is still working, but the glow of lanterns and the play of flashlight beams that let us know help is inside.

In my hope and excitement I begin to walk too fast and trip and nearly fall, but even as I try to slow down some I find it difficult to return to my earlier more cautious pace.

"Johanna," I yell, "I found a safe place for us to go into to get out of the wind and rain."

Without moving her face away from my back, she nods to let me know she's heard me, a moment later pumping her little arms in celebration.

Taylor beings to stir, and though I'm sure she's going to be frightened and disoriented waking in the middle of the pummel and pounding of the storm, I'll be very glad to have her conscious again.

I continue to move toward the lone structure as if I'm a ship lost at sea and it's a lighthouse leading me home.

For a moment it disappears and I think maybe I've imagined it, that it is the storm equivalent of a desert mirage, but then the wind slashes in a different direction and my rain-impaired vision clears enough to see it again.

"We're almost there," I yell. "Just a little bit—"

I stop abruptly—speaking and moving.

Not far from the house now, I have a better view, and can see through the large bay window in the front.

A man with a hood over his head is bound and bleeding. Tied to a wooden kitchen chair, he is being worked over by one man while another one holds a shotgun to his head.

I recognize the two men inflicting the torture from the suspicious group at Ace the other day with the stolen van that I had seen the burned body in this morning.

Ordinarily I would feel compelled to intervene, to sneak up into the house and attempt to rescue the man being tortured, but my first and only priority right now is the care and protection of my girls. That is all that matters. They are all that matter.

Rousing now, Taylor begins to cry.

I can barely hear her over the cacophony of the storm, so I'm reasonably sure the men in the house can't hear her, but I need to get her and Johanna as far away from the house and the men in it as fast as I can.

I begin to slowly back away, keeping an eye on the

window to make sure they don't see us, though how they could
through the wind and rain I can't imagine.

As I continue to back up, I not only keep an eye on them,
but search the area for somewhere safe for us to hide and ride
out the rest of the storm.

"He can't believe it. I mean . . ." Luc is saying, "talk
about stunned. You just can't fathom how gobsmacked
this angry young dude was. And he had to think fast
because if the others see the good man and his little girls,
they are dead. I mean there is no chance they see what's
going on in that house and get even one more breath. So
the angry young guy creates a loud distraction in hopes
that the good man will see what's going on and the bad
guys won't see him."

"And he did," I say. "And he was able to get away with
his daughters and he had no idea he had a young man he
met in hell to thank for it."

He nods and looks away again.

I actually tear up thinking about what might have
happened to Johanna and Taylor if he hadn't done what
he did.

"Thank you," I say, my voice breaking a little. "Thank
you for what you did to save my daughters."

"It was the least I could do for you," he says. "And I
hope to God if there is one, that someone somewhere
along the way will do or have done something like that to
save my sister."

"I do too, Luc."

"So, from what this hypothetical angry young man has heard, the good man who is a cop isn't working the so-called hurricane house case because it is located on the Bay County side of Mexico Beach, but the hypothetical angry young man wonders if the good Gulf County cop would like to give his Bay County brothers in blue some info on the whereabouts of these bad guys who robbed and killed the even badder guy in his so-called safe house during the storm. And if there might be a way to leave the angry young man out of it."

"Absolutely to both," I say, "but . . . what about the bad guys. Will they try to roll over on the good young man who saved the Gulf County cop's daughters?"

"They might," he says. "They probably will. Though . . . they have no idea who he is and he may have even been wearing a disguise, so . . ."

"So this hypothetical young man is not only good and heroic but smart," I say.

"Smart might be a stretch but he might be careful."

"So he can complete his mission," I say.

He nods. "It's the only thing that matters to him."

"I hope maybe one day I'll get to help him with his mission."

"You've got your hands full at the moment," he says. "But maybe one day."

"Did the big bad guy in the not so safe house have any information about the young man's sister?"

"Not that he divulged before taking his leave of this world."

"Sorry to hear that."

22

By the time I finish with Luc, Reggie is with Arnie and Darlene at their table and I walk over to join them.

"Who's the young man you were talking to?" Reggie asks.

She looks beyond tired and stressed. The deep, dark half circles beneath her bloodshot eyes look like bruises and her dull face resembles a damaged drumhead, its fine lines severely etched into her paper-thin skin.

Reggie has more on her than most, but everyone in this storm-ravaged region, coming off over a week of no electricity, no running water, and complete isolation from the outside world, is raw-bone weary and frayed to the point of breaking.

"Someone I used to work with at PCI," I say.

"We need to talk to you, John," Darlene says.

"And we wanted to do it in front of Reggie."

"Okay."

"They actually got me out of bed to do it," Reggie says.

The bar is mostly empty now, the storm-weary workers upstairs in their rooms attempting to rest and sleep before having to get up and do it all over again.

"We like you, John," Darlene says.

"Oh no," I say. "It's one of *those* kinds of *we need to talk to you*s."

"You're a very good investigator," Arnie says.

"A great one," Darlene says. "And I wouldn't even be here if it weren't for you."

"*But* . . ." I say.

"But we're good too," she says. "And we . . . we both feel like we don't get the respect or opportunities we deserve, we have earned."

"Reggie, you're our boss," Arnie says, "and John, you're our coworker, and we consider both of you friends, but . . ."

"We think John gets all the good cases," Darlene says. "And we get what's left, what he doesn't want."

"And you guys are so close, so . . ." Arnie says. "It's like there's no room for us, no way for us to be in the middle of you two."

"And it's not just us saying this," Darlene says. "Some

of the visiting cops from other agencies have noticed it too."

"*Some of*?" I ask. "Or one?"

"Well . . . it doesn't matter how many, does—"

"It was Ray, wasn't it?" I say.

"Well, you know it wasn't Phillip," Reggie says.

"Ray's been very generous with a lot of his helpful opinions."

"And he's the last person you should be listening to," Reggie says. "He means well, but all he's done since he's been here is stir up discord and get in the way. If you're going to listen to anyone, listen to Phillip."

"We were thinking this before he said anything," Arnie says.

"John and I are close," Reggie says. "And it's true that I lean on him—maybe more than I should—but you two are not being left out and John is certainly not getting all the good cases. I'm sorry if it seems that way. I'll try to do better at communicating with you about . . . well, everything."

"We'd really appreciate that," Arnie says.

"We would," Darlene says. "And that's something that's needed to happen for a long time now. We should've said something sooner."

"And that's on us," Arnie adds.

"But the real reason we wanted to talk tonight," Darlene says, "the reason we asked you to get out of bed and come down here is . . . We believe John is investigating some of our cases behind our backs. And we don't think this is the first time it's happened. Now, those other issues—y'all not communicating with us and John getting all the plum assignments . . . that's one thing, but . . . to have our investigations reinvestigated behind our backs . . . well, that's another. It's disrespectful and insulting and . . ."

Reggie starts to say something, but Darlene isn't quite finished.

"And I hate to say it . . ." she says, "but feel like it has to be said. Isn't John on trial in another county for . . . well, involving himself in other people's cases?"

I think about what she's saying, and perhaps she's right. Even if I was asked, it was another cop's case in another jurisdiction.

"I'm glad you have both expressed what you're feeling," Reggie says. "I wish you would've done it sooner and at the office, but . . . regardless . . . I'm glad it's out in the open."

"We did it here tonight because we believe he's here reinvestigating one of our cases," Darlene says.

"Okay," Reggie says, "in no particular order: Do yourselves a favor and don't listen to Raymond Blunt—or any other busybodies like him. John and I will both be more mindful to include you two in discussions and communicate to you what's going on and why. But the truth is . . .

John doesn't just get good cases. He makes his cases good. And part of how he does that is through hard work and his lifetime of experience and not blaming others and not being so insecure he won't ask for help or input. And the times anyone has looked at his work, he not only listened to what they have to say but he's reconsidered the evidence and his handling of it himself. See . . . that's the thing that bothers me most about what you're saying. You two ask John for help all the time. All the time. You just want it on your own terms and with you still controlling the investigation, getting credit. How many cases has John helped you on that he let you take all the credit for? And this bullshit about interfering in someone else's case is what he's on trial for . . . that's not just untrue it's low— beneath even the most insecure officer. John was asked to help and he got both my and the sheriff of Potter County's permission, and doing what he did, acting responsibly and even heroically, has cost him far more than you can even imagine. And as far as your current cases . . . John isn't reinvestigating them. He's—at my request—seeing if there's a link between any of these cases. That's a parallel and separate and different investigation—one that I was going to tell you about in the morning at our meeting. Guess I should've done it this evening when it came about. That's on me. Sorry. I thought in the morning would be plenty soon enough. Now, I'm gonna cut you some slack because we're all stressed and in shock and

overworked and overwhelmed, but . . . but if you feel that
. . . even given the current circumstances we're dealing
with, the environment we're all working in, that your
investigative work can't withstand another set of eyes,
well, maybe you're in the wrong line of work. And if it
happens again, I can assure you that you're in the wrong
department."

"I didn't mean—" Darlene begins.

"Save it," Reggie says. "Sleep on it. Think about what
I've said. All of it. And think about how very respectful
John and even I as your boss have been with you being
such an inexperienced investigator. And we'll talk about
it at our meeting in the morning. Now I know you don't
think you were given a fair chance in Marianna, but that's
not the case here. And no one has given you more of a
fair shake than John. I'm gonna be honest, after the way
you acted toward him when we were investigating Chris
Taunton's death . . . I'd've been done with you if I were
him, but not John. He's still worked with you and shown
you respect and given you many more chances. So think
about all that. And give me a reasoned response in the
morning at our meeting."

"Yes, ma'am," she says.

She looks downcast, but not as much as Arnie—who
also appears to be extremely embarrassed.

"Now, John," Reggie says, "since we're all here and
since when we meet in the morning you'll be in the Potter

County courthouse fighting for your life, is there anything you want to say?"

I nod.

"Okay," she says. "Let's hear it."

"I'm pretty sure we have a predator at work here," I say. "Since the storm hit he has been making his murders look like accidents—all in some way or another related to the hurricane. Philippa Kristiansen, Charlie West, and PTSD Jerry Garcia were all alive after the storm and were all killed with blunt force trauma that could be made to look like an accident. But none of these were accidents. They are murders. And I believe they were all committed by the same killer. I've looked at all the autopsy reports and all three of these victims have something in common. They all have a bone that was broken after they were already dead. I think that's his signature—or part of it. And I'm afraid that many of these missing persons we're looking for are going to show up with the same signature in circumstances that look like accidental death but are actually the work of a sadistic predator drawn to the pain and suffering of the most isolated and vulnerable among us, like an African lion to a wounded wildebeest."

TAMPA BAY TIMES DAILY DISPATCH

Hurricane Michael in Real Time

By Tim Jonas, *Times* Reporter

When is the Florida Gulf Coast going to get the funding it needs? Why isn't anyone listening? Why isn't Washington responding to this disaster? People, listen to me—I'm on the ground here. It's far, far worse than you can imagine, than anyone is saying. And no one is hearing us. No one is responding. Why is that?

Within 10 days of Hurricane Katrina, Congress had passed supplemental disaster relief funding. 10 days!

Hurricane Ike and Hurricane Gustav took only 17 days. For Hurricane Andrew, the last Category 5 storm to strike the United States, it took 34 days. For Hurricane Sandy, which sparked bitter debate in Congress, it took 74 days.

I know it's still relatively early days here, but nothing is being done and it doesn't look like there is going to be anything done anytime soon.

Hurricane Michael decimated everything here and there's still no supplemental disaster funding, and it doesn't look there is going to be.

Washington is playing politics with people's lives, with the survival of the Florida Panhandle, and this is absolutely not acceptable. Call your congressman or woman today. Demand more.

We can do better than this and we have to. You still haven't done right by Puerto Rico, still struggling to recover from Hurricane Maria in 2017, and now you're letting a big part of the Panhandle die.

23

"My name is Bernice Jones. I'm one of the custodians at the school."

It's the following morning and we are back in court—in a courtroom that is even more polished than it has been previously, something I didn't think was possible, and smelling even stronger of Murphy's Oil Soap.

"Which school is that?" Gary Scott asks.

Looking at him at the lectern, I realize who he reminds me of. His retro suits, his ankle boots, his longish feathered hair—he looks like a '70s-era Al Pacino, only with less charm, less intensity, and less movie-star swagger.

"Oh, sorry. The high school."

"Potter High School?"

"Yes, sir."

Bernice Jones is a large, older black woman with enormous breasts that lie across her belly, the ends of which hover around her waist.

"And were you there the morning of the shooting on April 23rd of this year?"

"Yes, sir, I was."

"Can you take me though what happened?"

"I's in the supply closet when all hell broke loose. *Pop, pop, pop*, and *bang, bang, bang*. Sounded like a war zone. Kids done a play on that Friday before had some of those same sounds, but . . . I knew right away this was different. . . was the real thing. And I seen on the television where kids take guns to school and start shootin' up everything. My husband said nothin' like that would ever happen here, but I told him you don't see what I see every day. No respect. Spoiled rotten. Actin' the fool. No manners. Told him . . . Big Daddy you just don't know . . . they's crazy white kids everywhere. And that's always who's behind it. I ain't tryin' to be racial or nothing, but truths is truths. People so scared of Muslims and immigrants and young black thugs, and they kids is building bombs and shootin' up everything."

As I listen to Bernice Jones speak, I wonder what the reporters from out of town must think of her. Like many impoverished, uneducated, small town, Deep South women from her era, she speaks in a way that is common around here but must seem like a different language to those who haven't grown up hearing it like those of us from here have.

"*Sure*," Gary Scott says, his nasally, whistling voice filling that one word with both condescension and patronization, "but getting back to the morning of the shooting..."

"Like I says, I knew it was a real school shooting," she says. "Right then and there I said my prayers. I's thinkin' it might be my time. 'Cause when it's your time it's your time and when it's not it's not. Nothing you can do about it. So I said my prayers and I went over and locked my door."

Since the storm, I've been trying to think of what the broken thick-bodied pines lining the highways in Michael's path remind me of. And it comes to me as I'm sitting here on trial, listening to Bernice Jones's testimony. Snapped about a third of the way up from the ground, the top two-thirds of the tree leaning over onto the ground, the swollen, splintered joint of the breakage reminds me of something I haven't been able to come up with. But now I realize that the fractured spot where the tree was broken looks like the busted and split-open seam of a pair of woven paper and thin wood kids' carnival Chinese finger cuffs given out at the school's fall festival.

As I'm returning my attention to Bernice's testimony, I

glance around the courtroom. To my surprise I see Rick Urich sitting in the gallery with the rest of the onlookers.

"And then?" Gary Scott is saying.

"I turned out the lights and got on my knees."

"To pray?"

"I already told you I had done that. No, was so I could see what was going on."

"I don't understand," Scott says.

"The door to the janitor closet—"

"I thought you said you were in the supply room?" he says.

"Same thing," she says. "Gots other names too if you wanna hear them."

"No, that's fine. Please continue."

"The door to the . . . ah, supply closet is like the ones on the classrooms," she says. "They're big solid wood doors but above the knob they's a little window."

"When you say 'little window' . . ." Scott says. "Can you describe it for the jury? Its dimensions?"

"I'd say it's about two and half, three feet tall and about six inches wide."

"Thank you," he says, "but if that's the size and shape of the window and it's above the door knob, why on earth would you get on your knees to see?"

"Oh, well . . . It's blacked out."

"Your window is blacked out but you got on your knees to see?"

"Yes, sir. The window is covered with black construction paper. If it weren't, kids be looking in on me all the time. Now, I ain't doin' anything in there I ain't supposed to be, but . . . I wants to eat my lunch or call Big Daddy on my break in privacy. Don't need no youngins staring at me while I do."

"Okay, but, surely if it's blacked out you can't see through it whether you're on your knees or not?"

"They's a rip in the paper down at the bottom," she says. "Plenty big to see out . . . and . . . with the lights out behind me I can see out but can't nobody see me."

"And what did you see?"

"Not much," she says. "Halls was a ghost town. Everybody locked in they classrooms even as bombs going off and all sorts of shooting. Every now and then somebody would run by, a kid or a cop. I saw the shooter . . . I froze and peed myself a little. Had to cup my hand over my mouth like this to keep from cryin'."

She demonstrates how she held her own mouth with the old, bent fingers of her arthritic hand.

"Had on one of them long black leather coats like a cowboy or a vampire and this spooky mask . . . all white and no expression and . . . was holding this big ol' shotgun . . . jackin' shells into the chamber and shooting up the ceiling."

"I'm so sorry you had to see that, that you had to be that close to death," Scott says.

"Not as sorry as I am."

"And while you were kneeling there looking out into the hallway did you have occasion to see anyone else?"

"Yes, sir."

"Who was that?"

"The defendant," she says, and points at me as if she has been told just how to do it—or has seen it on TV. "John Jordan."

"And what did you see him do?"

"He run by the first time, heading to the right," she says. "Had his gun drawn, looking like he wanted to shoot somebody."

"Objection, Your Honor," Anna says. "How does one look like he wants to shoot somebody?"

"Sustained," Wheata Pearl says. "Ms. Jones, please only tell us what you saw and not what you think other people were thinking or feeling or wanting to do."

Bernice nods. "Yes, ma'am. Sorry."

"He had his gun drawn?" Scott asks.

"Yes, sir."

"Where was he pointing it?"

"All around," she says. She forms the shape of a handgun with her thumb and forefinger and waves it about. "You know like how they do on TV when they raiding a drug house. Like sweeping it around before they yell *clear* or shoot somebody."

"Was he walking or jogging or running or . . ."

"Running flat out," she says. "Didn't even slow down to take the corner. I figured he'd stop at the corner and check both directions in the main hallway but he never even slowed down. If someone would've been there, he wouldn't've had time to tell who it was before they shot him or he shot them. I thought to myself at the time . . . he gonna get hisself killed running into that firefight like that."

"Or kill someone else before he knew what he was doing," Scott says.

"Your Honor," Anna says.

The judge holds up her hand as if there's no need for Anna to continue. "Mr. Scott, this is your final warning. Say anything like that again and you'll be in contempt and we'll see if a little time to reflect on your actions in a nice jail cell will improve your manners."

"Sorry, Your Honor."

"No, you're not," she says. "That's the most sorry-not-sorry apology I've ever received in this courtroom. But I promise you this . . . You will be. You will be very sorry if you ever pull a cheap stunt like that again."

Wheata Pearl pauses, takes a sip of whatever's in her rattlesnake mug, and then turns to the jury.

"Ladies and gentlemen of the jury, what Mr. Scott has just done is wrong and he knows it. He's trying to tell you want to think. He's trying to slip in his own testimony, and I'll tell you this . . . It has been my experience that when an attorney resorts to that it's because his or her case isn't going all that well and he or she thinks he or she has to tell the jury what to think because the evidence isn't doing it. This is a serious offense because Mr. Scott knew exactly what he was doing. It's a cheap whorehouse parlor trick that has no place in a court of law. You are to disregard his statement and try to completely forget you ever heard it."

"I am truly sorry, Your Honor," Scott says. "I got caught up and I was wrong. It won't happen again."

"See that it doesn't," she says. "Now, you can continue, but tread very carefully, sir. Very carefully."

"I do apologize, Ms. Jones," he says, "for putting words in your mouth. I was wrong to do that. What else did you see or hear during the shooting that morning?"

"Kept hearing explosions and gunshots and screams and crying and I saw the defendant running in the other direction a little while later. The main hallway is a circle. So first time I seen him he was running flat out to the right, and the other he was running even faster to the left and it was only a few minutes later."

"And then I heard somebody yell, *Don't shoot. Don't shoot.* But I heard shooting after that. A few quick shots. *Pop. Pop pop pop.*"

"Do you have any idea who yelled 'don't shoot'?"

"No, sir," she says. "I mean I didn't see anyone say it. I just heard it but . . . it sounded like a male student."

"You heard what sounded like a male student yelling 'Don't shoot. Don't shoot.' And then you heard several shots fired?"

24

"M s. Jones—" Anna begins.

"What's all this *Ms. Jones*? Call me Bernice. Everybody does. I ain't one to put on."

"It's just a sign of respect and some formality for the court," Anna says. "I just have a few questions for you. I know everybody's getting hungry and we need to break for lunch soon."

"That's all right by me," she says. "My belly sounds like they's a thunderstorm inside it."

"Now, you testified that from behind the closed and locked solid wood door of the custodian closet, with the lights off, you got on your knees and looked out into the hallway through a small tear in the black construction paper that's covering the six-inch-wide window in the door. Is that correct?"

"Yes, ma'am."

"How big would you say the little tear in the construction paper at the bottom is?"

"I don't know . . . Maybe three inches."

"Since none of us have seen it and no proof of it has been entered into evidence, we'll have to take your word for it, but let's do that. Let's stipulate that it is a three-inch tear—because even if it were the entire width of the window it would still be very, very narrow. So . . . from behind a solid wood door in the dark on your knees through a tiny three-inch tear in the construction paper at the bottom of the narrow window, you were able to see and hear all that you just testified to? Is that correct?"

"Yes, ma'am. Every word."

"Are you sure? It just seems quite extraordinary that under those conditions and in that situation with such a limited view and with explosions and gunfire going off you could see and hear all that. Are you absolutely sure?"

"Yes, ma'am. I am."

Without warning I am transported back to Potter High the morning of the shooting.

Withdrawing my weapon, I make my way up the hallway that leads to the main circular one beyond.

The acrid air is thick with smoke and the smell of burned gunpowder. Visibility is very low.

Through the fog, I can hear the dissonant sounds of disem-

bodied screams, the arrhythmic bursts of semi-automatic gunfire, the intermittent explosions of bombs, and the incessant blare of the fire alarm.

As I reach the main hallway, it gets worse—the smoke thicker, the racket louder, the terrified screams more piercing.

Unable to determine where exactly the shots are coming from, I take a right and head south in the main hallway.

Even if it wasn't dim and filled with smoke, the circularness of the hallway would make it difficult to see very far in either direction, its hard surfaces bouncing noises around, making it impossible to isolate or pin down the direction of any single sound.

"Well then let me ask you this," Anna is saying. "With as fast as you say John was running, how long would you say you actually saw him from that three-inch tear in the construction paper? Because it seems to me it couldn't have been more than a split second, and that if he was running as fast as you say he was, that he would've just been a blur. And yet you're saying you saw him long enough to not only identify him but to see what he was doing with his weapon and to notice an expression on his face. So how long would *you* say you saw him for?"

"I'm not sure exactly."

"Really?" Anna says. "You've been so sure about everything else. What would your estimate be?"

"A few seconds I guess."

"A *few* seconds? I wonder if I could get you to use

your hand and re-create the size and shape of the opening you were looking through for these few seconds?"

"Sure," Bernice says. "Be happy to. I'm just here to try to help get to the bottom of the truth."

She holds her thick hand up perpendicular to her face and with her arthritic fingers and thumb forms a small opening—and then actually looks through it.

It's a great visual for the jury to see.

"Thank you so much for your cooperation, Ms. Jones. I really appreciate it. Now how far away would you say John was from the door when he ran by it?"

"I'm not sure exactly."

"Well, the entire width of the hallway is only about eight feet . . . so if John was running up the middle of it, that would put him about four feet from you. If he was veering to one side or the other, that puts him either a little closer or farther back."

"I'd say he was somewhere in the middle," Bernice says. "Both times."

Reaching the first set of library doors, I see that they are shot up and shattered, large shards of glass hanging precariously over the jagged opening.

I pause and glance in. There is no movement, and though I'm sure there are students hiding inside, no one is visible.

As I round the first arching curve of the hallway, I can hear the live gunfire better and believe I'm getting close.

Another loud explosion close by, though I can't be certain exactly where, leaves my ears ringing.

Up ahead I hear shots being fired, and as I get closer, I can see Kim sitting on the floor in a pool of blood, leaning against the wall of a small alcove that leads to a dark, empty classroom, returning fire. On the floor a few feet away is her shot-up radio.

I rush over to her, crouching behind the same wall.

"So from about four feet away through a tiny three-inch opening you could identify who you were seeing, what they were doing, and the expression on their faces —even in the case of John who you testified was running at full speed?"

"Truths is truths," she says. "And that's the truth. What I say I seen and heard is what I seen and heard."

"A part of what you say you heard was a male student yelling 'Don't shoot. Don't shoot.' Is that correct?"

"Yes, ma'am, it is."

"And are you suggesting to the court today that that male voice was Derek Burrell? Because that seems to me like the impression you were trying to make—or at least Mr. Scott was trying to leave on the jury."

"Well, I guess I'm not saying that for sure . . . because . . . I don't rightly know for sure, but . . . but I believe that's who it was."

"Okay," Anna says. "Let me ask you this . . . Do you know how far it was from where you were—in that small supply closet behind that solid wood door with all the explosions and gunfire going off all around you—to where Derek Burrell shot at and was shot by John?"

"No, ma'am, not exactly. I guess I don't."

"Would you be surprised if I told you that it was over one hundred yards and around two big curves in the circular hallway?"

"No, I don't guess that would surprise me too much," she says. "I don't know how far it is . . . but I guess from what I heard about where that poor boy was killed that sounds about right."

"Do you think that no matter how loudly someone yelled from where Derek was to where you were, behind that solid wood door and with all the chaos and confusion and explosions and gunshots going off, that someone could hear what, if anything, Derek said?"

"I don't know . . . I thought that's who I heard, but like I say . . . I can't say for sure."

"So you're saying it's possible that you heard another student who was far closer to you. That's at least possible, right?"

"Sure, it's possible. Can't say for sure."

"Would you say that it's probable?"

"Can't say for sure. Could be."

"Now, I know you're a custodian at the school and not in maintenance or construction, but did you know that the ceilings of the Potter High School hallways have been treated to reduce noise? That they've been sprayed with a dampening material to keep the noise in the hallway down?"

"No ma'am, I didn't know that . . . but it don't surprise me none."

"Did you know I attended Potter High School back in the day?" Anna says. "And when I went there the hallway floors were some type of hard commercial Linoleum or some covering like that. But what are they now?"

"Carpet," Bernice says. "Been carpet for the last few years."

"So with carpet on the floor and dampening material on the ceiling, you're saying that from over one hundred yards away, around two big curves in the hallway, behind a closed solid wood door, you could hear something Derek Burrell said?"

"No, ma'am, I'm not saying that. I'm saying I thought that's who I heard but that I don't know for sure. I said that from the beginning—I don't know for sure."

"Yes you did. Thank you for that. Now, just a few more questions and I'm going to let you go and let us all go to lunch. You mentioned someone you referred to as 'Big Daddy.' Who is that?"

"That's my husband, Gerald Jones, Sr."

"So you must have a son named . . ."

"Gerald Jones, Jr. Yes ma'am."

"Have either Gerald Jones, Sr. or Gerald Jones, Jr. had

any run-ins with the sheriff's department in Potter County?"

"Objection, Your Honor," Gary Scott says. "Relevance?"

"Your Honor, I was about to get to that when I was interrupted."

"Overruled," Wheata Pearl says. "Okay, Ms. Jordan, get to it. Ms. Jones, you may answer the question."

"Yeah, they've had some."

"Has the Potter County Sheriff's Department ever arrested or charged them with crimes?"

"Yeah."

"And who was sheriff during those arrests?"

"Sheriff Jordan."

"Sheriff Jack Jordan? What if any relation is he to the defendant?"

"It's his daddy."

"Do you know if John helped in any way, either officially or unofficially, on the investigations that led to any of the arrests of Gerald Sr. or Jr.?"

"Don't know," she says, "but I'd heard he had."

25

During the lunch break, in a small conference room in the courthouse, while Anna preps for the afternoon I call an investigator friend of mine at the Bay County Sheriff's Office and tell her what Lucas Burke had told me the night before.

As I'm talking to her, I think about my experience with my girls in the storm that night and what Burke had done to save us.

Just as we're about to hang up something occurs to me, and when we finish the call I begin to think about it.

"What is it?" Anna asks.

I look up at her and say, "Huh?"

"I can see the wheels turning," she says.

"You know how it's hard to tell where Port St. Joe Beach ends and Mexico Beach begins?"

Highway 98 runs along the coast next to the Gulf of Mexico, and while some areas have obvious beginning and ending spots—natural barriers like the woods between Port St. Joe and Port St. Joe Beach or contracted barriers like the way Tyndall Air Force Base separates Panama City from Mexico Beach—other boundaries are not so clear.

"*Yeah?*" she says, and I can tell that's not remotely like anything she was expecting me to say.

"The counties are like that too," I say.

Port St. Joe Beach is in Gulf County and Mexico Beach is in Bay County.

She nods. "The division between them is even harder to distinguish."

"Yes it is," I say. "I feel like Mexico Beach is in Gulf County."

"It should be," she says.

"But it's in Bay County, which is why I couldn't work the hurricane house case—even though I saw it and one of the guys involved was murdered in Gulf County."

"The body found in the van in Dalkeith the morning of the storm?"

"Exactly. It's Bay County's case—they processed the scene. They took possession of the body."

"Yeah?"

"I've got missing persons cases and what I now believe

are linked murder victims in Wewa, Port St. Joe, and Port St. Joe Beach," I say.

"Okay," she says, and I can tell she's ready to get back to her prep.

"If I'm right about the cases not only not being accidental but actually being linked by the same sick predator . . . What if he went beyond Port St. Joe Beach and killed in Mexico Beach? It'd seem all the same to him, but . . . we'd never see the cases. Never even know about them."

"Sounds like you need to call Bay County back," she says.

I nod. "That's exactly what I need to do, but before I do . . . and I realize how anxious you are to get back to your—to what you're doing—I have to thank you again for what you're doing for me in there. You're extraordinary. And I'm—"

"How hard has it been today so far?"

"Hasn't been easy," I say. "At least not until it's your witness."

"You and the actions you took that day are easy to defend," she says. "The reason it has been relatively easy so far is . . . they just don't have a case—which is causing Scott to reach the way he did with Bernice. I'm not saying he doesn't still have some good witnesses to come . . . but so far it has been some weak-ass shit."

"Is that the legal term for it?" I ask. "So typical of you

attorneys . . . couch things in legalese so the rest of us have no idea what you're talkin' about."

She laughs and starts to write some more notes on the legal pad in front of her but stops and actually puts her pen down.

"You know what," she says. "I'm ready. I don't have to do any more. Let's talk instead. Tell me how you're really doing."

"You know what I keep wondering?" I say. "If anything would be different if I hadn't done anything. And the only thing I can come up with . . . is that Derek would be alive."

She thinks about it for a moment before responding. "You think . . ."

"If I hadn't run up that hallway . . . the same people would be dead and Derek would still be alive. I don't think I helped anything. The truth is . . . it was over by the time I go there. All I did was kill Derek."

26

After the lunch break, Gary Scott calls a handful of students and teachers who all testify to the terror they felt, the chaos and confusion of the environment, how none of them could tell the good guys from the bad guys because everyone, including me, was shooting.

"We literally had a school full of active shooters," one of the math teachers says.

Shots fired. Explosions detonated.

Tyrese on the radio. "Were those gunshots?"

Kim and LeAnn rushing out of their offices.

"Go look at the monitors and radio me where he is," Kim says, withdrawing her weapon. "And tell Tyrese to put the school on lockdown. Go. Hurry."

As LeAnn enters the back door to the main office, Kim runs through the commons, gun drawn, head moving about, scanning, searching, scouring.

Kim pulling her sheriff's department radio, calling dispatch. "Active shooter at Potter High School. I repeat, active shooter at Potter High School. SRO in pursuit."

Alarms blaring.

Tyrese on the intercom, telling teachers there's an active shooter situation, the school's on lockdown, it's not a drill.

More shots. Explosions. Smoke. Fire.

Loud, concussive bangs rattling the school, raining down debris.

The explosions rocking the building make the earlier shots sound smaller somehow—popguns by comparison, or Fourth of July firecrackers.

The big bangs of the bombs are deafening, jarring, overwhelming.

The high school has become a combat zone.

When asked if any of them ever heard me identify myself as law enforcement they all responded the same way—no, they had not.

By far the best line for the plaintiffs was said by a male student who was a friend of Derek's, when he said that I wasn't so much an active shooter as a loose cannon.

The gunman is wearing what could be considered the school shooter's uniform—long black duster, the collar up, black boots, black fatigues, black gloves, a black military-style cap—but with one significant addition. Unlike in any previous school rampage shootings, this time the shooter is wearing a mask.

And they all agreed that not only was Derek Burrell a great guy and hero trying to save his friends, but that no one with any sense at all would mistake him for a school shooter.

"It was obvious to everyone that he was there to help," a female student from his class says. "Shooting him was like shooting a cop responding to the attack."

Anna attempts to mitigate what they're saying but there is little she can do. Either the jury agrees with their perspectives and points of view or it doesn't. And if it does I'm going to lose this case.

Later in the day, Scott calls a forensics firearms and gunshot wounds expert named Dr. Barnard Chandler who testifies that based on where Derek was shot, I couldn't have been aiming to wound and disarm him like I had claimed. The only conclusion he can draw from examining all the evidence, including where the two rounds entered and exited the victim's body, is that I was doing one thing and one thing only.

"And what was that?" Gary Scott asks.

"Shooting to kill," he says. "This was an execution."

As Anna cross-examines him, I relive the shooting for what feels like the millionth time.

As I near the place I estimate the shooter to be, I can hear the blasts of his shotgun and the return bangs of Kim's sidearm.

I slow down, hoping to be able to sneak up behind him and take him alive, but as I round the curving hallway, he spins toward me, levels the barrel of his shotgun in my direction and fires.

The round whizzes by my head. I can hear and feel it.

In the split second before I fire back, I can see that not only is the boy not wearing a mask, but he's not one of the suspects we've been investigating.

He's big and blond and sort of soft looking, dressed in jeans, boots, and a T-shirt, and I don't think I've ever seen him before.

He fires another round.

I aim at the shotgun, attempting to knock it out of his hands, but his head is leaning down on the stock, sighting, and I'm afraid the round will hit him in the face.

Lowering my gun, I squeeze off two quick rounds. One aimed at his left hip, the other his left knee.

He spins around and goes down, his shotgun thudding heavily on the hard hallway floor as he does.

"Dr. Chandler, are you testifying that you can know the motivations and intentions of a shooter by looking at gunshot wounds?" Anna asks.

"No, but you can certainly make inferences," he says. "Draw conclusions based on the evidence."

"So you're saying you can tell by where a bullet enters and exits a body what the shooter meant to do?"

"In most cases."

"What if the shooter is a bad shot?" she asks. "Just misses what he aims for?"

"That's possible," he says, "though not often with well-trained professional law enforcement officers like the defendant."

"You're saying that professionals usually hit what they're aiming for?" she says.

"Generally, yes," he says. "I'm not saying they don't miss . . . Just that if they're aiming for the leg they don't hit the head."

"Ever?"

"I'm not saying that," he says. "The extreme cases are the exceptions that prove the rule."

"In this case," she says, "we have a round that enters the victim's lower left leg. What, if anything, do you conclude from that?"

"I think the other round is far more telling," he says.

"Really?" she asks. "You can tell which bullet matters most?"

"Yes," he says.

"Are you sure it's not just that one bullet proves your theory and the other contradicts it?"

"No, that's not it."

"Doesn't the round in Derek's leg back up John's story

that he was trying to stop him from shooting and not kill him?"

"I don't believe so."

"Really? Why is that?"

"I believe this is simply evidence of the defendant missing what he was aiming for," he says.

"Why can't the other round be that?"

"Well . . ."

"You can't know for sure it's not, can you?" she says. "You can't know that to a scientific certainty can you?"

"Well, that's a relative term, but I'm convinced, again based on the evidence, that the victim was being executed."

"Executed? Wow. That's a very strong and prejudicial word. Not at all a word that an unbiased scientist would use, is it? It's the word of someone who's willing to prove his worth to the plaintiff, isn't it? Speaking of . . . How many times have you testified as a so-called 'expert witness'?"

"I'm not sure."

"What if I told you it was over three hundred?" she says. "Would you take issue with that number?"

He shrugs. "Probably not."

"It is, in fact, how you make a living, isn't it? Being an expert witness?"

"I have books and—"

"Well, then let me ask it this way . . . what pays your

bills? Your books or testifying as a guns and gunshot wounds expert?"

"Using my expertise in important trials to get to the truth probably makes more than my books."

"Is that what you try to do when you testify in trials?" she asks. "Get to the truth?"

"It is."

"Then the truth must always be on one side," she says. "In every single case. Is it true that you are always an expert witness for the plaintiff?"

"Yes."

"You've never once in your life testified on behalf of a defendant?"

"Experts typically specialize."

"You've certainly done that," she says.

"A lot of reputable experts do," he says. "We live in a specialists society."

"That may be, but you can't say that truth is limited to one specialty, to one side every single time. Now, as you know, John's statement under oath is that he was attempting to subdue the person shooting at him and the school resource officer, not to kill him. He has consistently maintained that he attempted to shoot Derek in the leg and in the hip just to bring him down, to stop him before he killed an officer who was already injured and couldn't move. Is it possible . . . Is it possible that John's first round went into Derek's leg like he claimed shooting and that though he aimed at Derek's hip when he shot, that Derek was moving, already falling from the shot to the leg? And so instead of the round hitting Derek's hip, it hit where his hip was a moment before—his abdomen area. Is that possible?"

Hurricane Michael Hits Region's Tupelo Producers Hard

By Merrick McKnight, *News Herald* Reporter

Massive amounts of white tupelo gum trees in the Apalachicola and Chipola river basin areas of Gulf and Liberty counties were destroyed by Hurricane Michael, removing the main source required for bees to produce tupelo honey.

According to many area beekeepers, the bees are mostly alive and well, but the storm's impact on the environment is going to have a huge impact on them—particularly when it comes to the production of tupelo.

According the University of Florida, the Panhandle is home to nearly 500 commercial beekeepers and more than 1.2 billion honeybees—bees that not only produce honey but play a crucial role in the pollination of other crops in the area, such as blueberry, cucumber, and watermelon.

The Florida State Beekeepers Association has set up a GoFundMe campaign to assist beekeepers in the affected areas.

27

That afternoon after court I drive over to the Bay County Sheriff's Office to meet with an investigator named Pamela Garmon.

Because I have to go by my office in Port St. Joe first, I travel Highway 98 along the coast into Panama City, which takes me through the areas hit hardest by the hurricane.

Before I left the courthouse, I encountered Rick Urich who seemed to be waiting in the back to talk to me.

"I'm surprised to see you here," I say. "I didn't think you guys took breaks."

The forty-something African-American cell phone salesman who looks more like a professional athlete gives me a big, warm smile worthy of a Good Samaritan, his eyes sparkling, his teeth gleaming.

"I just wanted to come and say thank you again for looking for me yesterday and to apologize for wasting your time. I know how busy you are right now."

"You drove all the way out here to Pottersville to tell me that?"

"We were working at a little home in the woods back off the highway not too far from here," he says, "and I . . . I just . . . I wanted to ask you a couple of things."

"Okay."

"I just feel so bad for Betty. It's a real sacrifice for us to come here and do what we do. It takes a special person, you know? I want to help get her back. And I was wondering if maybe the person who picked me up yesterday is the same one who took her. What if he planned to kill or abduct me or something but decided at some point that he'd have his hands full with me."

I don't know how Rick is in a fight but he certainly looks formidable.

"That's an interesting idea," I say. "Did he act suspicious or do anything that would make you think—"

"No, not really. It's a farfetched idea. I . . . I just want to help if I can. Is there anything I can do to help find her?"

"The way you all are helping those in need with their homes is helping us all more than you can know. Let us focus on finding Betty and—"

"But I want to help find Betty. I just still can't believe

she was really taken like that. There's got to be something we can do."

"We're working on it, and won't give up until we find her. But if there's anything you can help us with, I'll certainly let you know. And if you give me the contact info of the man you helped yesterday, we'll follow up with him."

"I didn't get anything like that from him," he says. "I don't even know the address of his place, but I could probably take you there."

"Okay," I say. "I have somewhere I have to be right now, but maybe tomorrow or . . . I'll come by the church and pick you up when I can."

"But what if he's got her there?" he says. "Shouldn't we go now?"

"I just can't right now," I say, "but I can have a couple of deputies go with you."

"I'd rather it be just us," he says.

"I would take a deputy or two with us when we go anyway," I say. "Even if there's a chance he could have Betty."

"Oh, gotcha," he says and shrugs, his demeanor changing, and he suddenly seems disinterested. "Well, okay then. Either way."

"I'll call them," I say. "Can you go now?"

He purses his lips and nods noncommittally. "Yeah, sure. I can go. It's just . . . I wanted to talk to you. I heard some people talkin' about you and . . . well . . . I was wanting to become a police officer—but not just that. I really want to be a police chaplain and I thought I could ask you some questions on the way out to the place."

"Why don't you go with the deputies now," I say. "And I'll swing by the church sometime and talk to you about being a police officer and a chaplain?"

So as I'm driving toward PC two of Gulf County's finest are taking the Good Samaritan to talk to the man he helped yesterday.

My journey is slow and difficult with many dead stops along the way. There are several detours and spots where the traffic is one lane because part of the highway has been destroyed—either washed away by tidal surge or crushed with the rubble of crumbling hotels and restaurants.

Beginning at the east end of St. Joe Beach and continuing to the very west end of Mexico Beach, the coastline has been demolished.

Where once were sea oats–dotted dunes of pure, clean sand so white it looked like sugar, there is only a storm-flattened beach with dirty, wet compressed sand, veins of black running through it. The water is brown instead of green, the environment foreign instead of familiar, and I mourn for what have before now always been to me the most beautiful beaches in the world.

The buildings on both sides of the highway, the small

cottages, the colorful condos, the excessive mansions, the touristy shops, the gulfside dining establishments, and the last of the old fishing shacks are all gone to one degree or another.

Lifted by the tide, flung apart by the wind, the structures left even partially standing are detached from their foundations, out of square and leaning like at any moment they will finish their fall to the battered earth below.

Entire intact homes have been washed across the highway, coming to rest among other structures, vehicles, and debris like limbs and street trash caught on the steel bars of a storm water runoff drainage grate.

As if the remnants of a post-war province a world away, piles of rubble from what looks like bombed-out buildings litter the landscape.

As if an abandoned civilization in a post-apocalyptic desert world, sand drifts cover large swaths of the highway.

This is the first time I've been back to Mexico Beach since the day the storm hit, and I'm haunted by the echoes of that ordeal.

Landmarks that have been here for as long back as I can remember are no more.

The Lookout Lounge is a mound of broken cinderblocks.

What's left of Toucans restaurant blocks part of the

highway, still sitting where it landed after Michael lifted it off its cement pilings and washed it away.

Though still standing, the massive concrete and steel structure of the El Governor Motel is in tatters, the large back window of its rooms with the gorgeous Gulf view shattered, the contents of the rooms sucked out, some of it hanging from mangled balcony railings, some of it on the beach below.

The boats of the marina are capsized and tossed to the side, stacked on top of each other like a child's bathtub toys after the last of the water has drained out. The marina itself is filled with such an extreme amount of debris that it will never be clean again—houses and parts of houses and household goods, appliances and furniture, construction materials, vehicles, and what looks like enough 2x4s to frame the homes and businesses of an entire town.

As the debris field of what once was Mexico Beach ends, I enter the decimated pine forest flats that serve as the natural barrier of Tyndall Air Force Base. Tens of thousands of trees blown down, broken off, bent over, turned, twisted, toppled.

As the wounded woods recede, I'm not prepared for what I witness next.

Tyndall Air Force Base looks to have been ground zero of a massive successful terrorist attack. Perimeter fences down. Airplane hangars crushed like an old tin breadbox in a scrap metal compactor. Everywhere—in trees, on knotted and jumbled power lines, on bent steel frames—twisted and tangled sheets of tin flutter like ribbons in the wind.

Exposed military aircraft, from aging bombers to the latest fighter jets, can be seen in the wreckage and ruin, the damage extensive, permanently grounding.

Base housing, training and operational buildings, officers and enlisted clubs—either gone entirely or damaged beyond repair.

Coming down off the bridge near Tyndall into Callaway, I can see that the town has been hit every bit as hard as Mexico Beach and the air force base—businesses gone or boarded up, houses destroyed or damaged. Nothing open. Nothing operational. Rubble and debris everywhere, on every lot, lining every street, the untacked tarp corners of blue roofs flapping in the breeze.

The devastation is overwhelming. Depressing. Anxiety inducing. Difficult to comprehend.

The chaos of the environment, the mounds and mounds of debris, the piles and piles of trash make me feel anxious, angry, irritable, and claustrophobic.

Continuing into Panama City, I see that the low-income housing on 15th Street has been destroyed, its apartments vacant, the items left behind by those who'd been evacuated lie molding and mildewing.

All major chain restaurants and most of the smaller

independently owned ones are closed—as are all but a few grocery stores and gas stations.

The Panama City Mall is so severely damaged that it can't reopen—now and probably ever—wind and water damage leaves two of the three anchor stores and all the interior stores, restaurants, and kiosks ruined. Across the street from the mall, the Holiday Inn where Merrill and I recently worked on the Malia Goodman case looks as if an IED exploded inside, its glass windows shattered, wet sheets and drapes hanging out, waving in the wind.

When I finally arrive at the Bay County Sheriff's Office I am depleted, drained, depressed.

Inside I find Pamela Garmon, a middle-aged black woman who worked her way up from dispatch to patrol to now investigations, at the large table in the conference room looking through case files.

"I had about given up on you," she says.

"Sorry," I say. "That trip takes a lot, lot longer than it used to."

"Yeah, but at least it's got a beautiful view."

I try to laugh as I sit down across from her with my briefcase full of files, but nothing quite comes out. "Too soon," I say. "Too soon."

"Yeah, I guess it is, but better to laugh and cry than just cry. Hope you don't mind that I started without you."

"Not at all."

"You can double-check but I think I about got it all sorted."

"I certainly don't need to double-check," I say. "You know what we're looking for."

"Appears to me we got two deaths determined to be accidental that deserve a closer look in the light of what you've found over your way. And they're both in Mexico Beach. We got nothing in any other part of Bay County that's even questionable—they're either obvious homicides, suicides, or accidents."

"So Mexico Beach is as far west as he goes," I say.

"You think one perp's behind all these?"

"I think it's possible," I say. "And maybe for some missing persons we haven't found yet. Especially if the two in Mexico Beach have a bone broken post-mortem."

Her eyes widen. "They do."

"Mind if we take a look at them?"

"That's what we're here for," she says.

She slides all but two file folders to the side, then opens the two, turns them toward me, and pushes them across the table.

"David Cleary and Ellen Lucado," she says.

I examine Cleary's file first.

"Cleary was found in the rubble of the Gulfside Seafood Restaurant and Lounge," she says. "His body was in bad shape, but it seemed consistent with a building crashing down on top of him. The investigator who caught the case theorized that Cleary stayed during the storm instead of evacuating. When his house was destroyed he sought shelter in the downstairs bar of the Gulfside, and eventually it fell down on top of him."

I flip through the thin file.

"I'm'a be honest with you," she says. "We're workin' in emergency mode over here."

"We are too," I say. "Our entire area is."

"I won't be surprised if we missed something," she says. "Way things are right now . . . if it looks like an accident and quacks like an accident, we gonna call it an accident."

I nod. "I understand. Pretty much triage in every agency right now."

"But if we missed something I want to fix it," she says. "Don't want no sick bastard takin' advantage of our depleted state right now to get away with killin' our people when they already suffering the way we are."

The file depicts what she had described, and the autopsy reveals that the radius bone of his right arm was broken after death.

I put down Cleary's file and pick up Lucado's.

"Not much in there, I know," she says. "Ellen Lucado's body was found floating in the Mexico Beach marina. And even though she didn't drown, her death was ruled accidental because we figured she got struck in the head by debris flying around or falling before she went into the water."

According to her autopsy, the fourth toe on her left foot was broken after she was already dead.

I study the autopsy photo of her feet.

She has a tattoo on the top left side of her left foot—a simple black Chinese symbol that I think I've seen before but can't recall for sure and don't know what it means. She has attractive, well-manicured feet and her toenails are painted an electric blue that makes her seem both more human and more vulnerable somehow. From the photo alone I can't tell that her toe is broken.

"I was expecting to see more visible trauma on her feet or at least the toe that was broken," I say.

"No blood or bruising because she was dead when it happened," she says.

"I meant from the violence of whatever broke it," I say.

"Oh," she says. "Yeah. She's definitely in the better shape of the two."

I look at the file for a few more moments but there's nothing else to see.

"So you're thinking the pattern is . . . make a murder look like an accident caused by or related to the storm and break a bone after death?" she asks.

I nod.

"How many you got in Gulf County so far?"

"Three," I say, "but I'm betting more when we locate some more of our missing persons."

"Our boy's been busy," she says.

"That's what concerns me."

"How you wanna handle it?" she says. "Sheriff says it's up to me. I'll be liaising from our end. Says we can create a task force or just coordinate on it."

"Given how stretched everyone is," I say, "why don't we let our deputies and our investigators know what's going on—and we need to tell the Port St. Joe and Mexico Beach police departments too—and then just coordinate with each other. Task force would eat up time and labor neither of our departments have right now."

"Agreed," she says. "We give each other copies of the relevant files and both dig in on them and see what else we can come up with. Maybe by looking at them as suspicious deaths we'll come up with evidence that was overlooked before."

I nod. "Sounds good," I say, trying to keep the sense of futility I feel out of my voice.

"You're saying it sounds good but you don't look or sound like you think so," she says.

"I just get the sense that this particular sadist has perfected his dark deeds to the point of not leaving behind too much in the way of evidence."

28

On my drive back, I start calling the family members of the victims, beginning with Ellen Lucado's older sister, Diane.

"My name is John Jordan and I'm an investigator with the Gulf County Sheriff's Department."

"Yes?"

"Do you have a moment?" I ask. "Do you mind if I ask you a few questions about your sister Ellen?"

"Now's fine, but . . . has something new come up or . . ."

"It's just a routine follow-up," I say. "We try to do it for all our cases. Just take a second look at our investigations. It's one of our agency's best practices. Helps make sure we didn't miss anything."

"Oh, okay. What do you want to know?"

"Can you tell me why she chose not to evacuate?"

"She didn't," she says. "I mean she didn't choose not to, not that she didn't evacuate—although I guess she didn't, did she?"

I wonder if she's nervous for some reason or if she always talks so circuitously.

"She was supposed to," she is saying. "And I thought she did. We have friends who live on Overstreet—near the Wewa end—and she was going to stay with them but she never showed. I knew something was wrong because she didn't call them or me and that wasn't like her at all. She would've let us know."

"Any idea why her plans changed?"

"No, but she was a really good person. If I had to guess . . . I bet she got delayed trying to help someone or trying to save some pets other evacuees left behind. She was always doing stuff like that. Had several elderly neighbors she helped out and took in strays like a mother. That would be just like her. I'll tell you this . . . I'd give all the stupid pets in all the world to have her back."

"Was there anything unusual going on with her in the lead-up to the storm?" I ask. "Did she mention anything out of the ordinary? Anything at all, no matter how small it seems? Something suspicious? Someone new she met? Any conflicts she had with anyone?"

"Why?" she says, her voice rising. "Do you think she could've been . . . you know . . . that someone killed her?"

"Like I said, we just want to be sure. Please don't read anything into my questions. They're just some of the standard questions that we ask. What we try to do when we take a second look at a case is to question the original determination of cause of death. So since your sister's death was ruled accidental, I'm asking the questions we would have if it was suspicious. I'm sorry to put you through this but it really helps. Just please don't think that anything I'm saying means anything different than what you already know. If I discover anything in this second look we'll obviously let you know, but it's very, very rare that we do."

"I understand," she says. "Makes sense."

I'm glad it does to her because the more I say about it the less I believe it.

"No . . . she didn't mention anything odd or suspicious . . . I mean . . . her life seemed absolutely normal—same as it always did right up until the storm hit. She lived a quiet life. She was content, you know, the kind of person who never got mixed up in anything. She . . ."

Though she's very quiet about it, I can tell she's crying.

"Again, I'm so sorry," I say.

"Thank you," she says. "I . . . I just can't make myself think that it's real. Nothing seems real right now. The whole world is upside down. Nothing is like it was before the storm. Between losing Ellen and the impact of storm . . . I can't get my bearings. I'm just . . . lost."

"And I'm sure this doesn't help. I'm sorry to have bothered you. I really appreciate your time."

"It's fine," she says. "Thank *you* for looking into it again. It means a lot that y'all're making sure everything was . . . right or whatever."

"Well, take care," I say. "You have my number if you need anything or think of anything you need to let us— Oh, before I go . . . I wanted to ask you . . . I really like the tattoo on Ellen's left foot and I wondered if you could tell me what it means?"

"I don't . . . I don't understand. Ellen didn't have any tattoos. She didn't like them."

"Are you sure?"

"Positive."

"Could she have gotten it since the last time you saw her?"

"I saw her the night before the storm and she was barefooted and she did not have a tattoo on her foot or anywhere else. Is it . . . Do you think . . . Is it possible y'all have the wrong . . . Could it be someone else? But if so where would Ellen be? She'd still be missing or—"

"I'm so sorry," I say. "I keep making things worse for you. I'm sure I just got mixed up. Because of the storm . . . we're dealing with a lot of deaths and it's possible I confused some of the autopsy pictures I've seen. I'm sure that's what it is, just a mistake—and I'm so sorry for making it. But I promise you this—I'll get to the bottom of it and get back to you just as quickly as I possibly can."

The moment I end the call with Diane, I find one of the few places on the side of the road that doesn't have downed trees and pull over. As I open my briefcase and withdraw Ellen's file, I'm tapping in the number for Leno Mullally, the ME's investigator who worked her case.

When he answers he sounds like he has food in his mouth. The last time I spoke to him I thought he was eating because it was his lunch break, but now I'm wondering if maybe it'd be hard to catch him when he wasn't eating.

"You worked the Ellen Lucado case, right?"

"Refresh my memory."

"Her body was found in the marina at Mexico Beach."

"Oh, yeah," he says. "Attractive woman. Pretty feet. Real shame. She was found in the water but she didn't drown. Blunt force trauma. A power pole or a sailboat mast—something struck her in the head before she went into the water. But that's a Bay County case."

"Yeah," I say. "Investigator over there, Pamela Garmon, gave me the file. We're looking at a possible connection between a few of our cases."

"This like the other one you called about?" he says. "Think it might not be an accident?"

"I'm looking at the autopsy photos," I say. "Can you pull them up?"

"Sure, give me a sec."

He takes the sec to not only pull up the photos but take another bite of whatever he's eating.

"Okay," he says.

I describe the photos I'm looking at.

"Yeah," he says. "Ellen Tabitha Lucado."

"These show a tattoo on the top left side of her left foot," I say.

"Yep. See it."

"I just spoke to her sister," I say. "She says Ellen didn't have any tattoos. Didn't like them. Said she saw her barefooted the night before the storm and she didn't have a tattoo."

"Well, she had one when she was brought in here," he says.

"You're absolutely positive this is Ellen Lucado?"

"One hundred percent," he says. "Not only does her appearance match her driver's license photo, but we printed her. It's her. No question. It'd hurt like a son of a bitch to get one done there. Just bone under the skin. No meat."

"It's not red or puffy around it," I say. "And it's not peeling. It's not a new tattoo."

"Yeah, you're right," he says. "It's not new. Unless it's not a tattoo."

"What do you—"

"At least not a permeant one," he says. "Could be a temporary one. It wasn't a sticker. It was on the skin, but she could've just put it on as some kind of superstitious protection from the storm—which obviously didn't work."

"Can we check?" I ask.

"I love that you used *we*," he says, "like you'd come to the morgue and we could examine that foot together, but, no, her body was cremated a few days ago."

DURING MY CONVERSATION with Mullally I missed a call from one of the deputies who took Rick Urich to the home of the man he'd helped the day before.

"Sorry I missed your call," I say. "I was—"

"We're back," he says. "Couldn't find the place. He led us down several dirt roads up near the county line that he thought might be it, but . . . none of 'em were. Says he'll keep trying to figure out where it is and if he sees the guy again he'll ask him, but . . . nothing today but wasted time and gas."

"Okay," I say. "Thanks for taking him. Sorry it didn't turn up anything."

"Okay," he says. "Just letting you know."

Before I can say anything else he is gone.

29

I've almost made it back to Wewa when Pamela Garmon calls.

"I didn't expect to hear from you so soon," I say.

"I'm afraid it's not good news," she says.

"What's up?"

She clears her throat before she begins to speak and when she does I can hear the tension in her voice. "I shared everything with our sheriff and our lead investigator and they both have serious concerns."

"Concerns?" I say.

"Doubts," she says. "That there's really anything there. They think everything can be explained as accidental—including the deaths themselves and the broken bones afterwards. Think it's a real stretch to say we got some kind a serial killer on our hands."

I'm not just disappointed but deflated.

"Just wanted to give you a heads-up," she says. "Our sheriff's going to be calling yours to discuss it, so . . ."

"I appreciate it," I say, and I wonder if she can hear how disheartened I am.

"And hey . . . just between you and me . . . I'm still gonna look into it and we're not gonna ignore evidence. I promise you that. If we get more evidence or if another case happens that's similar enough to these to convince us . . . we will of course investigate it."

She had seemed so convinced before. Had she been and the sheriff and lead investigator really persuaded her that quickly and easily, or was she just being polite to me?

"You seemed pretty convinced earlier," I say. "They talk you out of it or did I read you wrong before?"

"I don't know . . . I'm conflicted about it. I really am. I can see it both ways, but . . . your theory requires a pretty big leap that the other one doesn't."

I don't say anything and we are quiet an awkward beat.

"The sheriff says he wonders if maybe you're trying to distract yourself from your court case and this is how you're doing it—imagining a serial killer. I'm not saying he's right or that I agree . . . but . . . it's probably worth considering. Have you considered that?"

"I have actually," I say. "More than once. And maybe I am. I'll certainly reconsider it."

"And hey, like I said . . . I'm still gonna look at it on my own and I'm not gonna let anybody over here ignore evidence if we catch another case with any similarities at all . . . You'll be my first call. Meantime . . . keep your chin up, partner, and good luck with your trial."

When we end the call I think about what she said and wonder if I am trying to distract myself from Derek's death, the trial, and what the eventual verdict will mean for me.

Maybe my subconscious is making a fool out of me.

There's definitely a case to be made for these all being sad accidents that have a few aspects in common.

I haven't finished thinking it all the way through when Reggie calls.

"Seems you made quite the impression over there," she says.

"Evidently," I say, and let out a sigh. "But not the one I was trying to. Did their sheriff convince you too?"

"No, I wouldn't say that. But . . . you even said yourself that these could be what they look like—tragic accidents."

"Sure," I say, "they could be. But . . . there's certainly some evidence that indicates it . . . could be murder."

"If they are accidental, no one would blame you for . . . seeing more."

"Sounds like the sheriff of Bay County is far more convincing than I am," I say.

"Give me a little credit," she says. "I'm not saying I'm convinced either way. Just . . . let's be cautious. Go slow. Consider everything—including your state of mind and whether you're searching for a distraction. All we can do is keep examining the evidence and follow where it leads. And I'm not telling you to do anything other than that. But . . . I mean . . . we're barely surviving right now . . . so just keep everything in perspective. You can keep looking into it and if you come up with anything else . . . let me know . . . but looks like you'll be a task force of one. Bay County's out and Darlene and Arnie want no part of it. And speaking of them . . . see if you can't patch things up. Be far better for the department if y'all can be friends again."

"I didn't realize we weren't," I say.

"Which might say something about the state of your mind right now," she says. "Given the storm and what you went through and with how things are now and with being on trial . . ."

That night I have a dark night of the soul.

For most of the evening I sit alone in my study, the flicker of candlelight from my altar the only illumination in the room, the interplay of its light and shadows dancing on my face.

I feel alone, isolated from every other person on the planet, my sense of separation intensifying with every passing moment.

The storm has been isolating—and not just because for a while we were cut off from the world outside our own, but because all the places that provided any opportunity for socialization, for gathering to break bread or have a drink, are gone. And not only that, but everyone is scattered, displaced, busy with day-to-day survival or early important recovery efforts. Merrill is busy with missing persons cases and other storm-recovery-related activities, but even if he weren't, the old gym on Main Street where we used to play basketball is now filled with the emergency supplies that pour into our little town daily—often by the semi-trailer full. The hurricane aftermath reality we're living means everything has been disrupted. Every. Single. Thing. Nothing is simple. Nothing is easy. Nothing is as it was before. I miss Merrill. I no longer see Dad and Verna and Jake and other family and friends on any kind of regular basis, and when we do see them it's for brief moments and everyone is exhausted and depleted, weary and rawboned. Home doesn't resemble anything like home anymore. And everywhere we turn there is trash, rubble, debris. Our trees are gone. Our homes and businesses are caving in on us. The chaos and confusion and uncertainty and disorganization closes in on us, causing claustrophobia, anxiety, and depression.

But it's not just the littered, lonely landscape that leaves me feeling cut off and alone.

The trial is also isolating—and not just because I'm trapped in the courtroom all day every day, far away from my normal routine and the familiar frames that give shape to my days, but because I alone am on trial. Even with Anna by my side, I alone am accused. I am the one being criticized and condemned. I alone am having my actions questioned and picked apart. I alone have to give an answer. And what can I say? I killed a kid. That's the bleak, bitter truth of it. No matter the mitigating circumstances, no matter the situation—no matter who set it up or who fired first—I killed a young man whose life was just getting started. Even if I win the trial—whatever that means—I've already lost. What I have done can never be undone. And I am alone in the unmerciful and unalterable fact of it.

The current case—or what I thought was the current case—is also isolating. Especially after today. I may just be making it all up, my guilt and isolation causing a certain subtle madness in my own mind that is imperceptible to me. Am I just imagining it all? Am I just craving something to occupy my mind, trying not to think about Derek, his death, his parents' suit against me for taking him from them?

I am alone.

I am isolated.

I am separated.

I am detached.

Anna is in the next room and would gladly come in here and offer me comfort and consolation if I would only ask her.

If I would just call him, Merrill would be over here in a matter of minutes—to sit with me inside this deafening silence or let me talk or rant or cry or anything I needed to.

Countless other friends would likewise be willing to help regardless of how inept that help might be, but right now nothing anyone could do would help.

What is this inconsolable condition afflicting me? Why do I find myself with this particular malady?

It's not because of Bay County's and then Reggie's response to my theory about the recent spate of accidental deaths—though that began the loss of altitude that has led to this nosedive.

And it's not just one thing—though it is one thing primarily.

It's not primarily the impact of the hurricane and the desolation it left in its wake, though that is part of it.

It's not that I'm all alone in my belief that we have a killer in our midst preying on us in our most vulnerable hour, but that too is part of it.

And it's not primarily the trial—though having to sit there and relive one of the worst and most regrettable experiences of my life is making a significant contribution to this cold, sad separation that has seeped into my every cell.

No, the primary reason I'm feeling the way I do—alone and miserable, detached and isolated, saturated with sadness and grieving so intensely I find it an effort to breathe—is because I shot and killed Derek Burrell. That is primary. That is everything—everything else is so secondary to it as not to even register when set next to it.

Rising from the floor where I was sitting in front of my altar, I begin to pull books off my shelves and search their pages for something I can't even completely formulate by candlelight.

I turn first to St. John of the Cross's "Dark Night of the Soul," but after just two stanzas give up on it.

Once in the dark of night,
Inflamed with love and yearning, I arose
(O coming of delight!)
And went, as no one knows,
When all my house lay long in deep repose
All in the dark went right,
Down secret steps, disguised in other clothes,
(O coming of delight!)
In dark when no one knows,
When all my house lay long in deep repose.

I then search other texts—some of them hundreds and others thousands of years old—the solitary expressions of men and women long since dead before my ancestors were born, but who were experiencing something akin to what I am in this dark hour.

I try many, many wise and true and profound writings, but it is not until I crack open my dusty old volume of the poetry of Hafez, the lyrical fourteenth-century

Persian poet, that I find the instruction my soul most needs in this moment.

Don't surrender your loneliness so quickly. Let it cut you more deeply. Let it ferment and season you as few human and even divine ingredients can. Something missing in my heart tonight has made my eyes so soft, my voice so tender, my need for God absolutely clear.

31

Melissa Burrell is crying softly as she takes the stand, dabbing at her puffy, red-etched eyes with a small white handkerchief.

"I know how difficult all of this is for you, Ms. Burrell," Gary Scott says, his soft tone nearly completely masking his voice's nasality, "and I'm so deeply sorry you're having to endure this—after everything else."

"We asked for this," she says. "And please call me Melissa."

"I think everyone the world over agrees that of all the profoundly painful things a human being can suffer, losing a child is far and away the most painful—that it is unimaginably excruciatingly heartbreakingly unbearably painful."

"I never have and never will experience anything as

devastating," she says. "Every single day since it happened I've wanted to die."

"I can only imagine," he says. "I'm so, so sorry."

He pauses for a moment.

Melissa wipes at tears and sniffles as he takes a quick sip of water.

"Was Derek your only child?" he asks.

She nods. "We didn't think we were going to even get one. We went through several miscarriages and a lot of fertility specialists. But . . . it was worth it. He was worth the wait. There's never been a better baby. It was like he knew what we had been through just to get him here and he was as grateful as we were just to be here. And then growing up . . . he was just always the most gentle thing. Kind and thoughtful. I can say before God that he never gave us one moment's trouble."

"I've heard very good things about him from all his classmates and teachers," Scott says. "They're all experiencing an enormous loss, but nothing compares to what you and your husband are going through and they know that. We all know that."

"Everyone has been so supportive," she says. "Well, almost everyone."

"What do you mean?" Scott asks. "I would think everyone would be extremely supportive and understanding."

"There are those—mostly online, but some in the

media and in our community—who blame him for his own death. And by extension me and Bryce. They say he should've never had a gun at school, that he and we knew it was illegal. That he should've never gone out and gotten it out of his truck and shouldn't have come back into the school with it and started shooting. Say he became a . . . a school shooter when he did that. Some actually go as far as to say that we owe the defendant an apology—that we put him in that terrible position and now he has to live with it for the rest of his life."

"How do you and your husband respond to that kind of . . ."

"I say at least he has a life," she says. "Derek doesn't. I'd love for him to be here having to live with something —anything."

"What about the fact that it's illegal to have firearms on campus?" Scott asks. "Even out in the parking lot in a vehicle. What would you say to those who say that if he hadn't climbed through the classroom window, gotten his gun, and come back in shooting . . ."

"Every young man I know around here hunts," she says. "Sometimes a rifle or a shotgun gets left in a vehicle. The boys forget it's there. Or they think they took it out to clean. They don't mean anything by it. Accidents happen. And as far as him going out to get it to help try to save the lives of his classmates . . . that makes him a hero. Nothing else. Nothing less. A young hero with his entire amazing life ahead of him and he had it violently taken away from him by an overaggressive killer cop who thinks he can shoot our children and get away with it."

"Is that why you've brought this suit against the defendant?"

She nods defiantly, glancing over at me for a moment then back at Scott. "Partly. I just couldn't let someone do that to my boy . . . to our family, and not do something. I'm so sick of corrupt killer cops being protected by the agencies they serve. The oversight and accountability is a joke. They always clear cops for shooting and they never criminally prosecute them. And it's not going to change until we the people do something about it. Our only recourse is a civil suit like this."

He nods gravely, pauses another moment, then says, "Now, can you tell us why you didn't sue the department the defendant works for or the one whose jurisdiction it is where this shooting took place?"

"Well, this isn't the reason, but think about that . . . the defendant doesn't even work for the department that has jurisdiction. If that doesn't let you know that there's something criminally off about the case, then I don't think you can be convinced. But the reason we brought this suit against . . . the defendant is as a way of begging for just some small modicum of accountability, of him being forced to admit some responsibility for murdering my only child."

"Most plaintiffs sue the agency the officer involved in the shooting works for because they have the deeper pockets."

"That's why we didn't," she says. "This isn't about the money for us. Not in any way. We're not keeping a dime of it, not one nickel."

"I noticed you sued for an extremely small amount—only fifteen thousand."

"That's the minimum for circuit court and we wanted it as low as possible to make the statement this isn't about money—it's about my son. This is about that man over there sitting at the defense table and only him being held accountable. It's saying you can't get away with this. That's why we're donating every cent of it to groups that are working tirelessly to stop police violence."

"That's very admirable of you and your husband."

She shakes her head. "It's nothing. It's . . . Our son is dead. Nothing else matters. Money can't bring him back and we don't want any money. We wouldn't use it anyway. We're hardly hanging on. We barely eat. We no longer have any interests or hobbies. No desire to travel or . . . anything. So we certainly don't need or want any money."

"What do you want?" he asks.

"For some court somewhere, with enough conviction and courage to actually do it, to hold the man who murdered my son accountable. To say to him you're not God. You're not the law. You're not above it. You can't do what you did and not be punished—even if it's just a measly amount of money in a civil suit. That's it. And short of my son being raised from the dead and restored back to us, that's all we want. And I don't think it's too much to ask."

"Neither do I," Scott says. "Neither do I."

He then turns and sort of stumbles back over to his seat as if he's so emotionally spent he is unable to walk.

"Nothing further, Your Honor," he says.

"Ms. Jordan," Wheata Pearl says, pushing back a stray strand of her strawberry-colored hair.

Anna slowly stands and deliberately walks over to the podium.

"Ms. Burrell, I have so many questions for you," she says. "But I'm not going to ask you a single one and I want you to know why. I know how you feel about my husband and I can only imagine that those feelings extend to me—especially as I am representing him in this case. So out of respect for you and as a way to keep you from having to interact with me or prolong your time on the stand I won't ask you the many questions I have for you, but instead will only say that both John and I are so very, very sorry for your loss—especially John, who wishes with every cell of his being that this had never happened."

Melissa leans into the mic and says, "Apology not accepted."

Anna nods and continues to look at her with sympathy and compassion.

"I'd've much rather you had kept your lame apology," Melissa says, "and asked me your many lame questions instead."

32

"I can imagine sitting through worse things than that," I say. "But not many."

Anna and I are driving back into Gulf County in the early afternoon.

"That was absolutely brutal," I say. "My heart would break for her under any circumstances . . . but to be the cause of that level of suffering . . . to be the child murderer she was describing . . ."

Because of the toll testifying took on Melissa Burrell, because of its emotional impact on the jury and everyone else in the courtroom—including Judge Wheata Pearl—the judge had decided that we wouldn't hear from any other witnesses today, but would instead reconvene in the morning. This was especially welcome news to me—and not just because of how I'm feeling, which had been bad long before I had to feel the utter brokenness of Melissa's being and experience the vitriol of her anger that was so singularly directed toward me, but because very soon my number will be up and it will be me that Gary Scott calls to the stand.

"It was nearly impossible for me to sit through," Anna says. "I can't imagine what it did to you."

"I'm sorry you had to sit through it," I say. "And stand up and talk to her afterwards, but I thought you handled it perfectly."

"I meant every word I said," she says.

"I know."

"But from a purely strategical standpoint . . . it was a no-win situation. There was nothing I could've asked her that would've done anything but inflict more pain and make me look like an insensitive bitch."

"As difficult as this has been," I say, "it has been incredible to see you work. You're such a talented trial attorney—and under nearly impossible circumstances. I mean, I knew you were brilliant and a good lawyer, but to see just how good a litigator you are in person . . ."

"You're sweet."

"I am but I'm not being sweet at the moment," I say. "Just truthful."

"I just wonder how the jury is hearing it," she says. "It's entirely possible that they will simply so empathize with the Burrells that nothing I do in the trial matters."

"Yeah, I can see that happening. And it'd be understandable."

"Based on what Merrick and Tim are writing," she says, "we're doing fairly well—and though Merrick may not be able to be, I would think Tim is objective and unbiased."

"Unless Merrick is influencing him."

"We should ask them how they think the jury is responding," she says. "I bet they're watching them far more closely than we can."

"For a home-cooked meal or an exclusive interview, they'll tell you anything you want to know. Or . . . we could ask the other observer who hasn't missed a moment since the first day."

"Randa?" she asks. "You're funny. The home-cooked meal I'd make for her might be seasoned with some arsenic and a dash of cyanide."

"If you did and were arrested you'd be the rare defendant who represents herself who doesn't have a fool for a client."

We ride in silence for a few moments, taking in the brutalized pinewood flats that were once part of the natural beauty that had made our homeland so distinct.

"You ready to talk about last night yet?" she asks.

I shrug. "Not much to talk about," I say. "I just gave in for a while."

"To?"

"You can probably guess," I say. "Guilt, grief, despair. All the classics."

"How are you now?"

"Not like that," I say. "Not giving in or up at the moment."

"Glad to hear that," she says. "But let me know what I can do. You're not alone in this."

33

I'm standing alone in the Gulf County Sheriff's Department conference room in our new building before a massive white magnetic dry erase marker board, re-examining everything we have on the storm-related deaths ruled accidental that I find suspicious.

I'm giving myself one last look, a final chance to find evidence that will convince the others before letting go and getting back to helping with the pressing needs of post-storm patrol, peacekeeping, and search and rescue.

Very little of the whiteboard in front of me is visible.

In addition to my handwritten case notes and questions, crime scene and autopsy photos hang from magnetic clips arranged as much as possible in chronological order beneath the timeline that runs across the top.

My messy, hand-drawn graph begins with Ellen Lucado, whose body was discovered in the marina in Mexico Beach on Friday, October 12th—the second day after the storm. Followed by David Cleary, whose body was discovered under the rubble of the Gulfside Seafood Restaurant on Sunday, October 14th. Then Charlie West was found in his room at the Boatman Inn on the next Thursday. The following day Philippa Kristiansen's body had been discovered in a cottage on St. Joe Beach. Then PTSD Jerry Garcia on Tuesday the 24th, the day of opening arguments in my trial.

I try to look at everything on the board as if I've never seen it before.

I move around as I look at it, changing my perspective, zooming in on specific pieces of evidence, zooming back out again to see how they inform the whole.

I scan for patterns and search for connections.

I examine the groupings of the discoveries—two within four days of the storm and then three in close proximity nearly a week later.

What, if anything, does that mean? Why did he stop? Or maybe he didn't and we just haven't discovered his other victims yet.

Thinking about his victims, I turn my attention to their individual identities.

No matter how long I look, I can't see anything at all that links the victims in any kind of profile or type. Unlike most murders like these—if that's what they are—there are no similarities among the victims. Not in age, sex, body type. Not in background or socioeconomic levels. Not in religion or ethnicity. Which is why there's probably no killer behind these deaths—and it's this more than any other single factor that most convinces me I've made this up, that a nameless, faceless predator exists only in my mind.

Have I just created a solution in search of a problem, a mystery where none exists, a pattern where there is only randomness?

I'm thinking about this when my phone vibrates.

Withdrawing it from my pocket, I see that it is Merrill.

"Mark two more off your list," he says, and gives me two more names from our missing persons list.

"Mark them dead or alive?"

"Alive," he says. "If not particularly well. One was in the shelter in Honeyville and the other at an aunt's in Campbleton. Neither knew anyone would be lookin' for them or even notice they were gone."

"That part's sad, but I'm glad they're alive."

"Not sure they are," he says. "Neither got a home or job to go back to."

That's the plight of probably nearly a third of our population right now.

"Speaking of being unhappy . . ." he says. "Why didn't you tell me Randa was out and staying here?"

Merrill had been guarding Daniel and his wife Sam when Randa kidnapped him, and he had never forgiven himself or Randa.

"I haven't seen or spoken to you," I say.

"That shit's worth a special call," he says. "Hell, I'a accept a collect call to get that info."

"I should've called you," I say. "Sorry."

"Especially since you haven't had anything going on," he says.

I laugh and apologize again.

"The hell she stay around here for?" he says.

"If I had to guess . . . I'd say she wants to join our family."

"Your—"

"Our friend circle," I say. "I think she wants to belong, wants what we have, especially since so many of us are involved in some form of investigation work—her favorite thing."

"I think you give her too much credit," he says. "You're assignin' her human traits and characteristics."

"That's certainly possible," I say. "On a bit of a roll in regard to that lately."

"In regard to what?"

"Getting things wrong."

"Let's talk about that over a game of b-ball sometime soon," he says.

"Our gym has been repurposed," I say.

"Outdoor courts at the high school have been resurfaced," he says.

"Not sure when I'll have any daylight hours free again," I say. "Probably no time soon."

"Then we'll rig up some lights. Middle of the night's fine with me. Not like you sleep anyway. And since I now have some free hours on my hands—daylight and otherwise—think maybe I'll see if I can't find out what ol' Randa's psycho ass is up to."

"Be careful," I say.

"I'm the last bastard you need to say that to—'cept maybe Daniel."

When we end the call, I return my attention to the whiteboard.

Either I'm missing something or there's nothing here to miss.

The timing? The grouping of the killings? The victims? The manner of death? The disposal of the bodies? The bodies themselves? The—

And then it hits me. It has been right there in front of me in every crime scene and autopsy photo all along—what my subconscious has been trying to tell me.

If this won't convince them, nothing will.

34

I'm still in our conference room, but now I'm joined by Reggie, Arnie, Darlene, Jill, Raymond Blunt, and Phillip Dean—and by video conference call, Pamela Garmon, Larry Butcher, the sheriff of Bay County, his lead investigator, Ernest Redd, and the ME's investigator, Leno Mullally.

"Let's get on with it," Butcher says. "Our towns are falling down around us and we all have other things we need to be doing."

"Okay," I say. "I'll be quick."

"I hear what you're saying, Sheriff Butcher," Reggie says, "but John is a first-class investigator and has earned the right to our undivided attention for a few moments this afternoon."

"Well, that's what he's got, so let's get on with it."

"As y'all already know," I say, "my theory is that we have a prolific killer here working among us, taking advantage of our vulnerability—and not just of his victims but of all of us, including our ability to respond."

"We've already heard this," Butcher says.

"I believe this predatory killer is murdering certain of our citizens in ways that can be disguised as accidents within the havoc the hurricane has wreaked on us. He uses blunt force trauma and his weapon is often some of the very debris he uses to conceal his murders within."

"We've already gone over this," Butcher says. "Nobody's saying it isn't an interesting theory or even out of the realm of possibility, but . . . there's no evidence."

"That's my theory," I say. "Here's my evidence."

I unclip one of the autopsy photos from the white-board and hold it up.

"Ellen Lucado has a tattoo on the top left side of her left foot. Her sister Diane swears that she didn't have that the night before her death."

I point to the thick black swirling strokes of the Chinese symbol on her foot in the photo.

After handing the photo to Reggie for closer inspection, I remove another from the board.

"Tom Willis, the homeless vet in Wewa who everyone knew as PTSD Jerry Garcia, has this tattoo on his right ankle," I say, pointing to the solid black circle with the arrows coming out of it.

I hand this photo to Reggie also, and remove another from the board.

"This image of swirling, snake-like arrows was on David Cleary's right shoulder," I say.

"Okay," Butcher says, "so all the victims have tattoos. Is that what you're getting at?"

"I checked with their closest friends and family members where possible," I say, "although it wasn't in the case of PTSD—I mean Tom Willis. But close friends and family members of all the others say they did not have these tattoos the last time they saw them—which in many cases was right before the storm."

"So they have new tattoos," Butcher says. "You're saying we've got a tattoo artist serial killer on our hands? That since you can't find anything else that links these extremely different victims, you're saying what they have in common is they all went and got tattoos right before or right after the storm? 'Cause I still don't buy it."

I shake my head. "No, that's not what I'm saying. I don't think these are even permanent tattoos. But I do believe the killer is putting them on his victims, that it's his way of marking them. It's subtle. It's virtually invisible —so many people have ink these days."

"I'm not trying to be difficult here," Darlene says, "but isn't the whole point of a serial killer to do things in series? He'd have a series of victims with certain similarities, right? These victims have nothing in common and aren't anywhere close to the same type. And if he was going to mark them, put his signature on them . . . they'd all be the same. He'd use the same symbol every time."

"I believe the whole point of what he's doing is directly tied to the storm," I say. "He's choosing victims that emphasize the chaos and confusion and disarray that our area, his hunting ground, is in right now. There are no patterns left here—no order, no center that can hold in this blood-dimmed tide we find ourselves in."

"Again, it's an interesting theory," Butcher says, "but it's just more of the same. This isn't evidence. It's just theory."

"You could even all it chaos theory," I say. "In addition to choosing his victims randomly, haphazardly, and killing them with remnants of the storm, he breaks one bone after they're already dead. I think this is meant to mirror the brokenness of our area. We're surrounded by broken limbs."

"But—" Darlene begins, but Reggie stops her.

"He breaks a limb of his victims and puts his mark on it," I say. "He breaks the right radius bone of David Cleary and places the mark on his right shoulder. The fourth toe of Ellen Lucado's left foot and marks her left foot. PTSD Jerry's right tibia and places his mark on his right ankle."

"I still agree with the girl there," Butcher says, all of us on this end stiffening at his dismissive name for Darlene, "they'd all be the same mark."

"They are," I say. "From different cultures around the world, these are all the symbols for the same thing—chaos. This is Chinese for chaos. This is Greek for chaos. This is Egyptian for chaos."

35

"Mr. Jordan, where do you work?" Gary Scott asks.

He's back in a three-piece suit—and he seems to be feeling pretty good about it.

"The Gulf County Sheriff's Office and Gulf Correctional Institution."

"I don't have to ask you what county you work in, do I? It's right there in the name."

It's not a question so I don't respond.

"So why, if you work in Gulf County, were you at Potter High School in *Potter* County on the morning of Monday, April 23, 2018, the day of the school shooting?"

"I was there for a meeting with some of the members of our makeshift task force," I say.

Scott looks at the judge but before he can say anything, she says, "You deserve that one, Mr. Scott."

He turns back to me. "Do you think this is funny, Mr. Jordan? This all a big joke to you?"

"No, I do not. And neither was our task force. It was a group of determined and dedicated professionals trying to prevent a school shooting. And this . . . this is truly a tragedy and my using your words was in no way to make light of anything but the words themselves," and, I think but don't say, the person who said them.

"So you just happened to have a meeting at a school that is not in your jurisdiction on the morning of the shooting?"

"I don't know," I say.

"You don't *know*? What does that mean? How can you not know?"

"I don't know if the meeting just happened to be when the shooting took place or if it was planned that way. I didn't set the time of the meeting or have anything to do with the shooting."

"But, in fact, you did, didn't you?" he says.

"No, I didn't," I say. "Just like I just said."

"How can you say that you didn't have anything to do with the school shooting when you were one of only three people who did any shooting at the school that day?"

I've asked Anna not to object unless she absolutely has to.

"I'm pretty sure you and everyone else in here knew what I meant and that you're intentionally being obtuse, but I'll explain it anyway since you asked."

Scott looks at the judge again.

She says, "Don't ask the questions if you don't want the answers. And don't pretend to be obtuse if you don't want to be called on it."

Without waiting for her or him to tell me it was okay for me to continue my answer, I start back as soon as she's finished speaking.

"When you asked about the 'school shooting,'" I say, "I took you to mean the active school shooter, not Derek Burrell or myself, who though we both fired shots that day, weren't *the* school shooter. I was no more a school shooter than Derek was."

"And yet in your statement you claim you believed he was, in fact, the school shooter."

"That's because when I arrived in the hallway that morning, he was shooting at the school resource office. I was responding to a school shooting. I came upon a student shooting at a wounded SRO. We both concluded that he was the school shooter."

"But you didn't return fire from where you were with the school resource officer," he says. "You ran all the way around the circular hallway to come up behind him and shoot him, didn't you?"

"The wounded officer wasn't able to move so we decided it best that I ran around to the other side and come up behind him, but I didn't run around there to shoot him. I had hoped to subdue him without getting shot or doing any shooting."

"But that's not how it worked out, is it?"

"No, it's not."

"We'll get back to what you did and why in a moment," he says, "but for now let's go back to where you work. Did I understand you to say that you have two jobs?"

"It's more like one and a half," I say. "I was a full-time investigator with the sheriff's department and a part-time chaplain at the prison."

"*Was?*"

"Hurricane Michael damaged Gulf Correctional so badly it's closed right now."

"Oh, but at the time you shot Derek, you had two jobs in Gulf County?"

"One and a half, yes," I say.

"I'm surprised you could find the time to shoot a child in another county," he says.

I can see Anna about to stand to object, but when our eyes meet I shake my head just enough to let her know not to.

I look at Scott but don't answer since it wasn't a question and was only him trying to score cheap points.

"There are two other investigators in your department, aren't there?"

"Yes."

"Do they have second jobs?"

"No, sir, they don't."

"So you're the exception," he says. "Do you think having two jobs divides your focus and attention so much that you don't do either job adequately?"

"No," I say. "I wouldn't do them both if I did."

"And you said one of them is as a minister?" he asks.

"Prison chaplain, yes," I say.

"So you're a religious man?"

"Yes," I say. "I am."

"Not many cops are also preachers," he says. "Not even part-time prison preachers."

I continue looking at him but don't respond.

"Well?" he says.

"Was that a question?"

"Yes. Are many cops also preachers?"

"I don't know for sure, but not in my experience," I say.

"And do you talk to God?" he asks.

"Sometimes," I say.

"Does he ever talk back?"

"No," I say.

"Sounds like a pretty one-sided conversation," he says.

Not unlike this one, I want to say, but am able to refrain.

"As a religious man, are you a good person?" he asks. "Do you do what's right?"

"I certainly try."

"Was it right to shoot Derek Burrell?"

"No," I say.

His reaction shows he wasn't expecting that response and he pounces.

"So it was wrong? You were wrong to do it?"

"Yes," I say. "It depends on how you mean it, but yes."

"Really? What kind of equivocation is that? I thought wrong was wrong."

"Most people would agree that shooting back at someone shooting at you is not in and of itself *wrong*," I say. "But when Derek fired at me, he was firing at the wrong person—meaning I wasn't who he thought I was. When I returned fire—something you could argue I didn't have much choice about—he had missed me twice. I truly did not believe he was going to miss again. What I'm trying to say is . . . as a law enforcement officer in an active shooter situation, I wasn't wrong to shoot back at someone shooting at me. But, like Derek, I was wrong about who I thought he was. And it's wrong that he was shot and killed. And I don't think any of that is in any way equivocation."

"I keep hearing your defense attorney, your wife, say that this was a tragic accident," he says. "I believe you've used the same term. Have you not?"

It's such an awkward way to ask, but I say, "I have."

"So you didn't mean to shoot Derek?" he asks. "It was an accidental shooting? Did your firearm discharge accidentally?"

"No," I say, "my weapon didn't go off accidentally. I've explained this, but I'll explain it again. When Derek shot at me and I returned fire we were both mistaken about who we were shooting at. We each thought the other was the school shooter. That's what made it an accident. That and the fact that I was aiming to wound and disarm him, not to kill him."

"But that's not really an accident, is it?" he asks. "Accidents are defined as something that happens unexpectedly and unintentionally, but surely when you ran around the hallway to come up behind Derek you expected to find him there. Both running up behind him and discharging your firearm were intentional acts. Were they not?"

"They were."

"And speaking of running up behind Derek and shooting him—"

"That's not what I did."

"Sir, that is *exactly* what you did."

"It's a circular hall and though he was firing mostly in the direction of the SRO, he was continually moving and shooting in every direction," I say. "But by far the more important point is that I didn't run up behind him and shoot him. I ran toward him and he shot at me and I returned fire."

"You ran toward him with a gun. Did you not?"

"I did."

"And did running toward a teenager while pointing a gun at him startle him?"

"I didn't run toward him while pointing a gun at him," I say. "My weapon was pointed down. And though I can't testify to Derek's state of mind, I think it's reasonable to say I startled him."

"Someone runs at me with a gun, you bet I'm gonna be startled," he says. "And I'm a grown man who's seen a thing or two, not a child acting heroically in a terrifying situation."

I don't respond.

"Mr. Jordan, did you roll Derek over and handcuff his hands behind his back as he lay bleeding to death?"

"I didn't know he was bleeding to death," I say. "But yes, I kicked his gun away from him and cuffed him to make sure he wasn't any longer a threat, and then I ran to check on the wounded SRO."

"And did you ever identify yourself as a police officer

—not just then, but, more importantly, before you shot Derek?"

"When I came around the northeast corner of the hallway he started firing at me," I say. "The only thing I did at that point was return fire."

"So that's a *no*?" he says. "You didn't identify yourself as police officer prior to shooting Derek. Is that right?"

I nod. "Yes, that's right."

"Did you identify yourself as police officer before you rounded that northeast corner?"

"No, I didn't."

"Did you at *any time*—anytime *at all* while you were running through Potter High School with a gun—identify yourself as a police officer?"

"No, I don't believe I did."

"Should you have?" he asks. "I mean according to policy and procedure and protocol, should you have identified yourself as a police officer?"

I nod. "Yes, sir, I should have."

"Now, you testified that Derek was wrong about who you were when he shot at you. Did you not?"

"I did."

"But aren't you saying now that that mistake could've been easily corrected if you had just followed protocol and identified yourself as a police officer?"

"I can't say for certain because there was so much noise and smoke, chaos and confusion from the explosions, and with how fast everything happened . . . but I should have done it and if I had it could've made a difference."

"You were wrong not to do it?"

"I was."

"And it's possible if you had, that Derek wouldn't have fired at you and would still be alive today?"

I nod. "Yes, sir," I say. "That's possible."

"So this wasn't an accident as you and your attorney keep saying," he says. "It's negligence, isn't it? You were negligent in your duties and a young man lost his life."

36

"He's right," I say. "I was negligent. This whole thing was far more a mistake on my part than some kind of tragic accident."

Anna and I are in the small room in the front left side of the courthouse during the lunch break.

"I didn't realize it until he asked me about it," I say, "but failing to identify myself may very well be the reason Derek is dead. Probably is. No wonder I feel so guilty. My subconscious knew I was to blame."

She says several things to try to contradict what I'm saying and comfort me, but none of them gets through.

I am devastated.

As horrible as I felt before, I feel even worse now. As responsible as I felt before, I feel even more responsible now.

I didn't just accidentally kill a kid. I failed to do something that might have kept us out of the situation in the first place.

"Can I just go back in and make a statement to the judge?"

"*No*," she says. "What kind of statement?"

"An apology and an admission of guilt."

"Baby, *no*," she says, jumping up from the table, grabbing my arms, and locking her intense dark eyes onto mine. "Listen to me. You've got to trust me. *Please*. I promise you'll get to say anything you want to before it's over. Okay?"

I nod but don't say anything.

She pulls me to her and holds me for a long moment.

Eventually I say, "I know you have work you need to do. I'm okay. Go ahead and . . ."

"You sure?" she asks. "I'm doing it for you, so if you'd rather talk or—"

"I'm sure. Go ahead. I need to think anyway. I'm gonna go for a walk."

"As long as it's not to the judge's chambers," she says. "Not that she would talk to you without me present anyway. Go clear your head. And . . . please just leave this to me. Let's see this to the end. You can always say or do what you want to—if you still want to—then. But I promise you'll get to in the trial itself. Just trust me."

"I do," I say. "Without reservation."

I SLIP out of the side door of the courthouse and head north on Main Street.

It's an interesting experience to be back in the small town I grew up in for the reason I am.

Main Street holds memories from my childhood like a magnolia holds its blossoms in early spring, and many of my memories here are not unlike those pink-tinged white flowers—graceful, delicate, and fragrant with the sweet smell of youth.

Main Street in a small Southern town is Saturday morning haircuts with your dad, community sidewalk sales, Christmas parades on cool Saturday nights in December, high school homecoming parades on pleasant Friday afternoons in October. It's driving around in beat-up clunkers as teenagers—often before being licensed—looking for your secret crush. It's riding your new bike down the middle of the street on early Christmas mornings in total emptiness. It's the main artery through which the life's blood of the town courses.

As I make my way along the cracked cement sidewalk, I'm overcome with a bittersweet sadness and longing that I associate with homesickness, but what I yearn for is not so much a time or a place but a state of existence. What I ache for is the hope and innocence and joy of an earlier time—the time before I knew there were such things as child killers and compulsive murderers and obsessive stalkers and school shooters.

Suddenly I am overtaken by anger—my hot blood seething with rage, and I wonder how it's possible to want to do so much good and do so little, how to hurt while trying to help, how to be one of the good guys and do something so bad.

"That really got to you, didn't it?"

I turn to see Randa walking up behind me, her pale skin looking odd and out of place in the sunlight.

"I could tell," she says. "The things Gary Scott was saying, the questions he was asking you . . . really upset you, didn't they?"

"I can't talk right now, Randa," I say. "I'm sorry. I need to get back to the courthouse."

"Just keep your head up, John," she says. "That's all I wanted to say—hang in there. And just know that even if no one else in that courtroom knows what it's like to be in such a desperate situation with no choices, I do."

Though I'm fairly certain she has followed me from the courthouse and only came to talk to me, when I turn to head back toward the courthouse she continues in the direction we had both just been headed.

"Don't let it get to you," she says as I move away from

her. "Very little justice happens in our halls of injustice, but . . . sometimes . . . outside of those courthouse doors, out here in the street, something just occasionally happens. Who knows, maybe that little prick in the three-piece suit will learn what justice means."

I continue walking without responding.

As I make my way back I try to do something to dissipate my anger. I control and focus on my breathing, say a prayer, take in the clear but hot afternoon. But nothing I try does much good.

I'm about halfway back when my phone rings.

Figuring it's Anna calling to check on me, I quickly withdraw it from my pocket. But when I do I see that it's the ME's investigator, Leno Mullally.

"So," he says, with food in his mouth, "you were right. I went back and took a look at PTSD, ah, Tom Willis's— the, ah, tattoo on his ankle. His is the only body that hasn't been buried or burned."

I would expect someone in his position to say *interned* or *cremated* instead of *buried* and especially *burned*. Of course, I'd also expect them to say it without food in their mouths.

"And you were right. It's drawn on—I'd say with a Sharpie or something like it."

"Thanks."

"But . . . now that we know there's a killer behind

these deaths . . . and not the storm . . . changes . . . I mean, breaking some of the bones he has would require incredible strength. It'd be extremely difficult to do. Probably looking for a very large, strong, and powerful man. Some of these big badasses who've come in to work cleanup and construction wouldn't be a bad place to begin."

TAMPA BAY TIMES DAILY DISPATCH

Hurricane Michael in Real Time

By Tim Jonas, *Times* Reporter

Among the many businesses affected by Hurricane Michael, perhaps no industry has been hit harder after the timber industry than the fishing industry.

Oystering in the Apalachicola Bay and shrimping in the Gulf of Mexico have been devastated and are at historic lows. This has also been the lowest monthly Gulf of Mexico shrimp haul since records began.

Hurricane Michael wiped out oyster houses, destroyed boats, its storm surge washed away docks and disrupted the Gulf and bay's ecosystem.

And Hurricane Michael is only one factor in that. These industries were already struggling from environmental pressures, including the lingering impacts of the 2010 Deepwater Horizon oil spill in the Gulf of Mexico. Many in the industry are increasingly transitioning to farming because things in the Gulf and bay are so bad. A decade ago, the industry was pulling in three million pounds of wild oysters a year. Today that number is down to a few hundred thousand.

37

"John, are you sorry that you shot, Derek?" Anna asks me.

"Profoundly," I say. "More than anyone can know. If I could undo one thing in my entire life . . . it would be that."

Court is back in session. I am back on the witness stand. And it's Anna's turn to question me.

"Do you feel bad about it?" she asks.

"Horrible."

"Guilty?"

"Extremely," I say.

"How about negligent?" she asks.

"That's not something I thought I was until Mr. Scott asked me if I identified myself to Derek this morning."

"And since then . . ."

"I have, yes."

"These aren't the usual questions an attorney would ask her client, are they?" she says.

"I wouldn't think so, no," I say.

"Do you know why I'm asking you them?"

"I think so," I say.

"Why?"

"You know how I'm feeling, what I'm going through," I say. "I tell you things a client wouldn't ordinarily tell his attorney."

"But even then . . ." she says. "Just because I'm in a position to know these things about you doesn't mean I necessarily need to ask you them under oath in a trial for which you are being accused of the wrongful death of a teenage boy."

"You know that being honest and open, expressing these things, is far more important to me than the trial."

"What is it you want to express—especially to the Burrells?"

"That I'm so, so sorry. That my heart is broken—and not just for what I've done but for them. It's hard for me to live with knowing that my actions mean Derek will never grow fully into manhood. Never experience a long-term relationship, children, adult life."

"Even though Ms. Burrell has made it clear that they don't accept your apology?"

"Yes. Of course. I don't blame them for not accepting

my apology. For anything. But it doesn't make me any less sorry."

"Now that we've covered that and you've gotten to say what you wanted to, I have some other questions for you. Okay?"

"Okay. And thank you."

"Do you know what constitutes negligence in a case like this?" she asks.

I shake my head. "No, not really."

"It means not acting as a reasonable person would act under the circumstances," she says. Did you act reasonably under the circumstances in Potter High School on April 23, 2018? Perhaps not perfectly, but reasonably?"

I nod. "Yes, I believe I did."

"And it's not just you who believes you did, is it?" she says. "A thorough and unbiased investigation by an outside agency—the Florida Department of Law Enforcement—concluded the same thing, didn't they?"

"They did."

"Professional law enforcement officers who investigate other professional law enforcement officers determined that you acted reasonably," she says. "That reasonable officers in the situation you were in would have acted as you did, didn't they?"

"Yes."

"And yet you feel horrible and guilty and responsible and would take it back if you could?"

"Yes," I say. "I do. I would."

"But feeling bad or even guilty and wishing you could take it back doesn't necessarily make you in fact guilty as far as the law is concerned, does it?"

"I guess not," I say. "Not necessarily."

"It's pretty simple," she says. "Did you mean to kill Derek or not?"

"No, of course not."

"And doesn't the fact that you kicked his gun away and cuffed him mean even afterwards you thought he was the school shooter, not just someone in the school shooting, no matter how noble or heroic his intentions were?"

"Yes, I thought he was the school shooter," I say.

"And still you just tried to disarm him—even after he had already shot at you twice?"

"Yes," I say, "that's true."

"Why did you think he was the school shooter?" she asks.

"When I arrived on the scene he was shooting at the wounded school resource officer," I say, "and she told me he was."

"He was shooting at a deputy who was already down from being shot, she told you he was, and when you approached him he fired at you twice?"

I nod. "That's right."

"And still you shot to wound and disarm, to stop him and save lives, not to kill?"

"Yes."

"You're certain of all those things and they are the truth and nothing but the truth so help you God?"

"Yes," I say. "I'm certain."

"Okay . . . now . . . let me ask you this," she says. "Are you absolutely certain you didn't identify yourself or give Derek the lawful order to drop his weapon?"

I think about it for a long moment. "No, I can't be positive I didn't," I say, "but I can say I honestly don't remember."

"Don't remember saying it or don't remember if you did or not?"

"I don't remember saying it."

"But with your training and experience it could very well be so second nature that you said it and now just can't remember whether you did or not?"

"That's possible."

"Was your badge displayed like it is supposed to be?"

"Yes, it was on my belt."

"And you weren't dressed like a student or anything, right? You looked like a professional, plainclothes police officer, badge on your belt, service revolver drawn?"

"That's right."

"You didn't have a rifle or a shotgun or any other of the weapons school shooters use?"

"No, I didn't."

"Weren't wearing a Pottersville Pirates hat or anything that could've made anyone think you were a student?"

"That's correct."

"So you round the corner and are shot at—*more than once*—and you return fire. And you can't be certain, but if right before that or during being shot at, if you didn't verbally identify yourself as a police officer, you don't think your badge and appearance was enough to identify you as such?"

"I just wish I had," I say. "Or wish I could remember for sure whether I had or not. That's all. It's possible I did. It's possible that it wouldn't make a difference anyway—there was so much smoke and it was so loud from the explosions and the gunfire and the fire alarm that had just stopped. My ears were ringing and I couldn't hear very well, and Derek had been in the hall longer than I had. And in the same way, he might not have heard me—even if I had yelled it. And given all the smoke and our movement, there's every chance that he didn't see my badge."

"Wow," she says, and just looks at me for a moment. "You're actually defending the actions of the young man who tried to kill you."

"A heroic young man who was trying to help save his classmates," I say, "who made a mistake. And what I'm trying to do is explain what it was like in that hallway—it felt like an urban warfare zone. The explosions. The gunfire. The alarms. The screams. And the not knowing what's going on or who's behind it or where they are. Only a few people know what it was like to actually be in that hallway that day, how bad it really was, and many of them are dead."

"Derek shot at you, could have killed you," she says. "Now his parents are suing you for, among other things, your character, integrity, and reputation, and you sit here defending him, justifying his actions. That's incredibly gracious of you."

I shake my head. "It's just the truth. I'm just trying to tell the truth about everything—including the Burrells' brave son."

38

"Thank you," I say.

Anna and I are on our afternoon drive back to Wewa. The commute has become both routine and ritual, giving us the opportunity to process what has happened and decompress from the day. It has become one of my favorite parts of day, the obliteration of the world outside our car unable to take away from what we're experiencing inside it.

"I *was* right that getting to say what you did is more important to you than winning the case, right?"

I nod. "There is no *winning* in this case."

She nods slowly and frowns. "I just wanted to get the best possible result for you—for your reputation, your future career, and to a lesser extent our financial future. If we lose it's going to a big hit. It's not like we have any extra money lying around. We can't cover their lawyer fees let alone the damages they're asking for. And there's another thing..."

"What's that?"

"The jury could always award them more than they're asking for," she says.

"*Oh*," I say. "Really? I hadn't thought of that, but still.."

"Even if the jury awards them a huge settlement and it ruins us, you'd rather have done what you did, today, right? Rather do what's right for your soul than the case?"

"Yeah. Sometimes when you lose you win."

Another Derek comes to mind, and I see British athlete Derek Redmond in the 400-meter sprint at the 1992 Barcelona Olympics when in the middle of the race he tore his hamstring but got back up in intense agony and tried to limp to the finish—something he was able to do with the help of his father who ran out of the stands to assist him. Derek lost the race that day, but he lost it in the right way and won all that matters most.

"*Sorry*," I add. "I just can't even care about—"

"I'm asking because I want to make sure the malpractice I committed today was at my client's request."

"It was," I say. "And thank you for what you did. I can't tell you how much I appreciate it—especially knowing what you thought about it and what it does to your case."

"I know what you mean, but it really is your case," she

says. "Far more so now. It's a reflection of you—your priorities, what matters most to you."

"Could we divorce?" I say. "Stay together, of course, but legally divorce so you, Taylor, and Johanna will be protected financially if this leads to my financial ruin?"

She takes my hand. "That's the sweetest request for a divorce ever, but I'd rather be with you in ruin."

"You'd still be with me," I say. "I'm not going anywhere. But you'd be—"

"End of discussion," she says. "Don't mention it again. Case closed. I've never been more proud or loved you more than I did in court today. I am a full partner in this and am honored to be. If they take all we have I'll help pack it up and load it for them."

Tears sting my eyes and the only response I can muster is to squeeze her hand.

We continue along in silence for a few minutes, during which I am able to compose myself.

Eventually, the slow-moving traffic on the rural route comes to a dead stop as grappling truck rigs like the one PTSD Jerry was found in block the highway in the process of gathering debris.

As we sit here something Anna said a few moments ago starts a chain reaction in my thinking.

"When you mentioned me having to play the Burrells' attorney's fees—"

"Us," she says.

"Huh?"

"*Us.* I mentioned *us* having to pay their attorney's fees. You're not alone in this. It's all *us.*"

"Oh. Well, thank you. Thank you so much for saying that—and meaning it."

"I do."

"It reminded me of something Randa said today."

"You spoke to Randa today?"

"When I went for my little walk," I say. "She alluded to something bad befalling Gary Scott. It was an offhand comment about how I might get lucky and win the case or something, but it made me think . . . You know how we can't connect our victims in the chaos killings?"

"Because the killer's MO is randomness," she says. "Chaos theory. Yeah?"

"What if I'm wrong about them and they're not as random as they appear? What if the killer is picking people he thinks deserve punishing?"

Her eyebrows arch above her widening eyes. "He could see the hurricane itself as punishment and is taking out those he believes should have been killed but somehow escaped their fate."

"Exactly," I say. "Of course, that could be giving him way too much credit. It could truly be random and that's his point, but it sure would help us if we could find some sort of link between the victims."

"You will," she says. "If there's one there to find."

As I start to respond my phone vibrates, and I pull it out and glance at it.

"It's Reggie," I say. "Mind if I take it?"

"Of course not. Answer it."

39

"I guess you heard from Mullally," Reggie says.

"Yeah."

"So we have confirmation that the killer marks his victims with these symbols after he kills them."

Anna and I are still sitting in traffic on Highway 71 as the huge hydraulic arm of the grapple truck is loading large piles of trees, limbs, and debris into its heavy-duty dump bed and the attached identical trailer, and I wonder if a year from now these big rigs will still be here, running up and down the rural roads between town and the laydown yard.

Next to me, Anna has opened her leather portfolio and is working on her trial notes for tomorrow—probably trying to figure out a way to attempt to mitigate the damage I did today.

"So now the question is," Reggie is saying, "how do we catch him?"

"I have absolutely no idea," I say. "Think about it . . . his MO is chaos, his choice of victim seems random, his method of murder flexible. We've got no pattern to follow, no victim profile to pursue, no evidence to test—"

"Until he strikes again," she says. "Sadly."

"Maybe not even then—or at least it might not be much. He keeps it so simple, keeps his work so subtle. He may not leave anything behind—except a psychological signature we're unable to identify or interpret."

"Damn," she says. "Doesn't leave much to—"

"There's a chance the victims are connected in some obscure way that's there if we look hard enough," I say. "Best place—maybe our only place—to start is with them. We need to interview the families and friends, learn as much as we can about them, compare it, and hope we come up with something. Anna and I were just talking about the possibility of the killer believing the victims needed to be punished. Since there are none of the other usual or obvious connections, it'll probably be one like this unless there isn't one at all, which is still probably the most likely. They probably are truly random."

"I hope not," she says. "I hope we can find something. Right now we have absolutely nothing. Hell, if it weren't for you we wouldn't even know he exists."

"I know how short staffed and stretched thin we are but ... we need to increase patrols."

"I know," she says. "I just don't know how."

"We've got a lot of cops here from other counties because of the storm," I say. "I think we're gonna have to use them."

"That's a good idea. And I think I'll request even more."

"That would be great," I say. "If we can't catch him at least we can try to protect our people from him."

"Speaking of ... what're your thoughts about going to the media with this?"

"We have to let the public know," I say. "Especially since we're not sure how long it's going to take to catch him. Merrick helped me at the Boatman and I promised him the chance to break it when it came time. I'm sure he'll help us, do us right. Especially if you ask him nicely."

"Hey, you're the one who promised him something exclusive," she says. "His and my exclusive days are done."

"Doesn't mean they can't be undone—or whatever that would be."

"Quit talkin' shit like that and makin' me awkward around him and you and I can meet with him this evening about releasing a story."

"Can't promise anything," I say. "Only sure way to keep it from being awkward is to get back together."

"Hey, he could be staying with me now but he's too busy with his new big town reporter buddies. I wouldn't be surprised if he winds up moving to Tampa and working for the *Times* before it's all over."

"All the more reason to step up your game."

"There's nothing wrong with my game," she says. "Next subject."

"Moving on," I say. "We've already got a curfew in effect because of the storm. We should keep it as long as we can, maybe even move it up some, and really enforce it. That, notifying the public, and increasing patrols should help save lives."

"The curfew begs the question how's he doing all this?" she says. "Between the curfew and conditions and—"

"I think he's using them," I say. "He thrives on chaos—uses it and our vulnerability against us. He's the kind of predator attracted to blood in the water or the cries of the wounded. Calls for help draw him, get him juiced."

"Given what we've been through," she says, "what we're still going through . . . It takes a special kind of sickness to—"

"Distress, disorientation, disability . . . are like mating calls to marauders."

"True."

"But don't forget, he's only done the two groupings of killings," I say. "At least that we know of. He did a few, stopped, then did more. And it has been a while since he has done any others, so maybe the curfew is helping. Certainly can't hurt. We add patrols and a well-informed public to the mix and we may shut him down altogether."

"We've still got three missing persons," she says. "Wonder if they're victims of his we haven't found? If they are . . . I wonder where they are?"

And then, as the grappler arms open and it drops its last load into the trailer below, an idea occurs to me.

"What if the grappler truck operator hadn't seen Jerry when he lifted that pile of debris?" I ask.

"Huh?" Reggie asks.

Next to me, Anna stops what's she's doing and looks over, her eyes seeming to grow bigger.

"If the body would've been positioned just a little differently," I say, "he wouldn't have seen him."

"You think the operator wanted us to find him?" she asks. "Is it him?"

"What? No. If he hadn't seen the body it would have wound up in the truck or the trailer," I say.

"Okay."

"And from there . . ."

"To the laydown yard," Reggie and Anna say at the same time.

"What if that's where his other victims are?"

40

"I got somethin'," a deputy yells from somewhere in the back.

I begin to move toward him, my muddy shoes sloshing in the water of the wet ground beneath my feet.

There are three laydown yards in Gulf County—one on Overstreet near Mexico Beach, one at the old dump near Port St. Joe, and one outside Wewa on Highway 71 not far from the prison.

We have search teams at all three. Darlene Weatherly is supervising the one on Overstreet. Arnie Ward is supervising the one near Port St. Joe. I'm with the team at the one outside Wewa.

Each search time is comprised of deputies from our department as well as some of the out-of-town officers from other agencies here to assist with protecting and serving the public in this post-storm world. I was lucky enough to get Raymond Blunt on my team. His partner Phillip Dean is on Arnie's team—though how he will notify anyone without speaking if he finds any evidence is a mystery to me.

"I think it's a foot," the deputy adds.

We have a six-member crew and have been searching for nearly an hour. This is our first find.

Often associated with construction sites, a laydown yard is an area outside at a worksite where materials, trash, debris, tools, equipment, vehicles, and other items are stored until they are needed or hauled off.

Our hurricane cleanup laydown yards are where the grapple trucks bring their loads of debris and trash and rubble and unload them.

Eventually, the loads that are dumped will be sorted, the wood chipped and hauled off to paper mills, the metal crushed and hauled to metal scrap yards, and the trash hauled to incinerators. But because this process has just begun, the sorting hasn't even started yet.

This particular laydown yard is in a fifteen-acre field set back off the highway and hidden by a hedge of trees, now mostly leaning or down, along the fence next to the road.

A little over a week into the cleanup and the fifteen-acre field is filling up fast.

Huge stacks of debris are piled in long, wide rows that allow for trucks and tractors to maneuver around.

As if a massive monument to a recently collapsed civilization, the laydown yard looks more like a burial ground for what used to be a once thriving community and the dense forest that surrounded it.

The mountains of natural and manmade materials are several stories high—some many times higher than the tops of the tall pine tree forest and the homes, businesses, hotels, and condos they used to be.

"Got somethin' over here too," another deputy yells. "Looks like the woman from the church."

"Everyone stay where you are," I say into my radio. "Don't touch anything."

When I reach the pile of mostly shingles and siding and household trash in the back where the first deputy yelled from, I see that he has indeed found a foot—and not just. It's connected to the body of an elderly black man.

Partially tangled in a torn blue tarp, the body is wedged sideways between the bent frame of an old futon and a small child's red and yellow hard plastic slide. Above, beneath, and around it is a precarious pile of sheets of tin, chain-link fencing, plastic patio furniture, interior hollow core wooden doors, large sections of ripped and jaggedly cut carpet, mildewed and molding rugs, and beyond those, thousands of other damp and dirty household items and materials from homes destroyed by the hurricane.

"Reeks like a son of a bitch," the young deputy says. "I'm trying not to breathe through my nose but it's like I can taste it in my mouth."

It appears the old man was wearing his pajamas when he was killed, and what's inside them has definitely begun to decay.

Though not visible from the little of him that's exposed, I have no doubt that somewhere on his mortal remains is a symbol that in some culture somewhere in the world stands for chaos.

"Okay," I say. "Tape if off and let's get forensics in here."

The second body, which is in a twisting and turning tangle of tree limbs, not unlike those PTSD Jerry was found in, is that of Betty Dorsey, the Samaritan's Purse volunteer who went missing from the parking lot of the First Baptist Church in town.

After cordoning off the two victims we found, we continue to search, but by the time the FDLE crime scene unit arrives we haven't made any other grizzly discoveries.

"It's not a laydown yard," Reggie says. "It's a graveyard."

I nod and look out over the bleak landscape, backlit by the setting sun.

The site looks like a post-apocalyptic trash city after the earth has been scorched and civil society is no more.

"How the hell is this now our new reality?" she asks.

I don't answer. I have none to offer. And we stand there in silence, her question floating between us as the sun sets on another of our altered, surreal post-storm days.

41

As the FDLE crime scene unit processes the scene and the medical examiner's office processes the body, all under the vigilant watchfulness of Raymond Blunt and Phillip Dean, Reggie and I step over to talk to Merrick, Tim, and Bucky.

"Do what you need to do," Ray says to Reggie as we're walking away. "I'll keep a close eye on the operation here."

The laydown graveyard is now bathed in the brilliant light of portable banks of LED work lamps, beyond which nothing is visible in the black night.

After realizing there are too many onlookers, Randa and Rick Urich among them, who are not so subtly trying to hear what we have to say, we decide to all climb into Reggie's SUV for privacy.

"John," Rick yells as we begin to move away. "John. You never came by. I thought you were going to come by and talk to me about—"

"I am," I say. "Just haven't had time yet. But I haven't forgotten."

"And what about this?" he asks nodding toward all the activity in the laydown yard. "Does this have anything to do with Betty?"

"We're just getting started," I say. "Don't really know anything yet, but as soon as we do we'll put out a statement. I know it's hard but please try to be patient. We will let you know as soon as we can."

He's not mollified by this but before he can let me know just how much, I tell him I'll be in touch and join the others already waiting for me in Reggie's SUV.

"This is me paying my debt," I say.

Reggie and I are up front, turned in the seats so we see each other and the three men in the middle seat—Merrick behind me, Bucky behind Reggie, and Tim in the middle.

"But this is a huge overpayment for letting me use your hotel room for half an hour, so we expect continued help and major cooperation."

"Of course," Merrick says.

"See those TV news crews over there," Reggie says, jerking her head toward the reporters and camera crews still among the gathered crowd on the other side of the crime scene tape. "They'd love to trade places with you right now, and they'd do anything we asked them to."

"We get it," Tim says. "We know how it works. And we appreciate this more than you know. We'll do you right. I swear."

"I'm not even sure how y'all can help us," Reggie says to Tim and Bucky. "This is a local story. How'd y'all get invited to this party?"

"It was our room," Tim says. "And because of our coverage of the storm and what's happened since—everybody in the state is reading us, including locals. I promise you we can be a big help. No matter what it is. Our dispatches about the storm go live online immediately and they get tons of views instantly. Our regional following on social media is higher than anyone's. We can put out a story that will be seen by a huge percentage of the people you're trying to reach in a matter of minutes."

"Okay," she says. "Well, just remember this . . . this story is just getting started. It'll be far better for you to be on my good side later than it is now, so don't screw me—"

"That go for Merrick too?" Bucky asks, snickering to himself.

"Nice," she says. "Very mature. Inspires a ton of confidence."

"He's an idiot," Tim says. "It's why he just takes

pictures. But he's good at that and I'll guarantee he won't say anything else stupid, because he won't say anything at all. And I promise you can trust us. We work with TPD all the time. You can call Sergeant Gibson or Lieutenant Silverman. They'll tell you."

"Sorry," Bucky says. "Didn't mean to be . . . I was just kidding, but it won't happen again."

"Okay," Reggie says. "As far as I'm concerned it's already forgotten."

"Thanks."

Since the storm, it has been unseasonably warm here, and tonight is particularly humid and muggy. With all five of us in the vehicle, the air becomes stale and hot very quickly, and Reggie turns in her seat, cranks the SUV, and taps the AC temperature down and the fan up.

She then nods toward me to talk.

"Okay, guys," I say. "What we've got . . . we believe . . . is a killer who has, since the storm, been murdering people in the area in such a way as to make it look like accidents."

"*What?*" Merrick says. "Seriously?"

"More than one?" Tim says. "How many?"

"Seven so far," I say.

"*Seven?*" Tim says.

"Oh my God," Bucky says.

"A storm serial killer," Merrick says.

"Technically, not a serial killer," I say, "and we certainly don't want to use language like that in the coverage."

"Why technically not a serial killer?" Tim asks.

"The serial killer classification requires a cool-down period longer than what we have here. This guy would be classified as more of a rampage killer. A mass murderer."

"Not unlike a school shooter," Tim says.

"Right," I say, and for a moment I see Derek Burrell lying bleeding in the Potter High hallway. "But you're right, Merrick. He's functioning like what most of us think of as a serial killer. I'd say the best, most accurate term we could use would be compulsive killer," I say, "but all these are so loaded we really don't want y'all to use any of these type labels to characterize this killer. We want to warn the public, ask them to be cautious and observe the curfew—not unnecessarily add to the extremely high levels of anxiety and uncertainty and stress that we're all living under right now."

"Is that what . . ." Tim says. "Is that part of why he's doing it—feeding on the . . . state the storm has left everyone in . . . and the condition the area is in?"

I nod. "We think so."

"This is a huge, huge story," Merrick says. "Thank y'all for trusting us with it."

"We really need your help," Reggie says. "Y'all have

an opportunity here. Think about it. Y'all can actually help save lives, but only if you get good information out as quickly and accurately as possible. Don't sensationalize anything. It's sensational enough on its own. Do this first story right and we'll give you more."

"I have so many questions," Tim says. "Mind me asking some of them?"

"It's very, very early in the investigation," Reggie says. "We don't have many answers yet, but you're welcome to ask."

"Can you tell us about the victims—both from the standpoint of who they are as human beings so we can capture them properly as people, but also what is it about them that makes him choose them?"

"We still have family notifications to do," Reggie says. "But after that we'll get you their info. I'll hold a press release in the morning. We're giving y'all a chance to break the story and warn the public prior to that."

"As far as how and why, when and where he's choosing them," I say, "we just don't know yet. We have yet to discern a particular pattern or preferred type of victim, which is why we want everyone to be careful, stick together, obey the curfew."

"Is this where he dumps his victims?" Merrick asks, nodding toward the lit-up laydown yard.

"No," I say. "He's been mostly staging the deaths to

look like accidents and leaving the victims in storm debris. The two bodies discovered here were inadvertently hauled here in debris piles."

"Thrown out like trash," Merrick says.

"*Yeah*," Reggie says, "let's not use lines like that."

Two Bodies Discovered at Hurricane Michael Debris Laydown Yard Near Wewahitchka
By Merrick McKnight, *News Herald* Reporter

According to Gulf County Sheriff Reggie Summers, two bodies discovered at a Hurricane Michael debris laydown yard near Wewahitchka might not be the result of an accident. The bodies of the two decedents are believed to have been in debris piles that were inadvertently picked up by cleanup crews and transported to the laydown yard. Cause of death is unclear so far, and the sheriff warns against jumping to conclusions, but at this point the sheriff's department is treating the deaths as suspicious. Officials are also searching for a connection with similar deaths in the area since the storm.

"We can't say for sure what we have yet," Summers said, "but I believe all our citizens should exercise caution until we know more. It's important that everyone abides by the curfew in place. And until we know more it would be wise to use caution in all necessary activities. The storm has not only disrupted life and many routine services here in the Panhandle, but its aftermath has caused our population to balloon. We are now not just dealing with our citizens but with people from all over the country. More people means more crime. Everyone needs to secure their property—keep your vehicles and homes locked—and be more aware of your surroundings than you previously had to be. I don't want anyone to panic, but I do want everyone to be careful."

42

"I'm Chip Jeffers," he says. "I've been a deputy with the Potter County Sheriff's Department for over thirty years."

Chip Jeffers is a middle-aged white man with a thick, wiry mustache, large, black plastic-framed glasses, and a pale, dome-shaped balding head haloed by brown-going-gray hair.

He's out of uniform—something I can only recall him being on maybe two occasions in all that time.

In a few minutes, Reggie will be holding the press conference about the Chaos Killer, but I won't know how it goes or what the response was until we break for lunch. It makes it difficult to concentrate on what's going on here in the courtroom.

"Mr. Jeffers," Anna says, "how did you come to get involved in the school shooting task force?"

"You could say I started it all," he says. "I was filling in for the SRO and the guidance counselor brought me a note the janitor had found in the trash of the boy's bathroom. It indicated there was going to be a shooting at Potter High, so I took it to the sheriff, Hugh Glenn, but to be honest, he's lazy and . . . far more a politician than a cop . . . so he was real dismissive about it. Told me I could look into it. So I did, and I enlisted some help along the way."

"Including the defendant, John Jordan?"

"Yes, ma'am. I've got tremendous respect for John. He's a great investigator."

"Did Sheriff Glenn know you asked John to help?"

"Yes, ma'am."

"And did he raise any objections?"

"No, ma'am. He was happy to have him. He told me so. And when we met, he asked John's opinion more than anyone else's. You could tell he really valued what he thought."

"The sheriff attended the task force meetings?"

"Yes, ma'am, some of them."

"And he asked for John's input?"

"More than anyone else's."

. . .

"MR. JEFFERS, are you currently employed by the Potter County Sheriff's Department?" Scott asks.

He's at the podium now, and Anna is back seated beside me.

"No, sir. I'm not."

"And is that because you were fired?"

"No, sir, it is not. I quit because—"

"You weren't fired for insubordination?"

"No, sir."

"Did you know your official employment file says you were terminated for insubordination?"

"No, I did not. But I'm not surprised. I quit because—"

"No further questions, Your Honor."

"Ms. Jordan?" Judge Wheata Pearl asks, knowing Anna will use redirect to let Jeffers finish what he was trying to say.

"Thank you, Your Honor," she says, standing and moving toward the podium. "Mr. Jeffers, why don't you work for the Potter County Sheriff's Department any longer?"

"I quit. I don't care what their corrupt asses wrote in my file after I was gone. I can show you my resignation letter."

"And why did you quit, sir?"

"Because I couldn't take Hugh Glenn's laziness and incompetence and lack of initiative any longer and I told him so. It's in my letter."

"Thank you," Anna says. "And thank you for what you did for our children and teachers and community."

Anna next calls the Potter High principal, Tyrese Monroe, and the guidance counselor, LeAnn Dunne, both of whom testify to what Jeffers did—I was asked to help on the task force and Hugh Glenn not only knew it but welcomed my involvement and solicited my input.

During the lunch break, I watch Reggie's press conference and read both Tim's and Merrick's articles about the case.

Both are about as good as we could have hoped for.

Reggie seems tired and rundown, which she is, and she shows more frustration and irritability with the reporters than usual, but it's nothing they don't deserve, and it's an effective and informative briefing.

She's in the hallway when we come out of our little room in the front of the courthouse, but I can't talk to her because she's this afternoon's witness.

"Reggie Summers," she says. "Sheriff of Gulf County."

"So, John works for you?" Anna says.

"Yes."

"In what capacity?"

"Officially, he's an investigator."

"And unofficially?" Anna asks.

"He's my rock. My confidant. My biggest supporter and best defender. I rely on him more than I should."

"And why do you do that?"

"He's the best investigator I've ever seen," she says, "but he's more than that. He's compassionate and caring and he's wise and discerning."

"Did he have your permission to be on the task force and help out with the Potter High School shooting?"

"Yes, he did," she says. "He had my blessing. And I'm glad you asked because early on something got misconstrued and I'd love the chance to set the record straight. I made a statement saying that John wasn't assigned to the Potter County Sheriff's Department and some people tried to twist that into meaning I didn't know what he was doing or hadn't approved it, but that's simply not the case. It wasn't an official reassignment and it didn't take John away from his responsibilities in Gulf County . . . so . . . it was informal but it was completely approved."

"Thank you. Now, I know how busy you are, how much you have going on so I'm not going to keep you much longer, but I did want to ask you about the shooting. Are you familiar with the fatal shooting of Derek Burrell by John during the school shooting?"

"I am," she says. "I've read all the reports, seen the interviews and read the affidavits."

"Great," Anna says. "Thank you for that. That's extremely helpful. Now, much has been made by the plaintiffs' attorney of whether or not John identified himself as a law enforcement officer before or during the shooting. John testified that he doesn't remember doing it. Doesn't mean he didn't, just that he doesn't remember. Can you tell us your thoughts on the situation?"

"We train to identify ourselves and to give lawful commands," she says. "Even out on the firing range. It's deeply ingrained in us, so I'd be surprised if John didn't instinctively yell it out, but . . . even if he didn't . . . If he rounded that corner and was immediately fired upon and returned fire to defend his life without yelling who he was or why he was there, no one could fault him. It's a bang-bang situation. If someone shoots at you, you don't have to identify yourself before returning fire in an attempt to save your life. And in that situation, the way he's dressed, his manner, and especially the badge on his belt is identification enough. It just *is* in that situation. The blame for the entire scenario is on the school shooter, but . . . the truth is . . . for as heroic and noble as Derek was acting, remember what he was out in that hallway doing—shooting at two police officers."

43

"Frannie Schultz," she says. "I was a classmate of Derek's. We were in class together the morning of the shooting."

"What was your relationship with Derek?"

"He was my friend and almost boyfriend."

"What do you mean 'almost'?"

"During the shooting, when we were huddled together in the back of the classroom and I thought were going to die, I worked up my nerve to ask him out."

"And he said yes?"

"He did. We agreed to go out if we survived."

"I'm so, so sorry you didn't get to go on that date," Anna says. "Did y'all talk about anything else while you were huddled in the back of that classroom?"

"Yes ma'am," she says. "I begged him not to do it."

"Not to do what?" Anna asks.

"Go get his shotgun out of the truck and go out into the hallway and start shooting. It would've been one thing if he had the gun in the classroom in case the shooters came in and tried to kill us, but he had no business out in that hallway."

Anna nods and starts to say something, but it's obvious Frannie has something else to say.

"Still," Frannie adds, "I'll always feel like the big dumb goof was my first boyfriend. And he'll always be my hero."

"He is for a lot of us," Anna says. "He acted very bravely—even if ill-advisedly. We all make mistakes, but to make one acting bravely . . ."

"That's the way I see it," she says.

"How do you view John Jordan?" Anna asks.

"The same way," she says. "He's my hero too. What he did for us. It's so easy to second-guess what people do. That's probably why more people don't step up. They stand outside and let kids die inside. But John ran in. Risked his life to keep us safe."

My eyes tear up the way they did the first time she expressed that sentiment to me.

"You don't blame him for Derek's death?"

"He's not to blame. And only someone who wasn't up there in the middle of all that chaos and confusion and explosions and gunfire would dare to. Those of us who were there . . . we know. We know Derek was brave but shouldn't've been out in that hallway. And we know what happened to him isn't John's fault. We don't blame him— not for some dumb, random, tragic accident. The truth is . . . I've wondered if I'm to blame. If maybe he was showing off a little for me. Until I told him I liked him and asked him out, he was just thinking about going to get his gun. Maybe he was trying to impress me."

"YOUR HONOR," Scott says, "something has come up that I'm not sure what to do about, so I want to just bring it before the court."

"Okay," Wheata Pearl says in her husky smoker's voice. "It's the end of the day, anyway, so I'm gonna go ahead and dismiss the jury and I'll hear what it is you have. Ladies and gentlemen of the jury, thank you for another day of your service. We'll see you in the morning with the promise that we can see the end from here. This trial will come to an end soon—and with it your service."

After the jury has filed out, Wheata Pearl looks down on Scott from on high and says, "Okay, Mr. Scott. What is it?"

"As Your Honor no doubt knows, we don't have any of the surveillance footage from the incident in question because the shooter's explosives took them out."

"Seems I recall something like that, yes."

"Well, we've received an email from an anonymous source who claims to be a PHS student who was there the day of the shooting, who's saying he or she has a video of the incident taken with their phone. And before Ms. Jordan objects to anything . . . I'm not asking for it to be admitted or anything else. I know how it looks, but this isn't late discovery on my part. I didn't know anything about it and I haven't even looked at it. I have no more idea what's on it than anyone else. That's why I'm bringing this to you, Your Honor. The court has my sincerest assurances that this is not a ploy or tactic to get evidence in at this point or anything else. I've already presented my case. And when I did I had no idea of the existence of this . . . footage. And even now . . . I have no idea what's on the—"

"Your Honor," Anna says.

"Yes, Ms. Jordan?"

"Two questions come to mind immediately."

"And they are?"

"Mr. Scott says he didn't know anything about it—my question is . . . until when? He left that part out. My second question is . . . is he saying that the communication that accompanied the footage gave no indication as to what the alleged footage shows?"

"What about that, Mr. Scott?"

"I literally just became aware of this when I checked my email as we were wrapping up," he says. "The court is welcome to look at my inbox. As far as the communication . . . It says essentially what I said. I can read it if you'd like?"

"I'd like," Wheata Pearl says.

"'Mr. Gary Scott, I'm a student at PHS and I was there that day. I filmed footage with my phone that you might find interesting for your case.'"

"Is this supposed footage attached to the email?" the judge asks.

"It appears to be, yes, ma'am."

"Okay," Wheata Pearl says, clearing her phlegmy throat, "here's what we're going to do . . . Mr. Scott, share all communication and footage with Ms. Jordan immediately. Y'all both look at it, test it, whatever you want to do with it . . . Then I'll hear from you both in the morning on what you want to do with it. Y'all make motions. I'll make rulings. And we'll all work to land this plane as soon and as safely as possible."

"Your Honor," Anna says, "during the investigation of the school shooting, investigators asked students and faculty for any photos or videos they may have taken. None of them showed the incident this case deals with. So . . . everything about this is suspicious."

"Highly," the judge says.

"I know my client is telling the truth," Anna says, "and we'd like nothing more than video and audio of the entire accident, but this seems like a stunt."

"Mr. Scott," the judge says, "if this is a stunt that you're involved in in any way, it will be a career ending one. It's not too late to come clean right now, but if it goes even one moment past this one I assure you it will be too late."

"Your Honor, if it were anyone else implying what you just did I'd be outraged and offended. But as I understand that the court is just wanting to ensure the integrity of this trial . . . let me be absolutely clear again. I am affirming to the court that everything is as I have described. I have no prior knowledge of this or anything related to it. I just received it in the manner I have described. I haven't watched it nor do I know anything about it. The only thing I've done is notify the court."

"Okay," Wheata Pearl says wearily. "I hope for your sake that is the whole truth and nothing but. We'll take this up in the morning. Court is adjourned."

44

"Do you believe him?" I ask.

"Scott? I don't know. He'd be a fool to try something like this . . . and he's not a fool."

We are driving back toward Wewa in the heavy late-afternoon traffic, surrounded by semis and vans and pickups and trailers.

As soon as court had let out we rushed into the small room, our room, in the front of the courthouse to watch the video, but the email never came, and eventually we gave up. After Anna left Gary Scott a particularly pointed voicemail, which included a threat to call the judge if she doesn't receive the email within minutes, we headed home for the day.

"But the fact that he hasn't sent it yet . . ." she says. "He could be up to something. How long does it take to forward an email?"

"I wonder if it's legit and why the student waited to share it if it is," I say. "It's going to be hard to watch, but if it's undoctored . . . I'm anxious to see what it shows and how it compares with my memory of what happened."

"The thing is . . ." she says, "even if it's the real deal . . . it's prejudicial. No matter what, for the jury to see you shooting and Derek getting hit and going down . . . It's one thing for it to be described. It's another for them to watch it happen."

"I know you have to think in terms of the jury," I say. "And I'm glad you are. But I'm just wondering what the jury inside my head will make of it."

"If it's real and the sender is impartial . . ." Anna says. "Why not send it to both of us?"

"Or give it to investigators when they asked for it?" I say.

"Everything about it raises questions," she says. "But the most pressing one at the moment is why Gary hasn't sent it to me."

After checking her email again on her phone, she calls Gary Scott and leaves another message.

"You asked us to accept in good faith that you're coming from a truthful and honorable place," she says, "but delaying sending me the evidence seems to contradict that. I'm not sure what's going on but if there's some valid reason why you haven't sent me the email yet, you should've communicated that. Since you haven't . . . and you haven't done what the judge ordered you to, I have no other recourse but to contact the judge and let her know. I'm going to wait another ten minutes before I do. So send me the video or call me and tell me why you haven't or just call the judge and explain it to her."

After disconnecting the call, she checks her email again.

"What did you think about the testimony today?" Anna asks.

I give her a small nod and shrug.

"What does that mean?" she asks.

"I thought it went reasonably well for us, but . . . it's supposed to, right? They were our witnesses. I guess I expected it to."

"It was a very good day," she says. "And that's not a guarantee even when they're your witnesses. Look at many of Scott's."

"That's true."

"I really hope you listened carefully to what Reggie said. She wasn't just saying that or making it up in some kind of misguided attempt to defend or protect you. What she said lines up with what every single law enforcement officer I spoke with told me."

"Thank you," I say. "I appreciate what you're trying to do. I really do. But . . ."

"But what?"

"If everyone in the world agreed that I did nothing wrong . . . it still resulted in the death of a teenage boy, so . . ."

"And that's truly tragic," she says. "Hopefully that's the worst thing that you'll ever have to endure in your lifetime, but . . . it wasn't your fault. He shouldn't have been out there shooting at you—shouldn't have been out there at all. It wasn't only illegal for him to have a weapon on campus, but he should've never broken out of the school and gotten it and come back in with it. And he should have never been shooting at two law enforcement officers. There's a reason why we have mitigating circumstances. It's a real thing. And this is it. You were in a no-win situation, but . . . we got the biggest win of all—the one I'll take every single time. You came home to me and our girls. You were fired upon. *Twice.* You could've so easily died. And you didn't. You should've never been fired upon. He should've never been out there. He was wrong. Not you."

"Thank you," I say.

"Stop thanking me and let what Reggie and the FDLE and everyone else with any impartiality or credibility is saying sink in."

"I'm trying."

"Try harder," she says. "You know, John, it's not the goal I started this case with, but I've actually reached the place where I feel like this was a successful trial if I can convince you of the truth of our case. Never mind the jury. I mean I hope to convince them. Hell, I actually think they'll be easier to convince than you, but you—or the jury inside your head—are the one I'm trying to convince first and foremost now. And if I have to choose one or the other, I choose you."

I have the urge to thank her again but resist it.

A few minutes later Pamela Garmon from the Bay County Sheriff's Office calls.

"Got any plans tonight?" she asks.

"Just trying to catch a killer. What's up?"

"That info you gave us on that home invasion and torture-murder in Mexico Beach . . ." she says. "We're making arrests tonight. You gave us these guys . . . plus we feel like we owe you for not believing you on the other thing . . . so we wanted to invite you along to take these dirt bags down."

I can't believe she actually used the term *dirt bags* unironically, and find it difficult not to laugh.

I have no desire to go on the arrest—especially since the guys they're going after are so violent and hardened. It's the perfect scenario for too much testosterone and an ensuing shootout, and I want no part of either.

"That's very thoughtful of y'all," I say. "Thank you for

thinking of me, but I'm good. I better keep working on the Chaos Killer case, see if I can get anywhere with it."

"Okay," she says. "But you're gonna miss out on what promises to be a wild ride. We'll let you know how it goes."

45

I 'm alone in the conference room of the new Gulf County Sheriff's Department again, studying the whiteboard when Reggie walks in.

"I thought I was the only one here," I say.

"You were. I just got here."

"Got a few minutes?" I ask.

"Yeah, but just a few. Merrick's picking me up. We're going to dinner."

"Good for you."

"We'll see. He may just want a story."

"He's not like that," I say. "I mean, he wants a story, but he wouldn't use you to get it."

"You sure?"

I nod.

"Hope you're right," she says.

"I was hoping *you* were right as I sat there listening to you testify today," I say.

"I was," she says.

"Thanks for doing it and everything you said."

"No thanks necessary," she says. "Just told the truth. You got a raw deal out of that thing—all the way around. Hope it finally breaks your way. You deserve it."

I glance back at the whiteboard, which has more information—notes, witness statements, and photos—since I set it up, and I feel like I'm on the fringes of the case. Being in court every day gives me very little time to work this investigation—and none at the same time the other investigators are working. Of course, I'm used to being an outsider, accustomed to working alone, but in this case it's heightened in a way it hasn't been since I've been an investigator here.

"How'd the press conference go?" I ask.

"Pretty well, I think."

"What has the response been like?"

"'Bout like what you'd expect. All over the place. But in general the media coverage has been fairly decent so far. I think Merrick's and Tim's pieces this morning set the tone. Did you read them?"

I nod.

"Speaking of responses," she says, "I got a call from Rick Urich, the Samaritan's Purse guy who went missing. He called me to complain that you didn't reach out to him personally about whether Betty was among the bodies found at the laydown yard. Said you promised him you would."

"I told him we'd release a statement once we knew something definitive."

"Says you also promised to come by and talk to him about becoming a police chaplain and that you haven't. Said it's a bad reflection on the department."

"Wow," I say, shaking my head. "I told him I'd come by at some point and talk to him when I could."

"I figured that was the case," she says. "Just letting you know he called. I told him between court and this investigation it would probably be a while before you'd be able to even think about getting back with him. Told him he might want to wait until he goes back home to Indiana where there's not a state of emergency and ask a police chaplain there."

"Okay," I say. "Thanks. Any word from crime scene or the ME from last night?"

"Nothing helpful," she says. "Except to confirm they were killed by the same guy. He's very careful. Leaves no evidence. Both victims were killed with blunt force trauma. Betty Dorsey had her left arm broken after death and this on the same arm."

She walks over to the whiteboard and points to an 8x10 photo of a close-up of a tattoo that is similar but more ornate than the earlier victims.

"It's the Druid symbol for chaos," she says. "Willie Green had his left ring finger broken after death and the infinity chaos symbol was on the back of his left hand."

She points to an image of a tattoo similar to the ones found on David Cleary and PTSD Jerry but with an added infinity symbol in the center.

"He's definitely got a signature," I say. "Operating based on some sort of pattern, but . . . the victims seem as . . . Sorry, I almost saw something, but it's gone. Hopefully it will come back. I was gonna say the victims seem as random you can get."

"ME's office said there were no signs of sexual assault —or anything else really."

I nod. "He's just killing them," I say. "Quickly and cleanly—and inconspicuously. I wonder how he feels about having his work so public now? Did he really want to remain hidden or was he hoping somebody would discover and appreciate what he's doing?"

"None of these guys really want their work to remain hidden for long, do they? Especially if they can find someone smart enough to perceive it."

"I think he's been at it a while," I say. "This or something like it. Seems settled, experienced, sophisticated. He may not have done this before, but he's been busy working his way toward it."

"I've put in a request to FDLE for help," she says. "And I've asked if anyone from the departments here helping with post-storm management has experience with this kind of thing. We would need the help anyway, but with you in court and limited time to work on it . . . it's vital."

I nod. "Good."

"And we've increased patrols in a big way—as big a way as we can manage right now. We're using some of the cops from other agencies to help with that—that and enforcing the curfew. We've run into a few issues, but—"

"Like what?"

"Some of them aren't used to our laidback small-town ways," she says. "Come off as rude and aggressive, and there have been a couple of cases of unnecessary altercations—pulling people from their cars and generally being pricks to them."

"All the volunteers and contractors and emergency service workers are helpful and right now we desperately need them, but . . . I can't wait until we get our little community back."

"Amen to that," she says.

"The background work on the victims turning up anything interesting?" I ask.

She shakes her head. "Not really. No connections. Actually, no similarities at all so far."

"If he's being as truly random as he seems," I say. "He's going to be extremely difficult to catch."

"Yeah, maybe we'll get lucky," she says. "Maybe he'll mess with the wrong redneck and get his face shot off."

When Reggie is gone I return the full weight of my attention to the evidence.

Once again I search for patterns, attempting to see something I've missed before.

Being alone like this suddenly feels right.

I've always been able to think better and work better alone.

I need and benefit from working with others too—especially in back-and-forth exchanges and insightful questions raised by smart, thoughtful people. But I need time alone to think about and process and study the evidence—to ask myself questions, to search my own mind even as I search the evidence.

I go back over everything we know, or think we do, so far—the victims, the timeframe of the killings, the location of the bodies, the means and causes of death, the psychological and physical signatures.

And then I begin to engage this shadowy, unformed figure in my mind, attempting to get him to reveal himself, to give up his secrets, no matter how begrudgingly.

What is it about chaos that draws you?

Does it mirror the chaos inside the hell of your own mind?

Are you trying to create some kind of order out of the chaos —an order known only to you?

I think about the mythology of creation, of God

creating chaos out of order, of how the chaos continues to show through.

Why are you choosing the victims you are? What is it about them that calls to you, that ignites your dark fantasies?

If your motivation isn't sexual dominance, what is it?

Why make your murders look like accidents? What is the point? Are you trying to stay hidden? Do you think we and the world we live in are all an accident?

Do you have a message—conscious or not? Are you saying something about the capricious nature of life?

In a superstorm like Hurricane Michael, why are some structures destroyed while those next to them go virtually undamaged? Why are some people killed and others spared? Are you playing God? Mother Nature?

Are you trying to exercise control where there is none?

What are you scared of? Are you motivated more by fear than rage?

Who made you the way you are? Were you neglected? Abandoned? Tortured? Trained to kill and destroy? Or were you born with no soul, no conscience, no compassion or empathy?How are you choosing your victims? Is it a conscious choice? Is it really as random as it seems? What is it about them only you can see?

How are you gaining their trust? Why do they let you get close enough to kill them? Are you charming? Handsome? Do you appear helpless or in need or approach them from a place of strength? How are you operating the way you are, given our current conditions and the curfew? Who do you hate more—yourself or those who created you?

Are you waging war against God? Or is it your mother and father that you are killing over and over again?

Who let chaos loose in your life?

When I circle back to how and why and where he is encountering his victims, I think about Willie Green being found in his pajamas—and remember that Betty Dorsey too went missing while in hers when she went to get her charger out of her vehicle. How many others were found in their pajamas?

Are you breaking into their homes? Spending the night with them? Do you creep in under cover of darkness, bringing chaos and death with you?

And then I realize what it is.

Given the curfew and how dark it is around here at night.

You aren't taking them at night at all, are you? You're an early riser, taking them in the morning when it's still fairly dark, when their guard is down, when they're less careful and less likely to perceive threats. They're in their pajamas because you come calling in the morning hours, don't you?

I look back at the timeline.

Why did you stop so soon after you got off to such a good start? Were you interrupted? Did you get overwhelmed? Or was it not up to you? Was it out of your control? Did chaos overcome you?

How did you get so good at this? What special skill set do you have that enables you to do what you're doing?

You've done this before, haven't you? Maybe several times. And because you use chaos and confusion and make your murders look like accidents, you've gone undetected, haven't you? You are as mature and experienced and sophisticated as you are because you've done this for a while now, haven't you?

Where?

Where did you have your apprenticeship? Ply your trade? Hone your craft? Was it in other disaster areas or war zones? Do you go from chaos to chaos, crisis to crisis, disaster to disaster? How long have you killed with impunity by hiding your chaos within the larger chaos of storms, fires, floods, wars?

Though still not fully formed, some of the edges of this dark traveler are coming into relief.

When I finish for the night, I text Reggie.

Need to talk when you can, I type. *Call me after your hot date.*

She immediately replies. *The hot part . . . if there is one . . . will be later. Having margaritas with the crew. Drop by.*

46

When I step out of the sheriff's department into the hot, humid night, I see that Randa is waiting for me by my car, her green eyes seeming to glow in the dark.

"Defendant by day," she says. "Dark detective by night."

"What're you doing here, Randa?"

"Waiting to talk to you."

"Why didn't you just call?" I ask.

"Wanted to see you in person," she says. "Didn't mind waiting. Gave me time to think."

"About?"

"Lots of things," she says, "but mostly about the serial killer you uncovered. I assume you uncovered him. Reggie said 'an investigator within the department' at the press conference . . . and I have a tough time believing it could've been Angry Dyke Darlene or Affable Arnie."

"You know I can't discuss it with you," I say. "And I'm pretty sure Reggie didn't use the term *serial killer.*"

"John, come on now. Doesn't matter what we call him. He's a prolific little prick. Lots of bodies in a short amount of time. You can use all the help you can get. And unlike the aforementioned ah, investigators, I can actually be of some help."

"I'm sorry. I don't make the rules, I just mostly follow them."

"You think if you followed them a little more or a lot less you'd be in court right now?" she asks.

"I haven't given it any thought," I say.

"Well, go ahead. I don't mind waiting."

"I've got somewhere I need to—"

"I'm a good investigator, John. I can help catch him."

"I'd be happy to hear any ideas or theories you have or about anything you find, but . . . all I can do is listen. I can't—"

"If I solve it or help you in a significant way will you tell Reggie to give me a job?"

"I don't tell Reggie to do anything," I say. "Who gets hired has nothing to do with me, but you know I'll gladly tell her if you contribute in any way."

"Understood," she says. "Well, I already have some theories. Would you like to hear them?"

"Sure," I say. "I just can't right now. Can I call you later tonight or tomorrow?"

"Okay. I just hope he doesn't kill anyone else between now and then."

"Everything okay?"

I turn to see Raymond Blunt and Phillip Dean coming out of the back door of the sheriff's department.

I had no idea they were even in the building.

"All good," I say.

"Roger that," Raymond says, walking to his car. Something in his voice has changed and he now sounds like he caught us doing something inappropriate. "Well, then, y'all be careful and don't do anything I wouldn't do. We're on our way to meet the boss and a few of the boys at the Mexican restaurant."

47

B y the time I get to Peppers', Reggie has very little of her massive margarita left. She has just lifted the alcohol ban and seems to be taking advantage of it.

Peppers', the Mexican restaurant on Reid, is the only restaurant open so far, its festive colors, loud musica Mexicana, and bright neon lights a stark contrast to the crumbling and permanently closed establishments all around it.

It has been packed since it reopened, its many booths and tables filled with the tired, hungry, and dirty work crews attempting to restore order to our area—cleaning up debris, replacing power poles, running new electric lines, erecting new cell towers, repairing roads, removing hazardous materials and dead bodies, and in general trying to create a sense of civilization out of the chaos.

Because of the approaching curfew, the crowd is thinning out, but there are still more tables full than empty.

In the center of it all is a long table of Samaritan's Purse volunteers in bright orange shirts, Rick Urich among them.

Reggie, Merrick, Ray, Phillip, Darlene, Arnie, Tim, Bucky, and a couple of other out-of-town cops whose names I don't know are at another long table by the boarded-up front window.

"I'm not too drunk," Reggie is saying. "Been here a while. Drinking slowly. Drinking a lot of water with it too. But don't worry. I'm not driving tonight. And I'm staying down here."

"I'm a DD," Bucky says, "and I haven't had a drop. I'll get them all home safe and sound."

"Me too," Ray says. "That's one of the services we provide in times like these—let the locals blow off steam. Be here to get them home."

Phillip Dean nods but doesn't say anything.

We all turn to watch as Randa walks in and takes a seat at the bar.

"She heard me say we were comin' here," Ray says.

Merrick, who if not drunk has a good buzz going, says, "That rat bastard Michael missed an opportunity.

Killed the wrong people." He turns to me and Reggie. "How can someone who did to Daniel what she did just walk around all free and shit? Walk right in here and have a drink with the good guys."

I don't say anything and attempt to change the subject, but Merrick does it for me.

"Reggie tell you we went on a date earlier tonight?"

"All of you?"

"No, no, no," he says. "We met these guys later . . . afterwards . . . later after . . . for drinks. Let the foreign press join us . . . 'cause they've done us right on the storm and killer coverage and . . . they're goin' home soon."

"Our editor is about to pull us," Tim says. "We're the only major newspaper still covering the storm . . . and we only have another day or two." He turns to Merrick and adds, "No offense."

"None taken. I know I'm in the minor leagues."

"Left us here longer than we thought he would," Bucky says.

"I worry about this area," Tim says. "I really do. Nobody realizes how bad it is and nobody's listening. Attention equals recovery money and y'all aren't getting much of either right now."

"Gives a whole new meaning to the Forgotten Coast," Merrick says.

"We won't forget you guys," Bucky says.

"Fuck no, we won't," Tim adds, his intense blue eyes growing even more intense.

"We're so grateful for what y'all've already done for us," I say. "Your coverage has been . . . not just informative but inspiring."

"We're gonna keep working on it," Tim says, "keep reminding people. Keep it in front of the people who can make a difference. Still can't believe the anemic response."

"I can't believe Uncle Santa isn't coming through with the funds," Bucky says. "It's surreal that there's no bill yet."

"It'll happen," Raymond says. "Just takes time. I've seen a lot of these and you just can't rush them. I know it's hard to see now, but this area will be back."

Phillip nods but doesn't say anything.

"Who's a big ol' ray mond of sunshine?" Bucky says, as if speaking to a baby or a puppy.

"That's me," he says. "But what about covering the investigation into the murders? I thought they'd leave y'all here for that at least."

"Sending in our crime reporter to take it over. It's too big for us."

The door opens and we turn to see Gabriel Gonzalez, the *Miami Herald* reporter, walk in.

"I'm back, bitches," she says.

Merrick, Tim, and Bucky jump up and hug her.

"How'd you get to come back?" Bucky asks.

"Told my editor either he lets me or I'm going to quit and go to work for the Associated Press. Told him the *Tampa Bay Times* is putting us to shame and we can do better."

"Welcome back," Tim says.

"Great work," she says.

"Where is Grover?' Bucky says.

"It's just me," she says. "I've got to take pictures too, but at least I'm here."

I get Reggie, Darlene, and Arnie's attention. "Can I speak to y'all for a minute?"

As the others stay and continue to drink and talk, the four of us make our way to the small private room down the short hallway past the restrooms in the back. On the way, I pause and assure Rick Urich that I will get with him just as soon as things slow down some. He responds like a petulant child, barely acknowledging I've spoken.

By the time I reach the small room in the back, the other three are waiting for me with an air of impatience.

"I just wanted to mention a few things to you since I'll be back in court in the morning," I say.

"Sure," Reggie says. "And thanks for including Darlene and Arnie too."

Darlene nods.

"Yes," Arnie says. "Thank you, John. And sorry again

about the other night. I hope we can let by Gods be by Gods."

I'm pretty sure he means *bygones* and try not to smile.

"I think he's doing most of his hunting in the mornings," I say. "Middle of the night to early morning."

I explain to them why and ask them to check to see if any other victims were found in their pajamas or if we can better pinpoint when they went missing.

"We have more patrols working the nights than the mornings," Reggie says. "Maybe we should switch that around."

"Or see if we can just add to the morning shift without taking away from the nights."

She nods.

I share a few of my other thoughts and theories with them, and then say, "But here is the main theory I wanted to share with you and ask for your help with. I think given the level of sophistication he shows, he's done this before—maybe several times. So here's my thought— what if he uses disaster areas to do what he does? What if in previous ones he's done the same thing he's doing here and no one noticed? He could be going from hurricane to wildfire to flood to tornado in order to do what he's doing without being noticed. He could easily be on one of these cleanup or construction crews or a cell tower builder or a truck driver who hauls in supplies or equipment, or any of a number of other workers or volunteers who descend onto a disaster area like ministering angels in times of greatest darkness. Would one of you be willing to start searching previous disasters in the morning, looking for deaths that were ruled accidental that might not be and for any victims anywhere with a chaos symbol tattoo?"

"I will," Darlene says, "but there's no way I'm waiting 'til morning."

48

Before heading home from Saint Joe, I go back to the office and work with Darlene for a while on the searches.

I find her at her desk already working on them.

"What did the reporters want?" I ask.

"Huh?"

"I saw you talking to them outside of the restaurant after everyone had left," I say. "They trying to get more information than Reggie is giving them?"

"Always," she says. "You know how it is. But they made some good points that I happened to agree with about public safety and their right to know. I was already planning on talking to Reggie about it anyway. But it can wait 'til morning. Let's focus on this."

I don't think I'm getting the full story from her but let it go for now and join her in working on the searches.

Because there is no magic database that allows us to enter in exactly what we're looking for and then mystically spits out the correct answer, we have to first figure out the best way to search for the information we're looking for that will give us the best chance of finding it.

We have a few different options and agree that ultimately utilizing them all is the best way to go, but beginning with those that have the greatest odds and most immediate chances of working is the wisest way to move forward.

We start with a SCMT search on FCIC/NCIC.

The FCIC/NCIC, or respectively the Florida and National Crime Information Centers, are electronic storehouses of crime data. The Florida center helps Florida law enforcement officials coordinate their activities and share information. The national center can be accessed by virtually every criminal justice agency in America every single second of every day of every year. It helps cops and other criminal justice professionals apprehend fugitives, locate missing persons, recover stolen property, identify victims and patterns of crime, and potentially prevents crime from happening.

It was launched in January 1967 with five files and 356,784 records. By the end of 2015, it contained 12 million active records in 21 files, and in that same year it averaged 12.6 million transactions per day.

The SCMT search is for scars, marks, and tattoos in individuals who have been arrested.

We're hoping to turn up something on the symbols the killer is marking his victims with.

Next we create an intelligence bulletin seeking information related to deaths during and following natural disasters that appear accidental but are in some way suspicious, where the victims involved have markings that resemble the chaos symbols we've found on our victims here. We send this out to the ROCIC or the Regional Organized Crime Information Center for the southeast region. Later, if we need to go wider we can, but our region is a good place to start.

We then compose a number of emails with the same information.

We send this to FDLE and request their help—both in searching for and disseminating the information.

If we discover that this same killer has operated during other disasters in other counties, we'll have to get FDLE involved anyway to deal with the multi-jurisdictional issues involved—and, of course, Reggie has already requested their assistance with the case in general.

We send a version of this same email to the Florida Sheriffs Association, requesting that they forward it to every sheriff's department in the state and asking that they then share it with their investigative units.

Most everything we've done so far focuses on Florida, but given the number of hurricanes and other natural disasters we have each year, it's not a bad place to start.

If all of these efforts don't yield any results, we can abandon the theory as flawed or escalate it by contacting the FBI.

During my drive home, Merrick calls me.

"I know it's late," he says. "But I also know you don't sleep. You got a minute?"

"Sure. I'm just driving back from St. Joe."

"Perfect. I just . . . I wanted to ask you about something."

"Of course."

"I feel like you're very, very good at what you do," he says. "And I just wondered . . . what keeps you here. Have you ever considered moving back to Atlanta or . . . anywhere . . . I think you'd be one of the best detectives in Atlanta or Tampa or Miami or even New York or L.A."

I know he's not really asking about me.

"What's brought this on?" I ask.

"Just . . . I've been around all these reporters from all over, you know, and I think . . . I'm every bit as good as them."

"You certainly are," I say.

"Tim told me he thought he could get me on at the

Tribune and Gabriella said the same thing about the *Herald*. And I'm tempted, you know?"

"It's only a temptation if it's something that would take you off your path."

"Why do you stay?" he asks.

"I'm home," I say. "This is where my family is, my friends. This is where I feel like I'm supposed to be. If it weren't . . . then I'd be searching other places . . . and I'd be open to relocating, but . . . not necessarily to bigger places. What we do is probably different in that way. I can certainly understand you wanting a bigger audience, more readers. I get that."

"That's part of it," he says, "though my podcast with Daniel had a huge audience."

Following Randa's arrest and the resolution of her case, Merrick and Daniel had stopped podcasting, telling their audience they would be back as soon as they found their next great case to cover, but so far they had yet to return, and I wonder if they ever will.

"Was that more fulfilling?" I ask.

"The case was," he says. "And I think that's the thing . . . I really want to write about crime . . . and in a small paper in a small town . . . I have to write about everything and there's less crime and fewer . . . for lack of a better word . . . *interesting* cases to cover. But moving might be very hard on my kids and . . . I'm pretty sure it'd mean giving up on any chance of me and Reggie being together."

"It's not easy for any of us," I say. "Finding meaningful, fulfilling work and having a meaningful, fulfilling personal life is . . . extremely challenging. Just a couple of things to consider . . . Always ask yourself what matters most—what's most important to your purpose and the quality of your life. And the truth is for most of us it's both. You'll be the happiest and most fulfilled and do the most good if you can manage to find meaningful work *and* a fulfilling personal life. For me—and I can only speak for me—the key is to never give up on having either. But if there's a choice, always choose your family and friends—or almost always. And remember that bigger doesn't necessarily mean better. In fact, I'd say it rarely does."

"Thanks, John."

When I get home I find Anna fast asleep at the kitchen table, her head actually resting on her law books and trial notes.

As I help her to bed, she tells me that Gary Scott never forwarded her the email and never returned her many calls, texts, or emails, and as far as she knows he must not have responded to the judge's attempts to contact him either.

"Should make for an interesting morning in court," I say. "Let's get some sleep so we'll be ready for it."

TAMPA BAY TIMES DAILY DISPATCH

Hurricane Michael in Real Time

By Tim Jonas, *Times* Reporter

In addition to everything else Hurricane Michael brought to the Florida Panhandle, it appears the super-storm also blew in a dangerous predator.

An official close to the investigation, which includes both Bay and Gulf counties so far, revealed that the departments are reexamining a series of deaths originally ruled as accidental.

As if the desperate people of this devastated region needed anything else to contend with. They're already dealing with so many issues relating to basic survival, a shortage in housing, a lack of grocery stores, gas stations, restaurants, and hospitals, record unemployment, dwellings that are falling apart and rotting around them, a presidential administration and lawmakers in Congress who have yet to do what needs to be done, fatigue, frustration, sleep deprivation—and now this.

49

"Your Honor," Gary Scott is saying, "we've decided not to introduce the video into evidence."

We are in the judge's chambers—Wheata Pearl seated behind her enormous antique desk, Anna, Gary, and I standing across from her in front of it. On the desk is a rattlesnake mug identical to the one on the bench in the courtroom.

The Burrells had the option of joining us but declined. This is probably far closer to me than they want to get, and I can't blame them.

"After reviewing the footage," Scott rushes on, "we have concluded that it is of no evidentiary value, will only upset the victim's parents and the jury—not to mention there's no way to validate its veracity with certainty."

"Well," Wheata Pearl says, "that settles that. Guess we're done here . . . because my instructions were for you and you alone to watch the footage, evaluate its evidentiary merit, and decide if you and you alone wanted to introduce it. Isn't that what you recall, Ms. Jordan?"

Anna smiles. "Your Honor," she says, "not only did he not follow your instructions to forward me the email with the attached footage, but he didn't communicate with me in any way and ignored repeated attempts to get in contact with him."

"Oh, you're not the only one he ignored," the judge says. "He ignored my instructions from the bench yesterday and my many phone calls last night."

Anna had made good on her threat to Scott and had notified Wheata Pearl about his failure to forward the email as ordered and refusal to answer her calls. From that point, the judge began calling him too.

"Your Honor," Scott says. "I'm very sorry for any inconvenience it may have caused but not only has my phone been acting up, but due to the stress of this case and its importance to my devastated clients, I haven't been sleeping well. I took a sleeping pill early last evening and was comatose until this morning."

"Let me tell you somethin' ol' son," the judge says. "You're gonna wish you were comatose for the foreseeable future when I get done with you. But for now that will wait. Just know that as soon as this trial is over your ass is mine. Now, while we're all here watching you do it, forward the email in question to me and Ms. Jordan."

"But—"

"Don't utter another syllable," she says. "Just do what I told you to do. *Now*."

He lets out a long sigh and begrudgingly complies.

My phone vibrates in my pocket and I pull it partially out to and glance at it. I've received a text from Pamela Garmon saying that the home invaders from Mexico Beach on the night of the storm are in custody—except for the one that is in the morgue. Drawing on the SWAT team, he chose suicide by cop rather than returning to prison.

After she and Anna have both confirmed they received it, Wheata Pearl says, "Have you received any other messages or footage or been contacted in any way by this anonymous sender?"

"No, ma'am."

"Or anyone else or received any other evidence of any kind?"

He shakes his head.

"Okay," she says, "I'm going to pull up the video on my monitor and we're going to all watch it together."

After she has moved her mouse around and clicked a few times, she turns the large computer monitor on the corner of her desk around to face us and joins us on this side of her desk.

"I'm sure this is going to be difficult to see," she says. "We ready?"

My heart is thudding against my chest, my temperature is spiking, and my skin turns clammy.

And then she clicks Play.

The video opens on a shot of a wooden classroom door.

Gunfire, explosions, and screams can be heard.

The camera moves up the door to the narrow pane of glass above the knob. At first it autofocuses on the steel mesh within the glass but then as it racks focus on the hallway beyond, the mesh nearly disappears.

Out in the hallway, Derek Burrell can be seen. His back is to the camera and he's firing his shotgun in the opposite direction.

Where Derek is standing is about twenty feet away from the classroom door the video is being recorded through.

Each blast of the shotgun thunders through the hallway, echoes through the school, its extreme audible peaks distorting the sound of the recording.

Anna reaches down and takes my hand.

The video not only shows Derek firing but being fired upon—presumably by the school resource officer, though she is not visible around the bend in the hallway.

Between the explosions and gunfire something

inaudible is said, perhaps by one of the students in the classroom. It's difficult to make out.

Suddenly, Derek jerks around this direction and begins firing. Two quick rounds as I come into frame.

I can be seen at the far edge of the frame returning fire.

As Derek falls, the kids in the classroom scream and whoever's holding the phone drops it and a moment later the recording stops.

"You okay?" Anna whispers to me.

I squeeze her hand and nod.

"Could we rewind to just before Derek turns and starts shooting at John?" Anna asks.

"Read my mind," Wheata Pearl says.

"And could we turn it up as loud as it will go, Your Honor?"

"Way ahead of you," she says.

Scott clears his throat and steps back away from us a few steps.

Unable to cue the video to the exact spot she's looking for, the judge starts the video over from the beginning.

This time, though, every blast is magnified and bounces around the judge's chambers.

"Wow, that's loud," the judge shouts, but doesn't turn it down.

This time when we reach the moment just before

Derek jerks around and starts shooting, we can hear what is said.

It doesn't come from the classroom but out in the hallway, and there's no doubt about who's saying it or what's being said.

Before Derek spins and starts shooting at me, I say, "Sheriff's investigator, drop your weapon."

They aren't the best or most beautiful words I've ever spoken but in this moment it feels like they are.

Before this moment, I couldn't remember if I had identified myself and given him a lawful command, and because of that I hadn't said I did in any of my statements, but in the fateful moment, my training and experience hadn't failed me.

50

"Heard things went well for you today," Merrill says.

Merrill Monroe has been my closest friend since childhood—and his recent absence in my life has left a huge void.

We are in the parking lot of a flower shop next to a collapsed commercial popup tent near the main intersection and only traffic light in Wewa. I had been examining the controversial tent with the crime scene tape around it when he passed by, saw me, and swung in. He's still in his black BMW and I'm standing next to his open driver's side window.

I nod. "At least for me personally," I say. "Not sure what if any impact it'll have on the case, but for me . . . it was a great day."

"Anna says that's our main objective these days," he says.

He and I have had so little contact lately I didn't know he was still helping Anna out with defense investigation work and by extension keeping up with the case.

"I didn't realize you were still helping her with the investigation," I say. "Thought everything was done. I really appreciate all you're doing."

"Don't mention it," he says. "Though I have to say I was particularly proud of finding that video."

"The *student video* we watched today?" I say. "*You* found that?"

"I said don't mention it."

I should have guessed the student didn't suddenly decide to turn in the footage on his own. Of course Merrill was the one to find it. Had to be the only one still looking.

"So you had seen it and knew what was on it and . . ."

I realize then the genius of what he did by sending it to Scott.

"Having the student send it to Scott was brilliant," I say.

"Well . . ." he says. "You might say *student* . . . or you might say *untraceable China hacker*. But yeah, thought having Scott think it gonna benefit him would mean he couldn't resist introducing it. He do that . . . We get it in *and* . . . save Anna having to deal with any discovery issues."

"Does she know—"

"She knows nothing about nothing," he says. "And neither do we."

"Thank you," I say. "You'll never know what seeing and, more importantly, hearing that footage did for me."

"You know, for being told *not* to mention something, you damn sure mention it a lot," he says.

I laugh and neither of us says anything for a beat.

"How'd the video play to the jury?" he asks eventually.

The judge had allowed the video to be entered into evidence, and despite Anna's earlier concerns about the jury actually seeing me shoot Derek, she had shown it in court this afternoon and questioned me about it, after which Anna rested and the judge dismissed court for the day, saying we'd have closing arguments tomorrow and then jury deliberations would begin.

"I couldn't look at them," I say. "Couldn't look anywhere. Just locked my eyes onto the screen and fought hard not to close my eyes, look away, or cry. Of all the difficult and painful parts of the trial . . . watching that footage with and in front of everyone was by far the most difficult and painful."

"Glad I could provide such an experience for you," he says. "You willin' for me to use your statement as testimonial on my website? Monroe Security and Investigations —we find footage that will fuck you up."

I laugh and turn to see Arnie Ward, the person I've been waiting on, pull into the lot and park across the way.

"The only grace at all," I say, "was that Bryce and Melissa weren't present for it. Left the courtroom because they couldn't bear seeing it."

"Was it worth it?" he asks. "The pain and . . . embarrassment . . . or whatever it was . . . in order to hear that you *did* identify yourself, seeing how quickly he fired, how little time you had to react?"

"No question," I say. "It's the single most important thing that's happened in the trial so far. It's no exaggeration to say that . . . what you did by finding that footage and getting it into evidence . . . may just have saved my life . . . and at the very least my sanity."

"Not even I can save somethin' that ain't there to begin with."

"I mean it. Thank you."

Arnie has yet to get out of his car, and I can see that he's on the phone.

"I know," he says. "You can't imagine how happy I was when I found that little punk with the footage. Little bitch tried to sell it to me too. *Shee-it.* Talkin' 'bout his side hustle is video. I's like, your side hustle gonna be tryin' to figure how to remove my boot from your ass if you don't produce that shit."

"I'm sure he was holding onto it for the documentary they'll inevitably make about the Potter High shooting one day."

"Exactly what he said."

We fall silent again.

Eventually, he says, "Harassing high school students ain't the only thing I been doin'. Been followin' your girl too. Bitch been keepin' some odd hours."

"Who?"

"How many women I tell you I gonna be keepin' tabs on?"

"Oh," I say. "Randa."

"Started to text you and let you know she was waiting by your car last night but wanted to see the look on your face."

"How was it?"

"Priceless," he says, "though if you were either surprised or happy to see her you hid it well."

"What's she been up to?" I ask.

"'Sides stalkin' you?"

"Yeah."

"She all over the place—all hours of the day and night when she's not stalkin' you in court. She up to somethin'. Just can't tell what exactly. She like followin' a bee, flittin' around from flower to flower."

"Where all is she going?"

"She's revisited every crime scene—or least where the

bodies were discovered—some more than once. She's been to the RV Park out on Overstreet, the couple of tent cities we got with volunteers in them. She keeps ridin' by and watchin' those night crews working on the lines. Like she window shoppin' or some shit."

"Well, let me know if browsing turns to buying."

51

For the past few days, the now collapsed popup tent has been a source of contention for our little town and has had many locals angry enough to threaten its owner and attempt to run him out of town.

The tent—which was set up during the first week following the storm when our town still didn't have electricity, running water, or cell service and we were all continuing to grieve the destruction and loss of so much we held sacred—houses a T-shirt vendor from Tennessee who was selling colorful shirts that read "I Survived Hurricane Michael."

Because we were all in so much pain, because we all knew people who hadn't survived the superstorm, because the hurricane that decimated our homes and savaged our surroundings, bringing with it death and destruction like had never been seen here before wasn't an amusement park ride, many among us viewed it as offensive and in extremely poor taste for an outsider, unaffected by the disaster, to rush in so soon afterwards to capitalize on our misery in such a crass and commercial way.

When hurting and resentful citizens had stopped by the man's tent and told him what they thought about him and that it best he left town, his callous response had been, "It's a free country. You don't like what I'm selling, don't buy one. I ain't goin' anywhere."

When some of these same citizens took their complaints to the mayor and board of city commissioners, they were patronized and placated—and the offending T-shirt tent remained.

It looked as if no one could do anything about the insensitive entrepreneur from Tennessee.

And then along came the Chaos Killer, who in the early morning hours, as the Tennessean was setting up for the day ahead, had clocked him in the back of the head with one of the galvanized tent poles, broke his right ring finger, placed his mark on the man's right palm, and had collapsed the tent around him to make it look like an accident.

Ironically, the tone-deaf Tennessean peddling the "I Survived Hurricane Michael" T-shirts had survived, and since no hospitals in the area had reopened yet he had been life-flighted to Tallahassee Memorial Medical Center. He's now in critical but stable condition after being placed in a medically induced coma while surgeons try to deal with his blood-swollen brain.

Someone with a wicked sense of humor and about as much empathy as the T-shirt salesman had already sent him a homemade T-shirt that reads, "I Survived the Hurricane Michael Serial Killer," with an accompanying note that said, "For you to wear if you actually survive."

"An actual survivor," Arnie says.

He has finally gotten out of his car and joined me at the scene.

"Maybe."

"Wonder if he'll be able to tell us anything?"

"Hard to imagine," I say. "Most likely attacked from behind. But even if he wasn't, I'd think the head trauma would prevent him from remembering anything."

"Probably right," he says, "but . . . it's a shame. Got no other witnesses or anything else to go on."

"Oh, but we do," I say. "We have everything we need to make an arrest and we need to let everyone know."

AN HOUR LATER, Reggie is standing in front of the crumpled tent giving a statement to the media, the crime scene tape flapping in the wind behind her providing great optics for the drama unfolding.

"It's moments like these," Merrick says softly, "that make you wish you worked in TV news."

I am standing next to him, Tim, and Bucky to the back left side, waiting for Reggie to begin.

"You just need a great photograph to accompany your words," Tim says. "I'll take Bucky's images over video footage any day. Why don't you have a photographer on this assignment?"

"You kidding?" Merrick says. "We have like two photographers in our entire agency that we all have to share. And only one of them is full-time."

"Give me that piece of shit camera you have," Bucky says, "and don't tell anybody—and for fuck sake don't give me a photo credit—and I'll shoot a couple good shots for you too."

Reggie takes a step forward and clears her throat, and everyone in the small group of gathered reporters grows quiet and still.

"We are very close to making an arrest," she says. "Not only do we have a witness to this brazen act of brutality right here in the middle of town, but the victim has survived and is expected to make a complete recovery. We're waiting for word from his doctors now about when we can interview him. All of which gives me great confidence to say to you that very soon this nightmare within a nightmare will be over."

They're all lies, of course. Every word—except maybe the ones about making an arrest soon. Those at least are aspirational.

Only a few people in our department know they are lies, and Reggie comes off as very credible and convincing, so hopefully this will work to both increase help from the public and rattle the killer.

"If you have any additional information you'd like to add to the strong case we are building, call the Gulf County Sheriff's Department. And to the man responsible for these vicious and insidious murders . . . you can call me directly if you'd like to put a peaceful end to this without a violent confrontation that could result in your death."

FOLLOWING THE PRESS CONFERENCE, Tim, Bucky, and Merrick ask to speak with me in private after everyone else is gone.

Now that everyone but us is, we stand near my car.

"We think we're not giving the public enough information," Tim says. "This was preventable. I know no one around here really cares that the T-shirt guy got it, but . . . chances are the next victim will be local."

I look over at Merrick. "Why not talk to Reggie about it?" I ask. "It's her call."

"We're not the only ones who think it," Bucky says.

"Officers in your own department believe the public should know more too," Tim says.

"I saw you talking to Darlene," I say.

"I won't reveal a source," Tim says, "but I can tell you it's not just one officer."

I start to say something but have to wait for a couple of semis to pass by. They are in a long line of heavy work truck traffic, and I wonder if our little town will ever get back to its pre-storm pace and quietude.

"Again, why not ask Reggie?" I say, looking from Tim to Merrick.

"Things between us are . . . complicated," he says. "You know that. But she'll listen to you."

"Actually, I listen to *her*," I say. "She's the boss."

"So you don't agree that we should be warning the public more?" Tim says.

"I'm not saying that. I'm saying this conversation should be happening with Reggie."

"Will you talk to her?" Merrick asks. "If you agree that—"

"We're not saying make everybody panic," Tim says. "Just . . . give them a fighting chance."

"It's her decision," I say, "and it's a difficult one. But . . . I'll talk to her."

"Thank you," Merrick says.

"And if y'all ever want to have a conversation like this again," I say, "have it with the sheriff—or at least include her in it from the jump."

WHEN I'M BACK in my car, I call Reggie and tell her what has just transpired.

"I'm disappointed in Darlene and Merrick," she says. "Darlene is capable of good work, but . . . if something's being stirred up . . . she's usually the one with the spoon."

"Yeah."

"And Merrick . . ." she says. "There was a time when he would've come to me before he'd even thought it all the way through himself."

I don't respond to that.

"What do you think?" she asks. "Should we be saying more?"

TAMPA BAY TIMES DAILY DISPATCH

Hurricane Michael in Real Time

By Tim Jonas, *Times* Reporter

Law enforcement officials believe a dangerous killer is at work in the aftermath of Hurricane Michael among the vulnerable people of the Florida Panhandle.

These same officials and members of the investigative team are conflicted about how much information to share with the public—wanting to warn those they have sworn to protect, yet not wanting to start a panic among those who can't handle any additional stress right now.

More than one investigator has asked me to disregard what their superiors are saying and inform you the public of just how dangerous a predator is at work among you at this decidedly dark and desperate moment in the life of the Panhandle.

And this reporter has also been conflicted, but ultimately decided to err on the side of caution and public safety—a responsibility I take even more seriously since this is my last chance to do so, my last article about the investigation before I return to Tampa and a new assignment.

Don't panic, but do use extreme caution and look out for each other.

During my time here covering Hurricane Michael I have gained a great appreciation for this part of the Florida Panhandle, and I care deeply what happens here —both in the fallout from the storm and with the prolific predator in your midst.

A source close to the investigation, which will soon include the Florida Department of Law Enforcement, revealed that investigators are at a loss because of a lack of evidence in the case. In fact, several victims whose deaths had been ruled accidental have been buried or cremated—and with them vital evidence that might have provided a break in the case.

According to one official actually involved in the investigation, at first only one investigator believed that the disparate deaths might be connected and might not be accidental after all, and initially his theory was met with skepticism and resistance. Now that the investigation is finally underway, area law enforcement are way behind and trying to catch up.

One factor making it particularly difficult to get anywhere in the search for the killer is there seems to be no pattern to his actions, no "type" of victim he's drawn to. Dubbed by some within the investigation the Chaos Killer because of the seeming random nature of his killings and his practice of marking their bodies with a symbol for chaos, he is suspected of having committed similar crimes in other jurisdictions. Other aspects of his ritual include killing his victims with materials and debris from the storm and breaking a single bone in their body after they're already dead.

Haven't the people of the Panhandle been through enough? Shouldn't the FBI be offering to help? Other federal agencies are letting the people of the Panhandle down. It'd be nice if at least one would step up and help out.

52

"We've got him," Darlene says.

She, Reggie, Arnie, and I are in the conference room of the sheriff's station with the door closed.

"I went back and looked at all the hurricanes that hit or affected Florida since 2000. If I had found anything in 2000, then I would've gone back further. I'm gonna tell you, it's staggering how many hurricanes and tropical storms we've had just in that time and how much damage they've done. I really had no idea. I guess living here you just sort of get used to hearing about them every year during hurricane season and you only really pay attention to the ones that hit you where you live."

"That's part of the reason we're not getting the help or funding we need," Reggie says.

"Well, at least we got Ray," I say.

Through the open blinds we can see Ray hanging around in the outer office, sneaking furtive glances over toward us, jonesing to join us. His partner Phillip is nowhere to be seen.

"It's unbelievable," Darlene says.

"That we got Ray?" I ask.

"*What*? No. The sheer volume of hurricanes that hit the shit out of us each year."

"Both are equally unbelievable," Reggie says.

"Speaking of unbelievable," Darlene says, "have either of you ever heard Phillip speak? I mean utter a single word?"

We both shake our heads.

"Where is he, by the way?" Darlene asks.

"He disappears sometimes," Reggie says. "He's just so quiet it takes a while to notice."

"He's like the perfect man," Darlene says.

"If he wasn't so creepy," Reggie says.

"Well, anyway . . . I didn't find anything—or think I did—until 2004," Darlene says. "But it was a false alarm. Or probably a murder someone tried to make look like an accident. I'm sure our guy isn't the first to do it."

"True," Reggie says. "We should contact the agency that handled that investigation and see what they've got. The first few he did could've been different enough not to fit the current pattern."

"Okay. Will do. I figured with as much hurricane activity as we had in 2005 it would make a great year for him to get his start. I mean between Tropical Storm Arlene, Hurricane Cindy, Hurricane Dennis, Hurricane Ophelia, Hurricane Rita, Hurricane Wilma, and Katrina, 2005 was a motherfucker and a half, but I didn't turn up anything. It wasn't until 2008 that I found what I believe could be positive matches—starting with Hurricane Gustav in August of that year. It was the hurricane that came after Tropical Storm Fay set a record by making something like four different landfalls in Florida. Anyway, Hurricane Gustav hit the Florida Keys and then continued on up into Central Louisiana and produced six tornadoes and some extremely heavy rainfall. But it's the strong rip currents throughout the state of Florida that are of the most relevance to us. The outer bands of the storm produced at least three water spouts each in the Panhandle, coming ashore near Valparaiso. Five people drowned in the rip currents and one of them had a broken toe and what the ME believed was a tattoo on his left foot. I believe the tattoo was actually a mark the killer made that looked like the Chinese symbol for chaos. I can't be certain, but I really think this could be his first victim. In September of that same year four other people were killed in rip currents related to Hurricane Hanna— two near Hollywood, Florida and two in Fort Lauderdale. One in each of those places is listed as having a tattoo that resembles some of the other chaos symbols we've seen."

"This is really good work, Darlene," I say.

"Yes it is," Reggie says.

"Maybe it'll make up for me being such an asshole the other night," she says. "Anyway . . . I also think he was responsible for one death in New Smyrna Beach during Hurricane Bill. And then in 2010—that was the year that tropical storm Alex passed through the area of the Gulf affected by the Deepwater Horizon oil spill and sent tarballs as large as oranges to wash up on shore in parts of the Panhandle in June—at the end of August and beginning of September of that year I think he killed three people in the wake of Hurricane Earl along the eastern coastline. And he's just getting started. If I'm right, in August of the next year he killed two people around Jacksonville Beach during Hurricane Irene and in October, following Hurricane Rina, he killed a surfer in Boca West. In 2012 he killed two more surfers around Jacksonville Beach during Tropical Storm Beryl, and then an elderly man in Key West during Hurricane Isaac in August of that year."

"Gets around, don't he?" Arnie says.

"In 2013 during Tropical Storm Andrea he killed people in West Palm Beach, Tampa, and Miami—three different people, two women and one man. One of them was staged to look like an automobile accident, the other was staged to look like an accidental drowning, and the third the result of accidental electrocution. All had a broken bone and some variation of the chaos symbol on them. In 2014 during Hurricane Arthur he killed two people near Daytona Beach. Both were made to look like drownings due to riptides. In 2016 . . . let's see . . . ah, yeah, in . . . September, during and after Hurricane Hermine made landfall near the Big Bend, he killed four people and made them look like drownings. In 2017 during and after Hurricane Irma on Cudjoe Key and then around Marco Island, he killed five people and made each of them look like accidents related to the storm, but all had a broken bone and his mark on them. And that brings us to Hurricane Michael."

"Were you here all night?" Reggie asks.

Darlene nods. "Couldn't've slept anyway. Now, I don't believe for one minute that these are all of his murders or that he only kills during hurricanes. I just started with them, but I'm willing to bet my left tit that he's done this same thing during other disasters and crises as well. I just haven't gotten to them yet. But they're next on my list."

"After a good night's sleep," Reggie says. "You've done enough for now. Excellent work. Really great job."

Arnie and I second that motion.

"Okay," Reggie says. "This is huge. We've got to notify FDLE—so many jurisdictions involved—and probably even the FBI. Fantastic work everyone."

"Wouldn't even be aware of it to work *on* if it weren't for John," Darlene says.

"That's true," Reggie says, "but what you did here is extraordinary."

"It really is," I say.

"This is so exciting," Reggie says, "but the thing about a case like this is . . . it's going to be taken from us. We'll still be involved, but chances are in a very small way. But —and this is the thing to remember, *the most important thing*—no matter who puts the cuffs on him, it'll be because of the work you've done. All of you."

"That may be somewhat true of what Darlene's just done," Arnie says, "but all I've done and what Darlene did originally is make the same mistake all these other agencies did—believed the murders were accidents."

Darlene nods but Reggie and I don't respond.

"Is there something I can do?" Arnie asks. "I don't mind pulling an all-nighter. Feel like I should. I know you say FDLE or the FBI are gonna catch him, but he's here, now, killing our citizens in our backyard."

Reggie looks over at me.

"You're right," I say, "he is. And we should do all we can to catch him. The sooner that happens the more lives we save. You could take Darlene's list of storms where the killer struck and try to come up with a list of who responded to them. I mean the first or very early respon-ders, because he was here right at or right after the storm.

So we're talking emergency services personnel, first responders, governmental groups, law enforcement agencies, search and rescue operations, even some of these big national volunteer organizations. If we can find who responded to all the storms—and it won't be many—we can begin to narrow down our list of possible suspects."

53

"If Reggie is right and you don't get to put the cuffs on him," Anna says, "will you be disappointed?"

Anna and I are lying on the couch in our living room, holding each other as we talk about what's on our minds. Taylor is in bed, long since asleep, and though there are things we both need to be doing, neither of us wants this rare-since-the-storm moment of intimate interlude to end.

I shake my head. "I truly just want him off the street," I say. "Unable to hurt or kill anyone else ever again."

"But—"

"And it's not just how I feel since shooting Derek," I say. "Though I'm sure that's part of it. It's that my gift and what I enjoy doing is investigating, not breaking down doors and taking down suspects. I could be okay with never doing that again. And when we put him in a cage where he belongs I'll know I had a part in that—no matter who actually escorts him into it."

"The most important part," Anna says.

I shrug.

She shakes her head and says, "Wonder how many predators like him are out there right now that nobody even knows about or suspects."

"Far, far too many," I say.

"Soon there will be one less because of you, because of the way you used your gifts."

"Far too many rapists and sadists, brutal men who do bad things to everyone misfortunate enough to orbit near the black hole of their soul."

"That's kind of poetic," she says.

"Speaking of poetic and gifts," I say. "The way you've used your many talents for me in this trial has been like watching poetry in motion. And no matter the outcome .. . you've given me a gift more valuable than you can fathom."

"It has been an honor," she says, "and though you've been my favorite client ever, I hope to never have you for a client again."

"No arguments here," I say.

"As much as I'm enjoying this," she says, "as much as I

wish I could lie here with you like this all night, I better go get back to work on my closing."

"Stay," I say. "You're ready. You've prepped enough."

"I don't want to, but I have to. This is it—our last chance to convince the jury. I've got to be ready."

"You already are, but okay."

54

"An accident is defined as an unfortunate incident that happens unexpectedly and unintentionally," Anna says, "typically resulting in damage or injury, an event that happens by chance or that is without apparent or deliberate cause."

Gary Scott has completed his closing argument and it's Anna's turn, and she stands at the podium with poise and peace, calm and confidence.

As she stands there in her navy dress, her hair pulled back revealing her sweet, beautiful face, I find her more attractive than at any other time in our lives. Her facial features and her figure show some of the typical signs of aging, but not many, and to me it's not that the bloom of youth fades as so many claim, but that in maturity the blossoming of true lasting beauty occurs.

"The shooting of Derek Burrell, a brave but misguided young man, who should have never been in that hallway with a weapon, let alone one he used to shoot at not one but two law enforcement officers, was a heartbreakingly tragic accident, but an accident nonetheless. An unfortunate incident that happened unintentionally and without deliberate cause. All the evidence in this case, all the testimony, all the physical evidence, all the expert witnesses, and most especially the actual video footage of the incident shows that John didn't deliberately kill Derek, he returned fire at the school shooter that was shooting at him. And make no mistake about it, ladies and gentlemen, in that moment that's exactly what Derek Burrell was—a school shooter. No matter what his motive and reasoning were, no matter how noble or heroic or understandable they were, in that moment he was a teenager with a gun shooting at law enforcement in the hallway of his school."

She pauses, giving an extra moment for the weight of her words to sink in. And they do.

"We're so quick to cast blame on the officers who huddled together outside of Columbine while kids were being shot to death inside. We criticize cops at Parkland and other places for not rushing in, for not doing their duty to put themselves in harm's way to protect our children in the most vulnerable situation they are ever likely to find themselves in—and then when one does, when a brave, noble, good man does what we have been saying for years those other officers should have done, we put him on trial. When he is cleared by objective state investigators who don't know him but base their findings only on the evidence, we bring him into court and put his every move under an enormous magnifying glass in slow motion and we sit in judgement. And what do we find when we do that? We find a man who acted bravely and honorably and nobly and professionally and correctly— not in slow motion but in split-second real time when lives were on the line. A wounded police officer was being fired upon and John ran around to confront the shooter, identified himself as law enforcement, told him to drop his weapon, and was fired upon. He was fired upon not once, but twice, and either round could have easily killed him, leaving me a widow and his daughters fatherless. And what does the fact that John was fired upon twice mean? Have you asked yourself that? Not once. But twice. He was fired at twice before returning fire, and that shows that not only was he not acting too quickly, that he didn't rush in guns blazing, but also that he was taking his time and attempting to aim and shoot in such a way as to wound and not kill, disarm and not destroy the young man who he believed was the school shooter—the young man who confirmed that belief for him by firing at him not once but twice. And still John took his time and attempted to save the young man's life.

Sadly, it didn't work out that way, but surely you can see that he tried."

She pauses again, but only for a moment.

"If John could take this accident back he would," she says. "He'd take it back before anything else in his life. And there's someone else who I'm certain would say the same thing. If, as could have easily been the case, Derek's round had hit John in the head and chest instead of barely missing, and John had died and Derek was on trial today, he would take it back if he could. He would still be a brave young man trying to help and do a good thing, who just accidentally shot a police officer because he thought he was the school shooter he was out there to defend his classmates against. It would have been an accident. And if I were here today as John's widow instead of his wife and attorney, and Derek was on trial for killing him, I stand before you and say that . . . even though Derek shouldn't have had a gun in his vehicle and even though he shouldn't have disobeyed his teacher and broken out of the school and gotten it, and even though he should not have gone out into that hallway and started firing at police officers, I'd say he didn't mean to kill John, he didn't knowingly kill a cop. It was a tragic accident and he would take it back if he could."

One final, brief pause and she continues.

"This reminds me of a dear, dear friend of mine," she says. "A truly good woman who has never knowingly hurt anyone, who is kind and caring and compassionate. A woman who had dedicated her life not just to taking care of her own kids, but educating the children of others. A woman who rises early to cook breakfast and check backpacks and fill lunch boxes not just with delicious and nutritious food but with nothing short of love itself—often expressed by a little note that reminds her children that no matter how difficult a day they are having, no matter how unkind or even cruel other kids can be, they are loved unconditionally and unreservedly, and in a few short hours they will be back in the arms of the source of that love in the warmth and safety of their own home. And on this particular morning that I'm thinking about, not only does my friend, this amazing mom and teacher, do all the early morning rituals that she does every morning but also, like every morning, she loads her kids into her minivan with all their stuff, and after dropping her son at kindergarten and her daughter at fourth grade, she goes to her own school and as she does every day, gives all she has to the kids in her classroom—some of whom don't have a mom at home like her. And it's not until the end of the long, hot North Florida day as she's about to climb back into her van that she remembers that her husband had a dentist appointment this morning, and instead of taking their baby to daycare like he normally does—since it's on his way to work—it had been her job to do this morning. But because she never does it and because her precious little baby fell asleep in the back of her van, this amazing, loving mom had forgotten she was back there—there where she still was and had been during the entire hot North Florida day. Her sweet little baby, her third child and the last she planned to have had roasted alive in the back of her van while she was inside her air-conditioned room taking care of other people's children. It was just an accident. A terrible, tragic accident that she would give anything in this world to take back if she could, but she can't. Like John, she can't. And like John, an investigation cleared her of any wrong doing, concluding that it was just a terrible, horrible, tragic, unimaginable accident. But unlike John, after that her husband didn't sue her for the wrongful death of his daughter. No one in her circle of family, friends, and community did anything but give her all the compassion they could come up with, knowing it was just a crushing tragic accident she would take back if she could."

55

B y the time Anna has finished her closing argument, tears are streaming down my cheeks.

And even without looking around the courtroom, I can tell that I am not the only one moved by her masterful, poignant, and persuasive presentation.

Even Judge Wheata Pearl takes extra time sipping from her rattlesnake mug and is careful to clear her throat before speaking.

When she does finally speak, she reads detailed jury instructions about the law that applies to this case.

"Members of the jury, you have now heard all the evidence, my instructions on the law that you must apply in reaching your verdict, and the closing arguments of the attorneys. You will shortly retire to the jury room to decide this case. But before you do, your eccentric old grandmother has a few last instructions for you. These are important so listen carefully. During deliberations, jurors must communicate about the case only with one another and only when all jurors are present in the jury room. You will have in the jury room all of the evidence that was received during the trial. In reaching your decision, do not do any research on your own or as a group. Do not use dictionaries, the internet, or any other reference materials. Do not investigate the case or conduct any experiments. Do not visit or view the scene of any event involved in this case or look at maps or pictures on the internet. If you happen to pass by the scene, do not stop or investigate. All jurors must see or hear the same evidence at the same time. Do not read, listen to, or watch any news accounts of this trial. Understand?"

The jurors nod, but they're not the only ones. Nearly everyone in the crowded courtroom does.

"You are not to communicate with any person outside the jury about this case. Until you have reached a verdict, you must not talk about this case in person or through the telephone, writing, or electronic communication, such as a blog, twitter, e-mail, text message, or any other means. Do not contact anyone to assist you, such as a family accountant, doctor, or lawyer. These communications rules apply until I discharge you at the end of the case. If you become aware of any violation of these instructions or any other instruction I have given in this case, you must tell me by giving a note to the bailiff.

"In reaching your verdict, do not let bias, sympathy, prejudice, public opinion, or any other sentiment for or against any party to influence your decision. Your verdict must be based on the evidence that has been received and the law on which I have instructed you. Reaching a verdict is exclusively your job. I cannot participate in that decision in any way and you should not guess what I think your verdict should be from something I may have said or done. When you go to the jury room, the first thing you should do is choose a presiding juror to act as a foreperson during your deliberations. The foreperson should see to it that your discussions are orderly and that everyone has a fair chance to be heard. Each of you must decide the case for yourself, but only after you have considered the evidence with the other members of the jury. Feel free to change your mind if you are convinced that your position should be different.

"I will give you a verdict form with questions you must answer. I have already instructed you on the law that you are to use in answering these questions. You must follow my instructions and the form carefully. You must consider each question separately. Please answer the questions in the order they appear. After you answer a question, the form tells you what to do next. If any of you need to communicate with me for any reason, write me a note and give it to the bailiff. In your note, do not disclose any vote or split or the reason for the communication. You may now retire to decide your verdict."

And with that the jury rises and files out to go determine my fate.

56

L ater that afternoon, as the jury deliberates and FDLE moves in and begins to investigate, Anna and I go to our bank to finalize the second mortgage of our home in preparation for the verdict.

That evening, after the jury has adjourned for the day and we know that no verdict will be coming, Anna, Taylor, Johanna, who has just come into town to stay with us for a few days, and I have dinner together. We then take a walk along Main Street, negotiating the piles of debris along the sides of the road, some of which block the sidewalks, and the additional heavy traffic that roars up and down the once quiet and mostly empty streets of our little town. Following our walk, we have ice cream and return home for games, baths, a book, then bed.

That night, after Anna, who is exhausted, and the

girls are fast asleep, I drive down to Port St. Joe to the sheriff's department to put in a little time with the whiteboard in the conference room and to see what all I've missed today.

It's late and the building is mostly empty—apart from dispatch, patrol, and a few random officers from other agencies here for a few more days to assist us—but I find both Arnie and Darlene in the conference room.

Neither of them look like they've slept or eaten or even bathed in a while.

"How'd it go today?" Darlene asks.

"I'm married to a truly brilliant woman and regardless of the verdict I can't feel anything other than being the luckiest man on the planet. What did I miss down here?"

They spend a few minutes taking me through the day's activities, including the arrival of FDLE and its integration into the investigation and the progress the two of them have made with the research they're continuing to do even at this late hour.

"While I'm trying to figure out which first responders were at every disaster where killings took place—" Arnie says.

"I'm searching for additional disasters he may have killed at," Darlene adds. "Not coming up with much. A series of wildfires in 2013 is it so far."

"And as far as which agencies or organizations were in first at all or nearly all disasters where he killed . . ." Arnie says. "There are not a lot. FEMA is never in particularly fast, and a few of these tropical storms were small enough that FEMA wasn't involved at all. And that's true of a lot of other national groups and federal organizations. It makes sense, but the most consistent early response around the state comes from local and state agencies in the state. The fire department in Orlando always sends volunteers. Police department in Sarasota. Marion County Sheriff's Department. There are exceptions—like the Red Cross, Salvation Army, and Cajun Navy—but otherwise . . . Oh, and the Samaritan's Purse organization. I'll tell you . . . I got emotional going through this, thinking about all the help we've received and what it has meant to us. Some of these amazing groups go out every single time."

And mixed in among them is an evil madman who comes to kill and destroy.

"Great work," I say. "Both of you."

"We've got a lot more to go through," Darlene says. "But . . . we're getting there."

"It's possible the killer isn't coming with a group, but on his own," I say.

"Or her," Darlene says.

"Or *her*," I say. "Statistically, it's most likely to be a man—and given the postmortem bone breaking . . ."

"The thing is," she says. "It could just as easily be a woman—if not more so in terms of gaining the trust of

the victims and surprising them when she attacked—
and when it comes to the breaking of the bones, it
doesn't have much to do with strength. It's not like even
a very strong man could snap someone's arm or especially a leg bone. The killer is having to use leverage to
do it—something a woman could do the same as a
man."

"Excellent point," I say. "You're right. It could be
either. But if he or she is coming on his or her own it's
going to be a lot more difficult to identify him or her."

For fraction of a second I get a glimpse of the killer,
but then it's gone and I can't get it back.

And then another idea occurs to me.

"Once you finish examining disasters, it might be
even more telling to see if we can find any victims whose
deaths look like accidents and have the chaos mark that
are *not* part of a disaster."

"Why's that?" she asks.

"Those murders may be a lot closer to home—let us
know where he's from. Help us narrow our search even
more and find him—or *her*—faster."

"Will do," she says. "That's . . . Maybe I should pull off
the disasters and go ahead and do that now."

"Just whatever you think," I say. "Both will help. Both
are just fields to use for comparison to narrow down our
lists until we just have one name on it—and right now we
don't have any names on it yet, so . . ."

"Cool," she says. "Should go faster tomorrow when we have more investigators from FDLE to help."

"Yes, it will," I say, and then something floats up from my subconscious.

Triggered by Darlene saying *or her*, it hits me that Randa went missing in 2005, so she was out there unaccounted for during the time of the killings. And now that she's out of jail, the killings are happening again here where she happens to have decided to stay. I'll have to check to see if any of the murders were committed during the time she was incarcerated.

"Can I get either of you anything?" I say.

They both say they're good.

"I thought I saw Reggie's vehicle when I pulled up. Is she in her office?"

"Was earlier," Arnie says.

"I'm gonna go check in with her. I'll be back to help in a few."

As I'm walking to Reggie's office, my phone vibrates in my pocket and I pull it out. It's a text from Merrill, and I try to read and respond to his text while I'm walking through the dim hallway.

Can't find Randa tonight. You seen her?

I haven't.

Holla if you do. I'll do the same.

10-4.

When I reach Reggie's office I find it empty, but I see that her phone is lying on her desk and it's lit up.

Finding it strange that she has left her phone—something I've never seen her do before, I walk over toward it.

Things get even stranger when I see that her service pistol is also on her desk.

I pick up her phone and take a look at it.

The screen is still unlocked and texts between Randa and Reggie are still being displayed.

Sheriff Reg, this is Randa Raffield. Do exactly what I say or someone you care very deeply for is going to have a fatal 'accident' tonight. Do I have your attention?

Yes.

Will you do exactly as I say? And nothing else?

Yes.

Make sure you do or the next time you see Merrick he won't have a pulse. Understand?

I do.

First thing. Don't tell anyone about this. If you involve anyone else, he's dead and your kid is next.

I won't. I promise.

Second, share your location with me so I can see exactly where you are.

Okay. Just did it. Do you see it?

You're in your office?

I am.

Can you see where I am?

The El Governor.

If you'd like to negotiate for Merrick's life, join us here at what's left of the El Governor. But do 3 things and only these 3 things. Come alone. Come unarmed. Leave your gun and phone there on your desk. Will you do as I say?

I will. You have my word.

You think you can take me, anyway, right? So you don't need a gun or backup anyway, do you? See you in 20.

57

I 'm racing down 98 toward Mexico Beach.

Beneath the starless sky and the pale half-moon, the night is dark, the beams of my head-lights surrounded by an inky blackness my blue flashers bounce off of.

I am alone in my car, alone on the road. I alone am aware of what Reggie is doing.

I have no idea how far I am behind her, but given the fact that her vehicle was in the parking lot of the sheriff's station when I first arrived and her phone was still unlocked when I entered her office, I can't imagine it's much.

Progress on the curfew-empty road is fast and easy and in less than ten minutes I am entering what's left of the decimated coastal town of Mexico Beach—the very same place I had spent the most intense hours of the hurricane.

Cutting my flashers and dimming my brights, I slow down some even though I am still a few miles from the hotel.

Eventually, I turn off my lights completely, driving only by the dim yellow glow of my parking lights. Soon I cut even them, and when I'm within a half a mile or so of the El Governor I park my car near the rubble of a stilted beach house and run the rest of the way.

All but completely wiped off the map, what remains of Mexico Beach is in lifeless pieces.

No electricity. No people. No signs of life. The once chill, charming seaside town now resembles the propped-up pieces of a fake town in an atomic bomb test site in the middle of the desert.

With no traffic and no human activity to compete with it, the tide crashing ashore is thunderingly loud tonight, every wave hitting the shore a mortar explosion.

The five-story El Governor Motel, which has been the biggest, tallest landmark on Mexico Beach for as long as I can remember, stands on the Gulf side of the street and has 120 rooms—each with a back view of the beach and the Gulf of Mexico beyond.

Before Hurricane Michael it had a heated pool on the side, a tiki bar along the back, and a gift shop filled with supplies and souvenirs off the lobby.

Now the beachside behemoth lies in tatters, its windows blown out, its railings missing or so pretzeled as to be unrecognizable, chunks of concrete lying around it like boulders around the base of a mountain.

On the side of the structure, all that is left of the huge black letters that once spelled El Governor Motel is *Gover or.*

Tattered drapes like battle flags hang through openings where windows used to be, flapping in the breeze blowing in off the Gulf.

Somewhere unseen in the darkness, pieces of metal clang against each other like the rigging of a sailboat lost at sea.

As I approach the dark, dead building, I see Reggie's SUV parked alone in the rubble-piled parking lot.

Ducking beneath a large hanging shard of glass, I step through the lobby door to find what looks like an explosives crime scene, window glass and souvenir trinkets crunching beneath the heels of my shoes. The room is damp and dank, its furniture overturned and piled together. All the papers scattered around the floor are wet and faded. The tiki bar from the back has been blown in through the back doors and windows, breaking the glass and crashing in to fill the entire back half of the lobby. Through the missing door of the gift shop, I see what looks like the bombed-out store of a terrorist attack on a mall. Thousands and thousands of trinkets only tourists would buy join beach T-shirts and hats and sunscreen and lotion and plastic bottles of soda and glass bottles of beer and a million other unidentifiable things on the wet, sandy floor.

Crawling back through the broken door, I step out into the parking lot and look up at the structure that looks as though it should not be standing.

As I stare up at the thrashed motel I see the beams of two flashlights moving in different places and in different directions up on the fourth floor.

I run over to Reggie's vehicle. The door is open but she's not inside.

With the dim light of my cell phone I search her SUV for a flashlight.

In moments I have one and I am rushing to the far stairs and beginning to make my way up them.

My progress is slowed and impeded by trash and debris, missing steps, and fallen, twisted railings, and it's going to take far longer than I thought to reach the fourth floor.

Several times my foot falls through the crumbling concrete step that is no longer there and I have to catch myself to keep from crashing all the way through. I'll be lucky to make it to the top without managing to break a leg.

It takes me a while to climb the rickety metal and crumbling concrete stairs, and as I do I think about what's going on here and why. I search for motivations, going over everything we've uncovered so far.

And in that moment I see something I haven't seen before—something clicks and the tumblers fall into place and the lock opens.

I now know—or think I do—what's going on. This is a setup and I doubt Merrick is even here.

When I reach the top of the stairs, there is nothing but darkness. The beams of the flashlights are off or have moved to different, unseen locations.

Most of the hotel room doors are open or missing, and I walk over and enter the opening of the room closest to me. Inside, I snap on the flashlight for a quick look around and then turn it off again.

From here it looks like the entire backside of the motel has been ripped off. What is left of the furniture in the room is in a molding and mildewing pile in the center, and through a large missing section in the interior wall I can see that the adjoining room is much the same —as is the one beyond it.

Stepping back over to the stairs, I hold onto a twisted piece of railing and lean out a little to see if I can locate the other flashlights again.

Scanning the external hallways floor by floor, I can find no beams of light.

And then I look up.

A beam of light is moving around up on the fifth floor.

Had I just been wrong and that's where it was before or had whoever it is moved from the fourth to the fifth by the time I made it up here?

I can feel the piece of railing in my hand start to give, so I reposition myself, let go of it, and begin to make my way up the next flight of stairs to the top floor.

When I step out onto the concrete hallway of the fifth floor, a beam of light in the third room over goes out.

Withdrawing my weapon, I rush over to the third doorway and step through its empty frame.

Holding the flashlight next to my Glock, I snap the light on and sweep the room.

It's as trashed as the one before—maybe more so. The rooms next to it, seen through the mostly missing walls, are in the same condition.

There's no one in the room, but through the empty metal frame of what was the sliding door leading onto the balcony, I can see an unconscious Reggie, tangled up in the twisted railing and leaning over the edge, the back of her head covered with blood.

The weight of her body leaning against the railing, which appears to be held in place by a single bolt or maybe two, seems to ensure that it will eventually fall. The question is how long does she have.

I start to rush over to help her but remember the beam of light from a few minutes before and decide to search the room and the ones next to it again before I do.

"John?" Randa says as she steps into the doorway behind me.

I spin around, pointing my gun and flashlight at her face.

The bright light washes her pale skin out even more but makes her intense green eyes seem to turn translucent.

She holds her hands up. "I'm not armed or shooting at you like Derek was," she says.

Raising my voice above the wind and surf, I say, "Keep your hands where I can see them. Step over this way."

When she gets close enough, I lean in to her and whisper, "You're being set up."

"No shit," she says. "I just woke up here a few minutes ago. No idea how I got here or who brought me."

"Will you help me?" I say.

"Of course," she says, her voice sincere, earnest, seeming to communicate *it goes without saying.*

"I'm sure he's nearby listening," I say. "He'll want to hear how this unfolds. I saw his light here a few moments ago. He can't have gotten far. Will you help me get Reggie in, then continue to talk loudly like you're talking to me while I go look for him?"

"Where is Reggie?"

I swing the light around and show her.

In the spill of the flashlight beam, I can see the dark,

narrow eyebrows above her wild green eyes arch in surprise.

"Sure," she says, already moving in Reggie's direction. "Come on. That looks like it could go any second."

"You're not leaving this room alive," I yell. "You're the one who's going to have an accident tonight, not me or Reggie."

We move over quickly and quietly to the balcony.

"What're you talking about, John? I don't understand."

We continue to talk like that to each other as we work to free Reggie from the railing and pull her back into the room.

"Tell me what made you do it?" I ask. "Are all these victims really random or are you punishing them for something?"

When we have Reggie lying on the damp floor of the moldy room, I whisper, "Take care of her and keep talking. I'm gonna go see if I can find him."

"Who?" she asks. "Who is it?"

"Tim Jonas," I say, "the reporter for the *Times*."

"What're you talking about?" she shouts as I turn off my light and sneak out of the room. "Why're you setting me up like this? I'm innocent."

Guessing that since we are on the far west end of the motel, Tim is to our east and plans to escape by the stairs on that end, I head in that direction.

It's so dark and I can see so little that I concentrate on trying to hear or smell him—a challenge made even more difficult by the sound of the wind and waves and the pervasiveness of the stench of mold, mildew, and rot.

In order to be close enough to hear us, he'll have to be in one of these first couple of rooms.

I make my way to the third doorway down and, crouching, enter the room.

As best I can tell in the moonlight, the room is empty.

I ease over to the opening in the wall to the west and step through it.

And see him standing there next to the hole in the wall on the other side, leaning in, listening to what Randa is saying two rooms down.

Quietly coming up behind him, when I am within three feet of him I click on the flashlight, identify myself, and tell him to show me his hands.

His diminutive stature makes me feel like I'm pointing my gun at a kid instead of a man, and I shudder as I have the feeling I'm back in the hallway of Potter High.

As he raises his hands I can see he has nothing in them and I wonder if since he uses debris and other natural resources and storm elements to kill, he doesn't carry a weapon.

"John?" he says. "I'm so glad you're here. I didn't think my text went through."

"Are you armed?"

"What? No. I'm here on a story. You won't believe—"

"Save it," I say. "I know it's you."

"What's me?"

"You're the chaos killer."

"The *what*?"

"Your paper sends you out on these assignments and you kill people," I say. "You're sent out sometimes to see if the storm will develop into something. When it doesn't, when it's just a tropical storm, you're still there—even though there's no need for the other agencies and organizations to show up—which is why there were murders in the smaller storms too. Your press credentials get you in anywhere—even past roadblocks and after curfew. You can easily approach people, pretending to want to do an interview, and the rest of the time you blend into the background. I wondered why the murders stopped for a while at the beginning. There had to be a good reason. It was because you returned to Tampa, but as soon as you convinced your editor to let you return, the killings started again. Now, very slowly place your hands on the back of your head with your fingers laced."

"John, this is crazy," he says. "Based on everything you just said, the killer could be any reporter or member of the press. Why not Merrick? Or Bucky? Or Gabriella Gonzalez?"

"None of them have been at all the other disasters where you murdered people."

"Bucky has."

"How do you know?" I ask.

"I mean, we always travel together."

"Which is what's going to make him a very valuable witness for us."

"You have no proof of anything and this is absolutely absurd. I'm not—"

"I'm willing to bet anything that the marker you used to draw the chaos symbol on Reggie is on you right now —unless you already planted it on Randa. Now, put your hands on your head and lace your fingers."

"Randa," he says. "That's who you need to be looking at. She's probably in there finishing the job on Reggie right now. Merrick said you have a blind spot when it comes to her that none of them can understand."

"Merrick would never give Randa Reggie's cell number," I say. "But he'd give it to you. But you're right— nothing I've said so far proves you're the killer, but what does and what will is your DNA on Reggie and Randa tonight, the burner phone in your pocket that was used to text Reggie, and the fact that you put information in your articles that only the killer could have known. You claimed sources close to the investigation revealed certain things to you, but no one told you any of those things. You were your own source. You knew because you are the killer."

"I can just argue that I did an interview with the killer, that she—"

"Last chance," I say. "Lace your fingers behind your head—"

"Or what? You'll shoot and kill me like you did Derek?"

He darts out of the room and I holster my weapon and follow him.

When I reach the open doorway I pause to shine my light in each direction to see which way he went.

He's heading east in the opposite direction of where Randa and Reggie are.

I follow after him—though not running nearly as fast as he is.

As I do, I call dispatch and request an ambulance and backup.

Using my flashlight to look for holes in the floor and debris blocking the hallway, I don't move as quickly or as recklessly as he does.

As I'm looking down at the floor, he disappears in the darkness up in front of me.

I can't be sure—did he make it to the stairwell or duck into one of the rooms?

Out of that darkness comes his disembodied voice.

"You think I'm a killer but you can't shoot me when you have the chance?"

I can't tell where the sound is coming from.

"Do you lack the courage of your convictions?" he yells. "That's not it, is it? You're haunted by Derek, aren't you? Wonder if you'll ever discharge your weapon again?"

I turn off my flashlight and listen for where his voice is coming from.

"So instead you're going to risk your life chasing me around this collapsing deathtrap. I like it, though. Leave it to chance, see how random all this really is."

His voice is being carried by the wind but it seems to be originating from inside one of the rooms.

I click the flashlight back on and begin searching the rooms.

Most have holes in the sheetrock that enables me to see in more than one at a time but some do not and have to be searched individually. In one such room, I step out onto the balcony, which is empty.

But as I'm turning to go back in the room I catch movement out of the corner of my eye, as in the pale moonlight, Tim is jumping from one balcony to another.

He's two rooms down from me heading back in the direction we have just come from.

Instead of following him from balcony to balcony, I run back through the room, down the walkway, and into the room that should be connected to the next balcony he jumps to.

Trying to rush through the room, I trip on an overturned table and hit the damp, soured floor hard.

By the time I'm up and out onto the balcony, he has already passed it.

But I'm there in time to see that as he lands on the balcony of the next room, the corner of the railing gives and he begins to fall.

Flinging his body around and trying to grab another part of the railing just causes him to fall at a much more awkward angle, and he hits his neck on the top of the railing below, causing his head to snap in a violent and unnatural motion that appears to break his neck before falling to his death on the beach below.

Slowly and carefully, I ease out to the edge of the balcony I'm standing on and look down.

His body is splayed like that of a suicide victim on the duneless beach, as not far from him the dim tide rolling in beneath the pale half-moon looks like blood.

58

The irony of the killer who made his murders appear to be accidents dying accidentally is lost on no one.

It seems as though every article written and every TV and radio report aired lead with it as if they are the first to do so.

It doesn't take long for members of Tim's own profession to rip off his mask of sanity and reveal the monster hidden beneath.

His early life had been a tortured, chaotic existence with a severely abusive alcoholic mother and a series of sadist stepfathers.

As could be predicted, Tim started setting fires and torturing and killing small animals in his youth. It appears in early adolescence he turned to a teacher, a social worker, and a priest for help, and was rejected, neglected, and sexually abused.

His history of violence and brutality are just coming to light, as are his various triggers, but it appears when his story is written he'll be among the most prolific compulsive killers of our time.

As is the case with killers like this, people—both experts and laymen alike—uncomfortable with ambiguity search for answers, attempt explanations. Is a predator like this born or made? Why did he do *what he did*? Why did he do it *the way he did it*?

Though the details are unclear and the reporting is intentionally vague, some have suggested that during Tropical Storm Barry, which hit Tampa Bay in June 2007, Tim experienced a life-altering event that inspired his particular brand of psychopathology. It seems that in a minor storm-related traffic accident, the only person to show Tim any kindness was killed while Tim, in the seat beside her, was completely unscathed—at least physically.

I'm sure by the time the final story is told, the blood on her face will have been said to have formed the shape of a chaos symbol.

People want answers, and in the absence of any— especially when it comes to the nature of evil—they fill the void with whatever they can find. But how can you explain the random killing of vulnerable strangers by a man who seemed on the surface about as normal as everyone else?

I cannot.

I will not.

What I *will* do is mourn his many victims and be grateful every day there will never be another.

"I STILL CAN'T BELIEVE IT," Bucky is saying. "I mean . . . I know it's true. I don't doubt it. I just can't believe it."

His shock is not unusual. But instead of a neighbor saying what a nice, quiet young man Tim was, it's the person who spent the most time with him, his professional partner that he traveled with, ate with, even shared a room with.

We are standing in the back parking lot of the sheriff's station. He has just finished his final interview and is about to head back to Tampa. I'm about to head home for some much needed time with Anna and the girls.

"I guess I am as dumb as he said I was," he says. "I just can't believe I had no idea. None. At all."

"Until recently no one was even aware there were murders to suspect someone of," I say.

He shrugs. "Yeah. I guess. But . . . to not suspect anything . . . At all."

"Sociopaths like him are very good at hiding behind

their mask of sanity," I say. "I doubt anyone in your position would have suspected him."

"How'd he even do it?" he asks. "We were together most of the time."

"We found most of the victims in their pajamas," I say. "They were abducted or killed in the middle of the night or in the early morning hours before dawn."

"So he just snuck out while I was sleeping and . . . went hunting?"

"My guess is he drugged your last drink of the night," I say.

"Oh my God," he says. "We always had a nightcap. Always. He insisted on it. And I always slept better when we were out on assignment. It was like this joke . . . no matter how shitty the hotel, I still slept great. He said it was his soothing presence. Fucker was drugging me so he could . . . go out and . . . do what he did."

I nod.

He shakes his head and frowns. "If I had just . . . realized what was . . . going on. I could've . . . saved so many lives."

"No one in any agency in multiple jurisdictions ever suspected anything," I say. "You're being way too hard on yourself."

"They weren't sleepin' with him. I mean . . . you know . . . sharing a room with him. He's gotta be one of the most prolific serial killers in the . . . in history."

"He was able to operate under all radars for so long," I say. "He really used the chaos and confusion and the devastation and depletion of these storms and their aftermaths in a masterful way. And when what he had been doing was finally brought out into the light . . . I think he was going to frame Randa for it all, leave the area, and continue what he had been doing—maybe even altering slightly his MO and signature if he could."

"Did you read the paper's statement?"

I shake my head. "Haven't see it yet."

"Was a sincere apology. Wonder what kind of liability they're looking at—sending him out to all these places to . . . murder . . . all these hurting and helpless people. Our leading crime reporter arrives today. Going to take over the reporting. They're letting me file our final story—something I've never done before. Merrick is helping me write it. But . . . what the hell do I say?"

59

Judge Wheata Pearl Whitehurst says, "I understand we have a verdict."

Her smoker's throat is phlegmy and she coughs and takes a long pull from her rattlesnake mug.

"We do, Your Honor," the foreperson says.

My heart is thumping in my chest and all I can hear is the sound of blood rushing through my ears.

I glance back at the full courtroom behind me for a supportive face. I find several. Dad and Verna. Merrill. Jake. Randa. Tyrese. Merrick. Reggie—who even with a bandage on her head is present to offer her support.

The foreperson hands the verdict form to the bailiff and the bailiff carries it to the judge. After looking over it without reaction or expression, the judge has the bailiff take it to the clerk to be published.

As we stand I am shaking slightly, and I take a few deep, slow breaths in an attempt to calm down some.

Anna reaches over and takes my hand.

"Now, before the clerk reads the verdict," Wheata Pearl says, "I want to remind everyone that this is a very serious matter. What this is *not* is a sporting event. I don't want to hear any cheering or outbursts of any kind. Y'all hearin' ol' Wheata Pearl on this?"

There are lots of nods in the courtroom. I am unable to because of how much I'm trembling.

The clerk holds the verdict form out in front of her, clears her throat, and says, "Did the plaintiffs prove their case? No."

Though the clerk continues to read I don't hear anything after that.

Anna proved her case not only to me but to a jury of my peers.

We don't celebrate. There are no hugs or pats on the back. If we show any reaction at all it is perhaps the exhalation of relief. The extent of what we do is squeeze each other's hand a little harder.

LATER THAT AFTERNOON, before we do anything else, we take

the money we borrowed, the money we would've had to pay if we had lost, and as we had previously agreed, we donate it to the charity that Bryce and Melissa had chosen and we do so under the name of Derek Bryce Burrell in his honor.

This act, which I knew I had to do the moment the idea occurred to me, will cause an even greater financial strain on our family, and Anna is an absolute saint to be so supportive of us doing it.

It isn't have been the charity I would have chosen, and that's the point.

This act is not one of contrition or penance, and it doesn't make me feel less guilty or give me the sense that I'm doing anything other than the least I can do.

As word of the verdict spreads, my phone vibrates nonstop from calls and texts and emails—mostly comments of congratulations from friends and family and requests for a comment or an interview from the press.

After only a few moments I power it off, and leave it that way until much later in the evening.

Three weeks to the day since Hurricane Michael ravaged our region, devastated our little town, and altered our lives forever, beneath a harvest-orange sun in a clear baby-blue sky, we work to salvage Halloween.

Since so many of the homes in town are damaged or destroyed, and so many of the neighborhoods are still unsafe, this year's Halloween festivities are confined to a community carnival on the campus of Northwest Florida Head Start and trick-or-treating on a closed-off section of 2nd Street.

Because no stores in the area that carry Halloween costumes are open and because our town is too torn up for most online deliveries, most of the kids participating are wearing homemade costumes or costumes that have been donated by outside organizations.

Anna and I take Taylor, Johanna, and John Paul to the carnival first and then down to 2nd Street. I carry John Paul, Anna pushes Taylor in a stroller, and Johanna walks between us.

The celebration, which seems to include most of the town, transcends Halloween and gives us all a chance to set aside, however temporarily, our fatigue and frustration and anxiety, and to join each other in enjoying our costumed children.

The carnival consists of face painting and bouncy castles and the kind of sidewalk games that school and church carnivals did when I was a kid—bobbing for apples, ducks in a barrel, and fishing through a cardboard-covered doorway. There are also cakewalks and hotdogs and hayrides.

Later, in the calm, cool evening, we stroll down 2nd Street speaking to our neighbors, bragging on their kids' costumes—especially the homemade ones, which there are more of this year.

The homes on both sides of this section of 2nd Street are close together and are close to the sidewalks, and we hit everyone—our sweet little angel, cop, and Beatle saying "trick-or-treat" and, after having candy placed inside their plastic jack-o'-lanterns, "thank you."

I notice that my neighbors and loved ones are as

tender since the storm as I am, many of them sniffling or tearing up as we talk about what we've been through.

Of all the touching expressions of love and resilience we witness, perhaps the most meaningful of all is how the empty lots along 2nd Street are filled with people who live in other parts of town, some of whom no longer have homes of their own, who have set up tents and decorated them with skeletons and scarecrows, ghosts and witches, and are passing out candy the way they would if they had a neighborhood.

The entire experience is encouraging and inspiring and communal and hope-giving in a way that does something for us individually and collectively to an extent the depth of which is difficult to explain.

"We survived," Anna says, and I can tell she's talking about far more than just the storm.

"Yes, we did," I say.

And not just us, but our family and friends, our neighbors, and our community as a whole.

We are wounded, but alive. We are battered and broken but not hopeless. Life will never be the same here. *We* will never be the same. But life will go on. *We* will go on.

As I think about what we've been through, what is still left to endure, some Yeats drifts through my mind.

Turning and turning in the widening gyre
The falcon cannot hear the falconer;

Things fall apart; the centre cannot hold;
Mere anarchy is loosed upon the world,
The blood-dimmed tide is loosed, and everywhere
The ceremony of innocence is drowned . . .

In our widening gyre, things fell apart as anarchy was loosed upon us and we lost our innocence, but in some ways—the most meaningful and significant and crucial ways—our center held and continues to hold, though nothing else does.

ALSO BY MICHAEL LISTER

Books by Michael Lister

(John Jordan Novels)

Power in the Blood

Blood of the Lamb

Flesh and Blood

(Special Introduction by Margaret Coel)

The Body and the Blood

Double Exposure

Blood Sacrifice

Rivers to Blood

Burnt Offerings

Innocent Blood

(Special Introduction by Michael Connelly)

Separation Anxiety

Blood Money

Blood Moon

Thunder Beach

Blood Cries

A Certain Retribution

Blood Oath

Blood Work

Cold Blood

Blood Betrayal

Blood Shot

Blood Ties

Blood Stone

Blood Trail

Bloodshed

Blue Blood

And the Sea Became Blood

The Blood-Dimmed Tide

(Jimmy Riley Novels)

The Girl Who Said Goodbye

The Girl in the Grave

The Girl at the End of the Long Dark Night

The Girl Who Cried Blood Tears

The Girl Who Blew Up the World

(Merrick McKnight / Reggie Summers Novels)

Thunder Beach

A Certain Retribution

Blood Oath

Blood Shot

(Remington James Novels)

Double Exposure

(includes intro by Michael Connelly)

Separation Anxiety

Blood Shot

(Sam Michaels / Daniel Davis Novels)

Burnt Offerings

Blood Oath

Cold Blood

Blood Shot

(Love Stories)

Carrie's Gift

(Short Story Collections)

North Florida Noir

Florida Heat Wave

Delta Blues

Another Quiet Night in Desperation

(The Meaning Series)

Meaning Every Moment

The Meaning of Life in Movies